Alicia
Enjoy!

MW00891820

IMMORTAL HEAT

A Guardians of Dacia Novel

Loni Lynne

Believe
In
Fate!

Loni Lynne Publishing

Loni Lynne

This book is a work of fiction. All names, characters, locations, and incidents are products of the author's imagination, or have been used fictitiously. Any resemblance to actual persons living or dead, locales, or events is entirely coincidental.

Loni Lynne, Publisher
First Edition: October 2014

ISBN:1502568381

ISBN-13: 978-1502568380

Dedication

To my amazing family and friends, thank you for all the love and support.

Chapter One

Mid-January—Timisoara, Romania

The brisk air hit Marilyn Reddlin in the face as she stepped out of the Traian Vuia International Airport terminal into a wintery Timisoara, Romania. Pushing her thick-lensed glasses up on her nose and squinting at her cell phone, the weather-app showed thirty-three degrees. Even with her warm woolen pea coat and accessories she couldn't help but shiver. Not many Americans considered Romania a bucket-list destination. But this was the homeland of her father, a place of mystery and magic steeped in tradition and history. Though never having met her father, Marilyn felt drawn to the country and its folklore.

Flashes of movement danced in her peripheral sight, putting her on edge. Someone was watching her. But who and why here? Blaming it on the paranoia her mother instilled in her at such a young age, she swore she wasn't going to let Diane Reddlin influence her adventure now.

Masculine spiced cologne of rich ambers and smoky musk assaulted her brain. Such a soothing scent. Inhaling involuntarily, she thought perhaps a man passing her in the terminal left his fragrance on her coat? The aroma settled into her brain and she tried to relax. Yet, why did her heart still race? Adrenaline kicked in chasing the sluggishness from her mind. The fine hairs on her arms stood up in awareness, magnetizing her nerves to a painful degree. Didn't her mother warn her of dangers lurking everywhere? She expected to see someone jump out at her. But there wasn't anything out of the ordinary.

People meandered, hailing the buses or cabs waiting for potential customers or going into the terminal to catch their flights. Shaking off the ill-ease, she rolled her suitcase along behind, wanting to get to the safety of the Hotel Elysee where Professor Vamier had her staying for the night. Her time in Timisoara would be short. Just a brief layover until her flight tomorrow evening. She'd been lucky enough to have Professor Aiden Vamier at the Babes-Bolyar University in Cluj-Napoca, take an interest in her paper on pre-Romanian history. He'd even asked for her to be his work-student for her final semester of her Master's Degree in History.

She rubbed at her neck where stiffness had settled in from the flight. She'd cursed her mother's insistence to have Dr. Jon Johnston prescribe her "relaxants" for her first time flying. She hadn't wanted to be drugged and refused to imbibe until queasy turmoil and sore muscles had her downing a pain pill and muscle relaxer with a can of ginger ale before she even left the tarmac in Newark for her flight to London.

Marilyn had hoped the medication would help. But all they'd done was made her sleepy, leaving her groggy and lethargic. Her sleep patterns were messed up enough without the drugs. She needed to get back on some sort of schedule soon if she was going to work with Professor Vamier.

There it was again, the odd sense of being watched. She didn't want to turn around for fear of someone standing behind her. Worse yet, she didn't want to turn around to find no one there. Pulling her suitcase closer, she patted her coat to make sure her purse was still secure under her wrappings.

"Knock it off, mother. I refuse to be a paranoid-psycho," she said under her breath before closing her eyes and exhaling all of her pent up frustrations. Her mother had battered her with years of being overly protective when all she wanted was to explore life.

Hailing a cab, she asked the driver to take her to the Hotel Elysee. She was anxious to get to Cluj to start her research of Romanian history and antiquities, but she could wait another day and recover from the jet lag she already suffered.

The less than fifty-pound suitcase clunked into the trunk of the cab, weighing down the back of the small vehicle, nearly touching the pavement. Would the car be sturdy enough to carry her to her destination? The cabby grinned at her, showing crooked but gleaming white teeth, his hand out to receive money. He wanted a tip? Perhaps it was customary to tip for taking luggage?

Tentatively, Marilyn placed money into his palm. The cabbie opened her door and waved his hand as if he were a footman to her personal carriage. Bundling her coat around her, she stiffened her spine and held her head up higher to show she knew what she needed to do. Confidence, even if she didn't feel it, would divert trouble elsewhere. Taking one last cautious look around, she slid into the warmth of the vinyl interior.

Buckled in, she waited for the driver. She needed to call her mother. The only way Marilyn managed to convince Diane Reddlin she'd be all right on this trip was to agree to call her when she arrived at each destination.

Knowing her mother the way she did, she would be checking incoming flights at every airport along the scheduled journey. Which she had. London was a battle—she'd taken a few minutes in the ladies room and found a pub that made authentic fish and chips when her phone rang only to have her mother nearly scream at her, trans-continentally, for not calling her upon *immediate* arrival.

Her driver pulled out into traffic without looking. A car horn blared behind them. Marilyn turned to see another cab breaking hard, giving her driver the universal gesture with his middle finger, before peeling into the vacant spot. The cabbie returned the greeting in the rear-view mirror, grinning at her and saying something about 'driving-assholes' from what she could translate. Marilyn only smiled and went to search her coat pocket for her cell phone so she could contact her mother before half the American Embassy and military forces were on the look-out for her.

Diane Reddlin picked up on the first ring.

"Your flight landed at six-ten. You've been on the ground for nearly an hour. What did I tell you about calling me immediately?" her mother badgered her. "That is so irresponsible of you. You do realize I have a meeting first thing tomorrow morning with the federal trade commission. I've been waiting for your call so I can go to bed."

Marilyn sighed. "I'm sorry Mama. I just wanted to make sure I got checked in through immigration, and it took longer than I expected for our luggage to be unloaded."

The cab veered to the right on two wheels, screeching in resistance to the torturous position the small vehicle endured. Marilyn squealed at the sight of cars whizzing by as if getting out of their way. Checking the view out her window, a cacophony of reverberating car horns signaled each other in their race to each personal destination as if their journey was the most important.

Her driver weaved in and out of traffic, like a drunken monkey, yelling the occasional profanity when other cars cut in front of him. Her fear of flying had nothing on her latest fear of Romanian drivers. She clutched the edge of the door and closed her eyes, praying the seatbelt was sturdy enough to hold her in and that she'd arrive at the hotel and not a hospital.

"What's going on, Marilyn? Are you still there?"

"Yes, I'm still here."

"I thought I heard you squeal. Are you hurt? What's wrong?" The panic in her mother's voice was evident. She would be jumping through the phone if she could.

Putting her shattered nerves back together, Marilyn tried to sound normal. "I'm fine, mother. Would you stop worrying?"

"My only daughter is half a world away, vulnerable and I can't do a damn thing about it—and you want me to stop worrying? You should have thought about that before taking this 'Aiden Vamier' up on his offer to study abroad."

"Mom, we've been over this. This trip is important to me."

Another hard right turn had her holding on to her phone and her empty stomach as if willing it to settle would keep her from getting car sick. The driver grinned at her in the rear view mirror. She feigned a small smile and held on to the door, making sure it was in the locked position.

"Why do you need to leave Frederick or the country for that matter? And Romania? Why it's barely out of the threat of communism!"

"That was twenty-five years ago, Mom. Things have changed."

"Not as much as you think." She was silent for a moment. "Your father was never heard from again."

There it was, the real reason for her worry. Marilyn couldn't blame her though. Her father had been an archeologist from Romania, working at the Smithsonian. He'd been sent on a research project to Cluj-Napoca when he went missing in the Hoia Forest, leaving her mother alone, six months pregnant with her.

"This trip will be good for me. I'm embracing the whole woman empowerment thing you've told me about over the years. How I need to find 'me.' Well, that's what I'm trying to do."

She had to take time to find out what she needed in life. She'd just been dumped by the one guy she'd given up everything for. It had been a disaster. This would be a fresh start with her to focus on her career and not a man.

"Yes, but I meant for you to find yourself here, in Frederick, Maryland not Romania." There was a derisive sniff from her mother. "You had your internship here at Livedel."

"Sorry Mama, I'm just not cut out to be a secretary."

"Administrative Assistant, Marilyn—and may I remind you it is what got you through your first two years of college. You had to go and fall in love with Daniel and follow him to Towson when you could have stayed in Frederick and gotten your degree right here at Hood or even Mount St. Mary's."

"Right now, that doesn't matter." Marilyn snorted. "I just want to focus on me. And this is the perfect opportunity."

"But in Romania?" Her mother's voice whined with true emotion. "You may as well be on the moon. I lost your father in Romania…why torture me like this, Marilyn?"

Frustration prickled. Always the same thing with her mother. "I'm not doing this to torture you. This is my time to shine. I can't follow in your footsteps. I need to be myself."

Her mother harrumphed.

Marilyn's upper body slid against the vinyl bench seat as her driver wove in and out of on-coming traffic to get around a slower driver. She closed her eyes as an echoing blast from a semi-truck alerted them of eminent doom if the driver didn't get back over in his lane.

This trip didn't bode well. Maybe she was doomed to death by a taxi driver instead of an airplane. Maybe her mother had a point. No…she wouldn't accept it. She would survive this trip, wild cab ride and all. Looking ahead of the car she took a calming breath. There were no cars in front of them now. She could relax or at least listen to her mother's ranting.

At times like this, Marilyn wished her mother would take a pill. The woman could try the patience of a priest. She'd been known to bring grown men to their knees in a board room but coddled her to suffocation.

"Couldn't you just be happy and excited for me, Mama? This is about my history, my heritage, a part of who I am. I want to explore the world and learn everything I can. I want to explore the ancient Dacian ruins and tour the Carpathian Mountains—I want to embrace the magic of Romania."

Her mother scoffed.

"I'm looking forward to studying with Professor Vamier." She wasn't sure what her future had in store for her. Whatever the situation, she wasn't going to find it sitting in a cubical at Livedel Enterprise the rest of her life.

Marilyn sighed and tried a different tactic. "You've taught me everything I know. Don't you think it's time I try to see if I really learned from your tutelage?" It was true. For all the smothering from her mother she'd also learned a great deal, she just never had the chance to use the skills she'd been taught.

She could hear her mother's deep breathing as if trying to hold back her true thoughts on Marilyn's beliefs. Finally she heard the switch in her mother's tone.

"How are you feeling? Did the muscle relaxants I had Jon prescribe for your trip help with the pain?"

"I'm fine," she lied, wincing when she noticed the speedometer on the cabbie's dash. Was there a speed limit in Romania? "But I think the difference in time is messing with me." She looked at her wristwatch. "It's six-fifty here and I finally feel awake, alert and raring to go."

"Are you taking your vitamins?"

"Yes."

"And your gingko?"

"Yes." Marilyn rolled her eyes. "Mom will you relax. You need to learn to start trusting me. I'm twenty-five now."

"Are you sure? What about your iron pills? I noticed you're looking pale and thin. You need more red meats, protein and iron rich foods. You might be anemic."

"I'm fine. Will you stop worrying?" Marilyn argued. She'd always been scrawny and pale, kind of non-descript. Her thick glasses and long, straggly, reddish-brown hair gave her a fem-geek persona. Being a book-nerd-history major didn't help her socially either. Her mother had tried to get her into society by having her attend Chamber of Commerce meetings and social functions with her since she'd turned twenty-one and could drink, but she was the gawky girl in the corner with a wine spritzer, trying to appear approachable.

"I know you have your meeting in the morning so I'll let you go, Mama. I'll call you when I get to Cluj-Napoca tomorrow night."

"All right. I have your itinerary so make sure you call me *as soon as you land*. You have your meds?"

"Yes. And I'll say my prayers before take-off."

"Good girl. I love you."

"I love you *more*, Mama." Marilyn made the natural effort to add 'more' to her closing.

Her mother said goodnight, letting her cell phone screen go dark. Lost in her own thoughts she jolted back to reality as her driver merged from an exit without signaling or giving the driver behind them room to let them in. She closed her eyes and prayed to arrive safely at her destination.

Maybe if she feigned sleep her cabbie wouldn't continue to grin at her as if he needed her approval to his asinine driving skills. Finally tires squealed on the pavement, and her body catapulted forward pressing the seatbelt into her breastbone. Well, it held. If not, she would've been upside down in the front passenger seat.

She looked out the side window and realized they were in front of the Hotel Elysee. A doorman dressed in a red jacket, black slacks and wearing a small cap opened her door and greeted her with a charming smile. Marilyn emerged from the car on trembling legs, thankful to have the aide of the doorman to keep her steady. The driver retrieved her suitcase from his trunk, and she paid him more than the trip cost. She didn't care, she was just happy to be alive and in one piece.

The doorman ushered a valet to see to her personal items and guided her up the marbled steps of the pillar-framed entrance of glass. Spiral topiaries stood sentry to the elegance of the reception area. Warmth and antique furniture greeted her. Bright chandeliers hung from Italian-Michelangelo paintings on the ceiling, giving the classic hotel a five star quality while she felt as limp and attractive as a haggard crone. Her glasses slipped down her nose.

"Ah, Miss Reddlin," the hotel manager greeted her from the lobby. "We've been expecting you. Mr. Vamier has taken care of all your needs while you are here. Dinner is on the house and Yves will escort you to your suite. If you need anything, please do not hesitate to let us know."

"Thank you."

Yves led her to the elevator that took them to the second floor where she was shown to a beautiful suite fit for a queen. The canopied antique bed and elegant Victorian furniture were wasted on her for a single night's stay, though. Maybe a quick, relaxing shower would renew her before going down to have dinner.

Marilyn tipped Yves, receiving a smile and a jaunty salute from him before he closed the doors. Placing a 'do not disturb' sign on the outside of the double doors, she locked them and stripped to the private bath, leaving her wrinkled travel ware and fatigue behind her as she turned on the various jet sprays of a soul-reviving shower.

#

The wine steward replenished her glass of merlot for the third time. Marilyn enjoyed the benefits of having someone take care of her. Professor Vamier was generous with his hospitality, even from afar. He'd guaranteed her exceptional treatment, gave her carte blanch for the night, and the staff treated her like a queen.

Though Marilyn never wanted for anything, except her father, her mother never let them splurge on frivolous things. She was a woman who pinched her pennies and those of the company to a degree she fought over with many of her board members. Diane Reddlin knew her job and got the company where they were. Though Marilyn's early life was taken care of by a nanny, her mother was always there at the end of the day. Working for Livedel and its generous CEO, Rick Delvante, provided a wonderful life. They'd never met Mr. Delvante personally since he was based somewhere in Europe, but still he treated them like family. When her father had gone missing, he'd sent his condolences, made sure her mother had the best medical treatment available through Livedel during her pregnancy and would always have a supporting job within the company. Now her mother was the chief financial officer of Livedel Enterprise and a respected member of Livedel both nationally and internationally.

Even with the pleasant lifestyle her mother made for them over the years, Diane Reddlin taught her not to take advantage of good fortune. Only blood, sweat and tears could get you where you needed to be in life. So having the opportunity to indulge in what a five-star European hotel had to offer, especially when it was bankrolled by a generous benefactor, made her feel special.

Professor Vamier had even taken the expense to book her a day in the spa before her flight. She looked forward to indulging in a prepared spa treatment tomorrow—it might help with her recent bout of aches and pains to get the whole Vichy shower, mud bath, facial and massage. It was a treat to be able to splurge on a vintage red wine much less a luxury spa day.

Taking a sip of said wine, Marilyn stopped with her glass half-way to her lips.

The odd sensation returned, like at the airport, as if someone watched her. She peered at the other guests. Only a few couples dined, engrossed in each other. Yet prickling awareness pinched the nerves in her spine. This was ridiculous. Her mother's foreboding had her paranoid. How could she control her half a world away? Rolling her eyes, she chuckled. Knowing her mother, if anyone could, Diane Reddlin would find a way.

Swirling the remaining liquid in the bowl of her glass, she let it bleed along the sides. The effect of the tannins took hold of her, making her giddy. Smiling within her own silent thoughts, she exhaled and downed the final sip of wine in salute to her new, adventurous life as she pushed her empty plate of meat juices away.

But the liquid called to her like a temptress. She'd soaked up much of the prime rib juices with her dinner roll but the remainder still sat there sinfully teasing her. The rare meat had tasted so good, filling a hunger she'd never experienced when eating.

She wasn't much of a meat eater but when she did, she liked hers cooked well. Perhaps it was the way the prime rib had been prepared? Pressing her lips together, Marilyn hoped her waiter would show soon to remove the offensive drippings from her sight before she made a spectacle of herself by grabbing the plate and licking it clean.

The server rolled out a dessert tray, and Marilyn automatically possessed room for the piece of decadent Belgian-chocolate cake whispering her name. She couldn't pass up the temptation. Besides, it was only a sliver of cake.

She needed something to absorb all the wine. The rich chocolate would complement the merlot and appease her craving.

The first bite hit her taste buds with the smooth, sinful flavor of Belgian chocolate- ganache. Marilyn sighed blissfully and closed her eyes, allowing the sweetness to pleasure her senses as she dragged the fork through her lips to capture every last molecule of taste.

Upon opening her eyes she saw a man sitting at her table, staring at her. She inhaled a crumb of chocolate cake, setting her to cough. Marilyn tried to breathe as her eyes watered behind her spectacles. The man handed her the water goblet and their fingers touched. Trembling at the jolt of electricity shooting through her hand, Marilyn took a sip to clear her throat.

She picked up the subtle scent of the amber and musk she'd noticed in the airport. Was it him? Was he spying on her?

He didn't blink. His electric blue gaze bore into her soul. Small tremors of the fear her mother had addressed for years came running back, but she sat immobilized, staring back at him.

Dressed all in black, his raven hair blended in with the black leather of his jacket and turtleneck shirt. Those blue eyes caught fire from the reflection of candle light between them. Little bubbles of sensual awareness boiled within her bloodstream, and her mouth went dry as if the cake she'd been eating left behind a sawdust residue. She tried to laugh away the nervousness, but what came out was more of a croak. "I think you have the wrong seat," she said in broken Romanian.

"You have to leave," he said.

He spoke in perfect, modern English with a hint of accent. She wasn't sure what kind. *You have to leave,* her mind echoed. She shook her head at the distracting sound of his voice. Like the Belgian chocolate ganache, the thick tenor drizzled delicious intent that could make a woman fantasize about what that voice would sound like whispering rich, sweet words into her ear. She needed to stop drinking red wine. It made her think silly things.

What would her mother do in a situation like this? With the stiffened spine she'd learned from Diane Reddlin, she met his gaze—difficult as it was to look into his eyes without melting. "This is my table. You are the one who needs to leave." She took another bite of her cake as if he weren't there. Whether the cake was more acceptable to bite into than he was would be a matter of decorum, but she bet he would taste yummy.

Hands joined in a single fist planted on the table, he leaned forward until his face was mere inches from hers. He studied her every move as she ate. The intensity should have unnerved her, and yet a wine induced boldness hit her, coupled with a determination to put him in his place, whoever he was. His good looks and dark, sensual appeal could only mean trouble.

The flickering candlelight created shadows along his jaw line, making him appear even more mysterious. His elegant European nose flared, the muscles in his jaw flexed. The mixed scent of the aroma she'd been alerted to at the airport and leather from his jacket again hit her senses. As much as she tried to fight her feminine instincts, her inner woman wasn't cooperating. Her nipples hardened, and a quiver started in her core. She shifted uncomfortably in her seat.

"You are in danger, Marilyn Reddlin. Leave now. . . before it's too late."

Those eyes penetrated straight through to her soul. She hoped to God he didn't know what her body was saying. Then his words and the fact he'd just addressed her by her name hit her like a bucket of icy water. She shook off the strange enchantment.

"Who are you? How do you know my name?"

"That's my business. Now, leave Romania...tonight."

Marilyn sat stunned, fighting the commanding lilt of his voice. There was an odd, suggestive pull. She fought it but he'd already left. She hadn't seen him get up. But when she looked, he'd walked out of the restaurant into the hotel lobby towards the entrance.

A few moments later she grabbed his hand, halting him. His eyes flared up at her, and then down to where her hand had attached itself to his wrist. She stopped and realized she didn't remember how *she'd* gotten from the table to being outside, trying to stop his departure. But here she was. They stared at each other for a moment, both astounded at the circumstances.

He jerked his hand from her touch and popped the collar on his jacket, glaring at her before walking away.

You will leave.

Did she just hear his voice in her mind or had he said that aloud? His back was to her, so she wasn't sure. She shook her head to get the sound of his voice out of her senses. This was too bizarre.

Like hell I'll leave, asshole, she thought while staring after him. Who did he think he was? Had her mother put him up to this?

Stopping dead in his tracks, he slowly turned around. Marilyn stood her ground, her hands fisted on her hips in defiance. Did she hear him curse? That was impossible, his lips hadn't moved, and they were now a parking lot away from each other.

A logistics truck pulled up through the circular entrance of the hotel, blocking her view, before driving away. When the view was clear, her mystery man had disappeared into the night, leaving only the echo of his warning behind in her head. She walked back to the dining room puzzled over the man's audacity.

She'd be damned before she turned tail and ran back home to Mama.

Chapter Two

The plane had less than fifty people on board. Not many must fly into Cluj-Napoca—or maybe not at this time of night. It was the last flight from Timisoara into Cluj for the day. Professor Vamier had reserved it to coordinate with his nocturnal schedule. He attended to other duties during the day and wouldn't be available until the evenings. He would need her help with his nightly workload as she attended his classes. Marilyn didn't mind. She would plan her day accordingly, so she could accommodate his time frame if needed. Adapting to schedules was the least of her concerns. Aiden Vamier had been generous enough, she could at least give in to his wishes.

Settling into the seat, she thought about reading for awhile. Happy nobody sat beside her, the dose of meds she took a few minutes ago would kick in soon, and she'd be able to curl up in the two seats. The overhead light instructed her to buckle the seat belt. With nails embedded into the armrests, she closed her eyes as the plane jerked forward for take-off. On an inhale of breath, Marilyn quickly went through her usual prayers in her head. It was always the same prayer, asking God to keep her safe, guide the pilot in his flight and if by some chance it was her time to die, to make it quick and painless. She never deviated from the routine, just in case it was that one time which disaster happened.

The plane leveled out as it reached altitude, and the security of knowing they were above any obstacles they could crash into helped her relax her grip on the arm rests. Opening her eyes, she gasped. Her mystery man sat right next to her in the empty aisle seat.

"What is it with you? Are you some sort of stalker?" she seethed.

"I thought I told you to leave."

"So you did."

"You didn't? Why?"

Marilyn stared at him. "I don't have to answer to you—Who are you? What do you want with me?"

"Draylon Conier. And you need to leave Romania."

Well he'd answered both of her questions. She couldn't fault him for that. Draylon Con-yea? The way he said his name made her think of velvet on satin. "Should I know you?"

It was a rhetorical question aimed at him, but he turned to face her. Even under the small cabin lights of the plane she thought she saw flames licking the sheer brilliance of his eyes.

"Should you?"

Okay, he was weird—sexy as hell, but weird. "I don't know who you are or why you want me gone, but I'm not leaving . . . and you can't make me."

That sounded juvenile but right now she didn't care.

"I've been sent to let you know you are in danger."

"In danger? From whom?"

"Vamier."

"You're crazy." She turned back to face forward, putting her book up to separate them. "Now, leave me alone. I'm not going anywhere unless you can give me some real reason."

She sensed Draylon relax beside her and he closed his

eyes. His breathing turned heavy but even.

Get on the next plane out of Cluj.

Drop dead. She turned the page in the book.

You will get on the next plane out of Cluj and leave Romania, Marilyn Reddlin. He stood up and left the seat to head towards the back. *Besides, I couldn't die even if I wanted to.*

She craned her neck around at his odd comment but got caught up in admiring the way his black jeans hugged his lean, strong thighs. So what if he was handsome as sin and built like a sex god? No man was that perfect. He was a strange guy—a would-be killer maybe? Marilyn refused to believe any of this. He was a psycho who could read minds. Or maybe she was the psycho since she thought she could read his?

#

The meds lulled her enough to relax in fetal position upon the two seats until they dipped over the Carpathian Mountains. The rocking and dipping of the plane as it hit turbulence brought her upright, clutching the armrest and squealing under her breath. She closed her eyes.

It will be all right, Marilyn.

Draylon's velvet smooth voice echoed in her head. Opening her eyes, she turned in her seat, forcing herself to look up and over the head rest enough to see further back in the plane. He was within sight, but he appeared to be asleep. His lips quirked into a semi-smile. Marilyn wondered how many hearts he'd broken with that grin. Her heart rate sped up as another dip took her stomach into a flip-flop swirl. The Caesar salad she'd eaten during her day spa threatened to come back up if they took another belly flopper.

Breathe. Relax.

She turned back around to face the front of the plane and found herself listening to his voice and doing as he told her.

That's it. Let go of the armrest.

She did.

Close your eyes.

She wanted to fight his voice. She didn't want a stranger controlling her mind. The vibration of his accent eased under her consciousness, held the power to lull her.

Am I a stranger?

Marilyn relaxed. The image of his hand caressing her face stamped itself behind her closed eyes. Lips whispered in a language she'd never heard against her ear—exotic, foreign, ancient in its guttural syllables. Like a soothing spa room set with aromatherapy and sounds of the ocean, she transformed into dreamland where she floated above the clouds in the arms of a dragon in black leather.

#

Disoriented, Marilyn lumbered off of the plane at Cluj Avram Iancu International Airport. The few passengers on her flight maneuvered around her to reach their destination as she tried to focus on just being able to walk. Tired, her brain registered a fuzzy mass of confusion and distorted visions.

She had her purse and knew she needed to retrieve her baggage from the luggage belt.

I must leave, she thought to herself.

She held out her passport to the official. He stamped it. She had a passport? What did the stamp say? Cluj-Napoca?

I must leave Cluj. I need to leave Romania.

But why? She was here for a purpose. She shook her head to clear it. Was she meeting someone? That's right, Professor Vamier. She should call him and let him know she arrived. But first she would get her luggage so she could find the ladies room and freshen up, call her mother before Diane Reddlin alerted the airport. Hopefully the baggage claim would be quick. There weren't many passengers around this time of night. It would be like her mother to have her paged over the public announcement system if she didn't call right away.

Suddenly propelled forward, her arm was nearly jerked from her socket, and she gasped in shock. Skidding to a halt, her assailant spun her around like a rag doll. Draylon held on to both of her arms, shaking her out of her stupor.

"Which bag is yours?"

"Let go of me," she hissed under her breath, trying in vain to shake her abductor. *I'll scream,* she threatened.

No you won't.

Marilyn was about to prove him wrong when his mouth clamped down on hers, stealing her breath, her scream, her will to resist. She went shock still as memories of her debacle with Daniel seeped into her brain. The pain…she hadn't been ready.

Pressed between the cold concrete pillar and the unrelenting heated solidness of Draylon Conier, fear settled into Marilyn's lungs, keeping her from breathing. He stared down at her, his brows screwed in confusion, his mouth a firm line of disgust.

He stopped what he was about to say and instead pulled her along with him.

Don't look. You're being watched.

You're full of crap. No one knows who I am…except you.

Following him, Marilyn felt like she was trapped in some James Bond movie, mistaken for someone else, except for the fact he kept referring to her by name.

Which suitcase is yours?

Scared, confused and still recovering from the meds she'd taken, all Marilyn wanted to do was crumple in a heap on the floor and sob.

His hand came up to cup her cheek. Its cool, solid strength startled her as his thumb brushed across her bottom lip.

Marilyn. Your life is in danger…that is all I know. I've been sent to keep you safe. Please tell me, which suitcase is yours.

"The large black, rolling case over there," she whispered aloud against the pad of his stroking thumb, pointing to the case just making the first turn.

Locking her wrist in his grasp tighter than any pair of handcuffs, he pulled her along behind him. She was about to protest when she sensed eyes on her from the few remaining passengers. A prickling sensation crawled up her spine. They approached, closing in on her. Turning around to flee, she saw a gaggle of blond groupies dressed in varying degrees of designer clothing approach. Fangs elongated as they opened their mouths, and the sound of a hundred snakes hissing erupted from them.

Draylon saw them too. She could hear his fierce hiss under his breath as he eyed them with territorial menace. Letting go of her wrist, he leapt at the leader of the group with graceful force. A sharp set of blades emerged from the cuffs of his sleeves. He tore across the face of their would-be attacker. Black blood spurted from his cheek, leaving him screaming in agony. Another leapt at them and Draylon went for his gut, shoving the blades through to the fanged creature's back.

While Draylon fought through the group, Marilyn ended up shackled in the unrelenting arms of two hissing women, their mouths opened and ready to devour her with ferocious looking fangs.

What the hell?

But before she could react, the two women dissolved into a smoking pile of ash at her feet. Frightened, Marilyn grabbed her suitcase and headed for the doors, letting Draylon handle the rest of the hissing, spitting mass of fanged-gothic humans. She needed to leave, get back to reality.

At the door, two more creatures jumped into her path. She took a step back, but they reached out and grabbed her arms only to explode like small firecrackers on the Fourth of July.

Freaked out she ran, trailing her rolling suitcase. She

made it to the arrival area where only a few taxis waited to take passengers to their destination.

"Miss Reddlin?"

A young man stepped forward to greet her. His dark suit contrasted with his blond hair and silver eyes.

"Yes?" She gasped for air, catching her breath as well as her nerves.

"I'm Mr. Vamier's driver. He wished for me to pick you up."

"Oh. Thank you!" Relief flooded through her as she stepped forward to let him help her with her luggage. Their hands touched. His perfect blond features disintegrated like sand through a sieve until only grains remained at her feet.

She screamed and took a step back as the wind whipped his remains helter-skelter. A hand grabbed for her, and she squealed in fright. Draylon. He looked from her to the pile of ash at the edge of the curb near the open black tinted sedan.

Before either one could move, another group of blond haired vamps ran up the sidewalk towards them. This *had* to be some drug induced freaking nightmare. Doc Johnston would have a helluva lot of explaining to do when she called home.

"Get in!" Draylon yelled, shoving her into the front seat and tossing her luggage into the back. She watched, stunned as he appeared to fly across the hood of the car, his great leather duster jacket opening as he did so. He got in the driver seat and ripped the manual transmission from park to first gear, peeling out into congested traffic, nearly running head first into the front end of a bus as it pulled out into their lane.

Marilyn couldn't look. "Are you nuts?"

"Put your seatbelt on. Things might get a bit touchy."

Avoiding the empty passenger bus by a hair, Marilyn turned around to see not one but three darkened sedans like theirs barreling down on them as they jockeyed around another innocent car. The driver blew his horn at them.

Her heart raced. She fumbled with her seatbelt, fighting to secure herself in the crazy ride. Her cell phone rang. Crap! She hadn't had time to call her mother. Retrieving her phone from her pocket, she fought her panic to alleviate her mother's fears, but right now she wasn't sure how she could alleviate her own.

Draylon grabbed her cell phone and tossed it out the window. She watched the slip of silver technology skim across the pavement, sparking and flipping until it smashed to smithereens under the tires of one of the cars chasing them.

"That was my mother calling! She's going to be pissed."

"Would you rather she be pissed that your phone is gone or pissed because you're dead?"

She couldn't think of anything to say, so she said the only thing that came to mind. "Screw you and the horse you *didn't* ride in on. I was fine until you came into my life."

"You've never had a life to be fine or otherwise," he muttered before his attention went back to the road and an oncoming car.

Marilyn covered her eyes. Peeking between her fingers, she saw the two sedans pull up along the sides, sandwiching them. Both cars tried to slam into them at the same time. Screaming, she just wanted to wake up.

Seconds later the car on the left swerved to avoid a head on collision with an oncoming semi-truck. Draylon turned the steering wheel hard right, ramming the other car off the road, into a shallow ravine.

There was still one more car.

"Nope...we have more." Draylon had read her thoughts, and she turned around to see he was right.

One revved up, keeping pace with them. Barely missing the on-coming car, the driver launched over them, taking a flying, Hollywood stunt car leap and landing upside down in front of them like an Acme anvil in a Looney Tunes cartoon caper.

Draylon veered at the last minute, flooring the gas to avoid running into the upside down mangled mass of metal. The closest car tailing them hit it head on and spun out of control, doing wild donuts across the highway and into a ravine.

"Why aren't they shooting at us? They're just chasing us."

"They don't want you dead...they just want you."

"Who?"

"Moroii...vampires, Vamier's goons."

"Why?"

"Hell if I know. I'm just following orders. Unlike you."

"Orders from whom?" She glared at him. She'd had enough of this roller coaster dream and wanted off. "Pull over."

To Marilyn's shock, he did. Draylon turned the steering wheel hard left as if trying to do a NASCAR spin in the winner's circle and slammed on the brakes.

The other car rammed into them, whiplashing Marilyn towards the veneer dash. The car's airbags went off. She was amazed to still be alive, uninjured in what should have been a catastrophic accident. Damn. She'd wanted adventure in her life, but this was too extreme.

Draylon ripped off the crumpled driver's door, uninjured and unfazed. He walked up to the driver's door of the other car, which had steam and smoke billowing out from its hood. Marilyn couldn't see much through all the humid mist, but Draylon pulled the driver out by his shirt front and beat the shit out of him.

The screech of ripping metal had her screaming again. Her passenger door ripped from its crumpled hinges. Gloved hands grabbed her and pulled her out, holding her with his arm around her throat.

"I'll take her!" The man next to her ear yelled across the night at Draylon as he lowered his mouth towards her throat. Marilyn could hear the hiss of his breath so close to her ear.

Why wasn't this guy crumbling into a pile of ash like the others had? *This wasn't happening. Oh God, just let me wake up, please.*

"Aiden would kill you," Draylon's said as if this wasn't an odd occurrence at all. The body he'd been beating against the car dropped to the ground.

"He'll never know."

Duck, Marilyn.

She obeyed the muted echo of Draylon's calm voice in her head. Feinting into the man he fumbled with her body to hold her dead weight and lowered her.

Free of his grip, she ran to Draylon's side. Better to be with the stranger you did know than one you didn't. Burying her face against his leather jacket, she inhaled his scent, the one she couldn't describe. It was him. The fragrance relaxed her over taxed, trauma induced senses. His arm came around her protectively, and he kissed the top of her head as if to comfort a frightened child, just a simple reassuring gesture, nothing more.

"We don't have much time." He gave her a gentle nudge. Going over to the car, he ripped off the crumpled back passenger door to retrieve her luggage. "We need to leave now."

Marilyn stood there in shock at Draylon's strength. It could have been the adrenaline rush making him so strong.

"Come on. We haven't got all night. It's not going to take long before the others recover enough and come looking for us."

She nodded, running towards him, stopping long enough to pat her coat and make sure her purse was still securely around her.

The toe of her boot caught on something, and she tripped over the leering face of her earlier abductor—just his head lay there, in front of her like the popped-off head of a Malibu Ken doll her friend Tina had in their youth.

Screaming, she held her mouth to keep from being sick as she tried to scramble away.

Draylon reached out to grab her.

"Oh my God. His head...y...you...he..."

"You can't kill a Vamier any other way. Severing their heads is the only way they die."

Marilyn found his lack of remorse and shock appalling. "You killed him."

"I killed them both. Otherwise you would either be in a shit load of trouble or on your way to a shit load of trouble. I made a promise to keep you safe...I don't fail."

"Who are you?" She backed up, shaking her head. She still didn't know who or what he was, or what these fanged freaks were.

Draylon cursed, raking his fingers through his hair. "I'll explain everything when I get you to safety. Right now...we are a little rushed." He tried to maneuver her wheeled suitcase through the brambles on the side of the road but finally gave up and carried the over forty pounds of black zippered mass over his shoulder. "Are you coming or are you going to stand here with the decapitated bodies? I don't really want to wait for another Vamier to come by and make me decapitate him too."

In a trance she stepped around the bodies and heads to take Draylon's proffered hand, helping her up the slight embankment into the night along the other side of the road.

"Where are you taking me?"

"Some place safe."

"Where is that?" Somehow she couldn't imagine any place that would be safe right now.

Draylon's head tilted down, and the wisp of dark hair covered his right eye. His teeth gleamed pearlescent in the dark as a devilish grin peeked out from his curled lips.

"Have you ever had tea with a witch?"

#

Rick Delvante had some explaining to do.

Who in the hell was Marilyn Reddlin, and why was she in danger from Aiden Vamier? He knew she had to be related to Diane Reddlin, the CFO of Livedel, but 'the bitch from Hell' was human. The Dacian clan tried not to associate with humans unless the mortals were in need of protection from Vamier's vampires.

But Rick had sent him on this mission. The man had never asked for anything from him ever—until now. Shit wasn't making sense.

The rough hewn chalet nestled against the outcrop of the mountainside like it had for so many generations. Marilyn looked dead on her feet from their short trek. Her shoulders slumped in exhaustion. Her hair had come out of its tightly wound knot at the base of her head and dangled in frizzy locks around her shoulders and face. She was young. There was too much immaturity in her. She hadn't come out of her shell and needed protection from the big bad world around her. It was bad enough she was so naïve. He knew it, could sense it. But to have Aiden's moroii tailing her, trying to abduct her…she needed his protection. He snorted. And she thought this was all a drug induced dream?

Still, he liked her gumption and sass. She could give as well as she got. With some professional training she might even make a good Shield, a personal immortal protector, if she ever wanted a job.

Marilyn continued to glance over her shoulder, looking for danger. She hadn't spoken or complained since they'd hoofed it. Even having been through so much in the past few hours, not only was she still standing, she'd kept up with him. As confused as he knew she must be, she hadn't badgered him with any more questions. He tried to get inside her head if for nothing more than to soothe her, but she'd gathered her defenses and the mental block she'd thrown up had him mystified. No woman had ever been able to block his probing.

"Where are we?" she finally asked.

"Nonni's." He picked up his pace again, opening the wooden gate that fenced in the yard. "We'll be safe here for awhile until I figure out what I'm supposed to do with you."

Marilyn glared at him but held her tongue as the half door opened and an old gnarled face peeked out into the dark.

"Is that you, Draylon?" the old woman called.

"It's me, Nonni. I've brought someone with me."

Nonni looked around as she hustled them into her home. Draylon bent down to kiss the wrinkled cheek of the old woman. Nonni was ancient. No one knew how old. But then, aging was a concept his kind didn't have to dwell on.

The heavy wooden door creaked shut behind them. Nonni replaced both the top and bottom part of the door and secured a wrought iron bar across the entrance, blocking all the elements from the cottage and any danger that might try to come in.

"You did not bring the Vamiers with you, Dray?" She eyed him.

"No, ma'am."

She didn't say anything more but turned to Marilyn and studied her for long moments, beginning to walk away and then turning and examining her again as if she were going to change her appearance if she turned away too long.

Draylon fought not to burst out laughing as Marilyn shied away, took a step forward when she thought it was safe, only to have the old woman turn on her again. It was bad enough he'd told Marilyn that Nonni was a witch.

"Come…eat."

"I'm not hungry…" Marilyn said.

Shit.

Draylon learned long ago it was best not to argue with Nonni. If she told you to do something, you did it. No questions asked, no disagreement.

Nonni turned on Marilyn, sending her backing into him. "I did not ask if you were hungry. I said 'eat.'"

Draylon nuzzled her ear. "It's okay. Do as Nonni says."

Marilyn nodded and they followed the old woman to the grand table in the middle of the chalet and sat.

Nonni still cooked on the hearth of the stone fireplace that took up the whole side of the house. He'd bought her a wood burning stove/oven combination to cook with nearly a century ago. She used it occasionally but preferred cooking over her open fire. The heavy oak table still held its rustic authenticity. Marks and nicks marred the stained wood. Two rough hewn logs split into two separate lengths created matching benches supporting up to eight guests on each side and two massive arm chairs dominated the ends. There was a reason for such a table. One never knew when guests would show up at Nonni's.

The rest of the interior was as massive. Two wolves lay sleeping on the braided rag rug near the other fireplace. Even their huge forms were dwarfed by their surroundings. The furniture, rustic as it was with its rough hewn logs and twine for frame work, were cozy and comfortable with their over-stuffed, goose down cushions.

There was no electricity in the house. Nonni didn't believe in it. Electricity was the work of Satan. It made man lazy and domestic. What was good a thousand years ago was still good today, was her motto.

Draylon was thankful tonight wasn't as busy at Nonni's. He could deal with the two pups.

"Here—eat. You are too skinny. You must eat to prepare

for your journey."

"My journey? I'm not going anywhere. I'm supposed to meet with Professor Vamier in Cluj."

Draylon gritted his teeth against what was about to happen. Though he couldn't read Nonni's thoughts, he knew what she thought.

Petite and wrinkled old lady that she was, Nonni had a temper that would make the devil whisper, "Oh shit—she's pissed."

Nonni got in Marilyn's face to spout ancient Dacian. Cringing and flinching, Draylon knew what every word meant. And Nonni wasn't heaping "happiness and joy" on the brunette. Then Nonni got in his face, shaking her crooked finger fractions of an inch away from his nose then punctuating her irritation with that same finger in his chest.

All he could do was nod his head in agreement and back up until the solid wall was behind him. If a four foot-six inch woman could make any man feel smaller—she would be the one to do it.

"Nonni, I'm just the messenger…no, I'm not letting her go with Vamier…Rick warned me…I know, I know."

Nonni spoke heatedly to Marilyn, first talking about her lack of manners and then laying down the law to her. But Marilyn stood her ground. Draylon couldn't read her mind. That thick blanket continued to block him from her inner thoughts. Then he thought he heard a low throaty growl come from her. It never burst forth from her mouth but it was there.

Nonni stopped, mid curse and lowered her finger. Her eyes widened, at first with shock and then interest and then a sudden calm broke over the old woman. Her eyes closed, chanting something Draylon couldn't understand. Opening her eyes, Nonni relaxed and walked away.

"What the hell?"

"Who's got Nonni in a tiff? I'll kill 'em."

Two naked men stood near the table. Draylon looked at the floor where the two wolves *had* been sleeping.

"Relax Ren, you don't need to kill anyone today." He looked over to see Marilyn checking out the two men's physiques. A slight pang of protectiveness clouded his vision. "Would you two go and put some clothes on. You're in the presence of a lady."

"So?" Ron, the other shrugged, making a point of crossing his meaty arms over his chest and flexing them.

Draylon took a deep breath. "Just put on some clothes."

"You gonna make me, Dray? You and whose Army?"

About to retaliate the way they always did, Draylon was shoved aside as Marilyn muscled past him. Ron and Ren's voices growled deep within their chests at her approach. Ron's eyes turned a stunning blue as his lips peeled back in a snarl.

Stepping in between the two, Marilyn squared her jaw and growled back at the naked man, setting him to back off.

The clink of something metal hitting the ground caused all of them to stop their ruckus. Draylon rushed to Nonni's side as she grabbed at her chest. Marilyn hurried over, too. She picked up the metal ladle Nonni dropped and looked to see if she could help.

"Is she okay? We need to get her to a hospital."

"No...no hospital," Nonni rasped, tossing her head from side to side. "That is where old people go to die."

Draylon supported the woman's head on his lap as she fought for breath.

"Are you sure, Nonni? You look pale and you're in pain."

"Pain is fear leaving the body...fear is gone now...time for this woman's work to be done." She nodded to Draylon. "Help me. I need to do what needs to be done."

Draylon wasn't sure that Nonni would be okay, but he helped her to stand and got her to at least sit in her rocking chair then placed a quilt around her frail body.

"Get her some water." Draylon glanced around to see the two men still standing there like naked sentries. "And damn it, would you two put some clothes on."

"I've got the water. Go get dressed," Marilyn commanded the naked twins. She leveled them a look, and her voice growled low as they tried to defy her.

Both men appeared to understand her tone. Looking at each other, they went to do her bidding. Draylon watched until they left—so did Marilyn, her eyes never leaving their retreat. Her nose twitched and her lip curled around the edges. Or was that his imagination?

Finally, she turned and pumped out a dipper of water from the hand pump fountain at the sink. Bringing it over to Nonni, she sat at the woman's feet, holding the dipper out to her as an offering.

Nonni's hands trembled as they reached out. Draylon worried about this new side to the old witch. He'd never seen her so shaken. Something passed between the older and younger woman, as if they were reading each other's thoughts. Then he saw it—whatever *it* was. Marilyn's intense stare, her eyes, turned emerald green, the rims around their fiery irises black as night. The change was only momentary and then, gone as if he'd imagined it all. He was not one to imagine anything—not when he himself was a mere creature of fantasies and folklore.

When Nonni had her fill of the water she sat back in her chair, weariness pinching her weathered features. She closed her eyes and chanted in tongues. A language he'd never witnessed her speak. It sounded ancient—like a prayer perhaps, and then she became quiet and a soft snore erupted.

Marilyn lowered the dipper and smiled. "Nonni is something else."

So are you, Draylon thought to himself. But he wasn't sure what.

Chapter Three

The room was small but tidy. The rustic wooden bed and large armoire were the main pieces of furniture and they took up most of the room. No television or any other electronics and only an oil lamp on a small bedside table gave her enough light to prepare for bed.

Glancing around, Marilyn removed her clothing and folded them. She changed into her oversized Baltimore Raven's football jersey, the only good thing she'd gotten out of her last relationship, and crawled into bed.

The half-medallion weighed heavy against her breastbone where it laid, the silver chain tangled in her hair. She didn't feel safe taking it off in the company of strangers. She rubbed the jagged edges and traced the detailed relief of the wolf's head. She knew the image intimately by touch as well as sight. The open jaws of the mighty wolf swallowing the serpentine tail of a missing beast.

It was one of the reasons she was here in Romania, to find the missing piece. On her twenty-first birthday she'd received a package from a friend of her father's. There'd been no name, no return address, just a letter explaining this had been an ancient Dacian artifact that her father had found, and he wished for her to have it when she turned twenty-one. She was to keep it a secret from everyone, but it would protect her and be the answer to her heritage.

Why would her father want her to have it? According to her mother, her father never accepted the fact she was his. Her father had accused her mother of being unfaithful because he was infertile. He'd never be able to have children. He'd left her mother claiming he'd divorce her when he returned from his trip to Romania...but he never returned.

And now she'd been sent this piece of Dacian history from a stranger who claimed *her father* wanted her to have it. This from a man who claimed she couldn't be his daughter? Maybe he'd had a change of heart at the last minute and never had the chance to apologize to her mother before he went missing. Or maybe he was still out there somewhere, hiding. But from her research into the Hoia Forest where he'd disappeared...it wasn't uncommon. People who ventured in sometimes never returned. The place held a paranormal aura that scientists were still baffled over.

Her interest in her heritage, the medallion and Romanian history in general led her to contact one of the top history/archeological professors in the country, Aiden Vamier. Her interest and the paper she'd done on Ancient Dacia and what background she knew had piqued the man's interest, and he'd offered her a chance to spend this semester, finishing her Master's Degree, learning at his side.

She never expected any of *this* to happen. What was it with exploding vampire-like creatures, wolves that morphed into naked men and Draylon Conier? She had to be in some crazy drug induced dream from the medications Jon gave her for her recent pains and sleep issues. The muscle aches, cramps and dizzy spells she suffered were too much to deal with. She'd talked to her mother about her conditions, and she'd suggested going to see Doc Johnston for an examination.

Yawning, Marilyn rolled to her side. She knew she should sleep. It was bad enough this was a dream. She didn't want to sleep within a dream and not know the difference between reality and fantasy. The press of the heavy bronze jagged edge digging into the side of her breast irritated her. Finally giving in, she slipped the chained emblem off and wrapped the necklace around the palm of her hand, lacing it through her fingers. No one would be able to take her medallion without waking her up. She wouldn't lose the only connection she had to her heritage.

#

Sunlight dappled across her face. Focusing on her surroundings, Marilyn's eyes tried to open but felt heavy, her lashes matted and crusted. Turning her head from side to side, prisms of light and pain shot behind her lids.

"Rest. Rest easy, zmeoaică."

"Thirsty…" Marilyn mumbled.

Cool water dribbled past her parched lips. Nothing ever tasted so good.

"You've been on a long journey, my friend," the kind voice whispered. "I knew you would come eventually. But your journey is not over."

A door creaked open and the bed weighted down. Wet snouts burrowed beneath her hands. She rubbed their noses.

"Get those two mutts off the bed, Nonni. They don't need to be up there."

The heavy male voice sounded familiar. If only she could remember …

"They are fine, Draylon. They are not hurting anyone—except you."

There was silence but Marilyn picked up on troubled thoughts. Not hers but someone else's.

"How is she, Nonni?"

"Her fever broke this morning. But she is still weak."

Nonni. She'd heard the name recently...yes? She couldn't remember and thinking caused her head to pound. She inhaled the spicy musk to calm the thumping. It reminded her of something...no, someone.

"All right, all right—" the woman stated with exasperation, "Therron, Kurren...shoo! Go sleep by the fire."

The weight by her side shifted and was replaced by a different weight. A hand brushed a strand of hair out of her face. A finger swept along her cheek.

"Are you sure she is going to be okay?"

"Yes. She's young and healthy—just adjusting to...things, Draylon."

Ah, Draylon! Yes, she remembered the name.

"But she's been sick for two days. It can't be jet lag. There is no fever with jet lag. Something is not right, Nonni. I'm calling Rick."

"No!"

The outburst from Nonni brought her awake, peeling her burning eyelids open. She watched as the old woman and the young man dressed in black stared holes in the other.

"He wouldn't know what to do with her. She's a woman. Besides, if you think Therron and Kurren are an issue, what do you suppose putting her in the wolves' den would do? No, she must be kept safe...and away from others."

"What do you purpose then? Keep her here?"

"No, she won't be safe here for long. Vamier would find her. You know what you must do. Follow your natural instincts."

Marilyn couldn't make out his mumbled words. She was so tired and weak. What was wrong with her? She heard the door open and close and sensed that Draylon had left. Nonni returned to her side and smiled a toothless grin down at her.

"He is so old but so young, too. But you will show him

the way."

What was she talking about? She spoke in English but what she said didn't make sense to her. She raised her hand only to have it drop across her chest. Chest…hand…her medallion! Panic set in.

Nonni gentled her. "It is safe within your belongings, my child." A cool cloth fell across her heated forehead. "You must have a care with it, though. It must not fall into the wrong hands. Keep it on you at all times when you leave. Keep it close to your heart, and it will lead you home."

More nonsense and riddles. Her brain wasn't equipped with enough neurons to figure out what she said. She sensed her brain working, keeping her inner organs alive. But using it for thinking or focus drained her completely.

"Rest…rest, zmeoaică. You will be home soon."

#

Follow my natural instincts? The one thing about the old woman was she talked in riddles and Draylon didn't always have time to figure them out. If he could just have someone tell him what he had to do, he'd do it. Someone like Rick. Rick always gave it to him straight. He knew where he stood with his old friend.

Rick Delvante had saved his life many years ago. During a battle in which his family had been destroyed, Rick had found him and nursed him back to health. He owed the man and promised to find a way to pay him back. But the man never accepted his offers over the centuries…not until three days ago when he sent him to intercept Marilyn Reddlin and keep her from getting to Aiden Vamier.

What was it about this young woman? Why after centuries of strife, wars and issues Draylon could've taken care of for Rick, why was it now—and with this woman?

Okay, she was the daughter of the most influential executives at Livedel, Rick Delvante's medical research facility. He'd heard about Diane Reddlin. No wonder Marilyn had issues. If she had Diane for a mother, it was a wonder the girl could think for herself. He'd heard the woman ate testicles for a mid-morning snack and washed them down with the blood of every man she'd bested behind the desk. Rumor had it she even had the United States Senate and half the Representatives by the gonads. She ate, breathed and pissed power but because of her, Livedel was the dominant international industry it had become in the past couple of decades.

Rick needed him to keep Marilyn from Romania. She needed to go home then. She'd refused him, wouldn't follow his command, verbal or telepathic. Something told him she still wouldn't listen to him. But right now, she was weak and vulnerable. With Vamier's goons hunting her down she wouldn't be safe. His instincts told him she needed to get back home, away from the immediate danger. That is what Rick wanted. Draylon knew what he had to do.

#

"What do you mean she's gone?" Aiden Vamier bellowed from behind his ornate desk.

Gerlich smirked. All he could think of was, "Another One Bites the Dust" as Trevor faced the music. What a putz! The idiot couldn't handle a simple female and bring her in?

"My lord, we had every one of the sentries out, but we were intercepted."

"Intercepted by whom? No one is capable of getting in our way."

Fool. Who do you think? Gerlich didn't need to put two and two together. He knew Aiden didn't either but still, playing dumb didn't make him a great leader. The man lived in a different world. He only saw what he wanted. He never looked to a bigger picture.

"Draylon Conier, my lord."

Aiden rubbed his smooth shaven face. The man was older than Moses by a decade or two, but he still looked like the fresh faced punk who had changed his world with a sword and ego.

"What does my brother's 'pet' want with the girl?" He stopped rubbing his face and stood to stalk down the three steps from his grand "office."

Vamier believed in power...the higher, the fewer. He thought having a desk, a dining table, a bed, a castle, higher than anyone else made him more powerful. He was no better than the Wizard of Oz, only here everyone paid attention to the "man behind the curtain."

"I...I...don't know, my lord," Trevor stuttered.

Gerlich stood at attention, wishing he could see better peripherally without losing his militant bearing. He lived for moments like this.

"You mean to tell me twenty of you were stationed at various posts waiting for her at the airport and not a single one of your sentries nabbed her. Was Draylon alone, or did he have those mangy wolves with him?"

"He was...alone, my lord." Trevor's voice quaked.

The inevitable is upon you, shit for brains. Suck up your last breath while you can.

"Alone." Aiden paced back and forth in front of them, his head down, his hands clasped behind his back.

The deadly calm signaled the approaching storm. Gerlich had seen it too many times.

"I don't think I understand. Did he take every one of my troops out by himself? Was there some sort of mass command of destruction he used? What?"

"No, my lord...it was the girl. She was untouchable."

Their leader stopped in front of Trevor, the blue vein popping out of his forehead, contrasting with his golden hair. His nostrils flared with disapproval. "I want to question the rest of your personnel."

"There…there is no one left, my lord. Devon and I are the only remaining. We were only injured in a car accident, the rest were either killed by Draylon or…"

"…or?"

"Or they turned to ash upon touching Ms. Reddlin, my lord."

Gerlich sobered. What? His shock had him almost lose his military bearing…almost. But the look on Aiden's face was frightening. He hadn't seen such a look in a man's eye since he had been with the SS back in Germany during World War II. It was evil and hungry, hungry for power just out of his grasp, and he'd be willing to sell his soul to Hades to get it.

The man smiled and took Trevor's face between his palms in a slap. "Trevor, Trevor, Trevor…that is such wonderful news. Good job."

Gerlich prepared himself but loved the sound of a fellow unit leader gasping his last breath as he tried to scream. Such a messy thing, but it brought him closer to the power he wanted for himself.

The thud of Trevor's lifeless remains echoed through the cavernous room. Still, Gerlich stood at attention until he was addressed. Aiden came into his frontal view, his lips and lower jaw coated with the red/black blood of his former unit leader.

"You are now in command Gerlich."

"My lord," he hailed in response, clicking his heels together.

"You Nazi boys always had a spark to you."

Aiden took out a pristine white handkerchief from his Armani suit pocket and dabbed at the blood on his face.

"I want you to prepare the other unit leaders to go into the battle fields for more recruits."

"Yes, my lord. Will that be all?"

"Then return to the United States and oversee the work

being done at the blood banks. You are now in charge over there."

"Do you wish me to do anything about Ms. Reddlin, my lord?"

Aiden sighed, his breath rasping in and out through his nose. "No, not just yet. I'll let you know when I change your tasks."

"Yes, my lord."

"Oh and Gerlich, have someone dispose of Trevor's remains and clean up the pool of blood. It stains the marble floor if it sits too long."

"Of course, my lord, right away." He clicked his heels and turned about face to do his master's bidding. What Aiden didn't see was the determined smile on Gerlich's face. He had grand intentions to move up the chain of command and take over...everything.

#

Diane Reddlin had been pushed far enough. She hadn't heard from her daughter since their phone connection had been cut over two days ago. Having exhausted all of her diplomatic connections in every country, and even insisting the president send out Navy SEALs to search for her daughter—even though she had no idea where to send them—she was at her wits end.

She hadn't been home in days. There were too many memories and reminders. It was worse than losing Richard all those years ago. At least she'd had Marilyn to raise and protect. Now she was alone.

Rubbing her gritty eyes, her mascara smeared on the backs of her knuckles, she looked over at the emergency phone again. She didn't want to have to rely on him. Rick Delvante may be her boss, but she had carte blanche to run the show as she saw fit. As long as profits were made, new contracts arranged and everyone remained happy, he never questioned her abilities to run his operation.

Though she'd never met the man, he had his finger on every pulse point of the business. He knew everything that went on. Sometimes she felt as if he had spies keeping an eye out for him. It amazed her when he would call her up out of the blue before she'd gotten recent reports out to him, already informed on the situations.

Biting her lip, she set her shoulders. This wasn't about business, this was about her daughter. He had informed her, years ago, that if she ever needed anything, for her or her daughter that all she had to do was call him on this phone. She'd never had to do so. But she was at her last hope.

"Yes, how may I help you?"

She hadn't even dialed. This was his private phone she'd picked up but it was a woman's voice. His wife maybe?

"Um…yes." She took a steadying breath. "I'm looking for Mr. Rick Delvante."

"Of course, Ms. Reddlin—I'll put you right through."

Okay, personal receptionist.

"Diane? What's wrong? You've never called this phone."

"I've never had to, sir." She could feel the sharp edge of emotion trying to battle its way up her throat. "I'm desperate though, and I don't know what else to do."

It was true. She'd never needed to rely on anyone, and now she had to rely on the one man who had made her what she was today.

"That's why I told you to use this number whenever you had an issue concerning you or Marilyn."

There was no doubt the man knew everyone's name. He was after all, Rick Delvante.

"So how may I help you?"

"It's…it's my daughter, Marilyn. I haven't been able to contact her for a few days, since she went to Romania. I'm afraid something has happened to her. I've tried every embassy, consulate and diplomatic connection I have and either no one can help me, or they haven't even tried. I'm calling you as my last hope."

"I want you to stay strong, Diane. I'm sure she is fine," his voice soothed. "In the meantime, I need you to send me all of her most recent information, copy of passport, credit cards, and most recent photo. You've got to trust me. I'll find her. I'll keep you posted on a regular basis."

"Please, if there is anything I can do…" Diane sobbed. Talking about her daughter got to her.

"I want you to relax and let me take care of you. We'll find her, Diane…I promise to you with all my heart, she'll be safe."

Chapter Four

"Why don't I just send her back home to the states?"

"You mustn't. That is the first place Vamier would look. Besides, Trevor is his lackey. Do you want that scum to get his hands on her?"

"Hell no."

Marilyn woke up to a heated discussion on the other side of the door. She'd had enough of this. Why wouldn't they just let her be? All she wanted to do was get to Professor Vamier and begin her studies. She had no contact with her mother or anyway to contact the professor with her phone gone. That was why she was here. She wasn't going home or anywhere until she had answers.

Tossing back the covers, she realized she was naked. Panic set in, and she snarled with frustration.

"Where are my clothes?" she called.

The door opened to reveal Nonni and Draylon standing there. Nonni stepped inside.

"Draylon, wait out in the other room…"

He didn't budge, just stared at her as if he'd never seen a woman in bed. Marilyn could only imagine what she looked like right now. When was the last time she'd showered or brushed her hair? Images of her as a wild, hot mess in front of strangers raised an unusual level of anger in her. To have them stare at her in such a state set off a defensive, adrenaline rush within her that had her wanting to attack.

"Draylon…now!" Nonni commanded.

Marilyn leapt out of the bed with a wild burst of energy and raced towards Draylon to attack. Before she could get to him though, Nonni slammed the door and backed away from her. *I have your things, zmeoaică. You have nothing to fear.*

The woman's mouth never moved, but Marilyn heard her speak the words.

My name is Marilyn.

Zmeoaică is who you truly are. You've come home. After so long, you have returned. It's just as Zamolxis ordained.

Nonni made no sense to her. Nothing made sense to her. She ached, worse than when she'd gone to see Doc Johnston. Muscles tightened in her arms and legs, muscles she never knew existed. They'd developed over night. She could see their definition. Marilyn's face felt swollen and dry, her head hurt and her eyes burned. Without any mirrors in the room, she couldn't see what was happening to her or how she looked. She'd moved too fast, the room spun and nausea threatened her stomach. She sat back down on the edge of the bed, trying to get her body and thoughts together.

"I want my things, Nonni…please."

"Do you promise not to leave?"

"If it's the only way to get my things back…I won't leave, yet." She looked up from beneath her wild mass of knotted hair.

Nonni tried not to crack a smile but the toothless grin came out anyway. "I get your things. We talk. No men—I send them away."

Mentally Marilyn felt better when Nonni brought in her

clothes, laundered and fresh. The woman had her sit in the
rustic, straight back chair near the washbasin as she applied a
soothing balm to her arms and legs to help with the aches.
After she dressed in jeans and a sweater, Nonni brushed out
her hair, applying a sweet, berry scented serum to smooth out
the knots. Marilyn let her run the boar-bristled brush through
the tangled mass. She still felt naked though. Her hand
instantly went to her throat. Her medallion was missing.

"It is safe. I tucked it away in your suitcase. It is most
impressive. Where did you get such a thing?"

"It was a gift from a friend of my father's for my twenty-
first birthday," she whispered.

"A gift, from your father's friend? Why did your father
not give it to you?"

"I never met my father. He went missing before I was
born."

"How sad for you. What did your father do?" Nonni asked
as she plaited her hair into a thick braid.

"He was a Romanian archeologist working for the
Smithsonian. He was well known and went on various digs
around the world, but he always loved the history and artifacts
from here." Marilyn turned to view Nonni. "I read some of his
papers and became as fascinated by the history as he'd been—
much to my mother's dismay."

"And your father? Who was this man?"

"Richard Reddlin."

Nonni stopped braiding momentarily as she appeared to
ponder the thought of her father then returned to braiding her
hair. Nothing in her features showed Nonni had any
recollection of the name.

Marilyn tried another tactic. "You said you wanted to
talk…without the men. Did you send them away?"

The old woman nodded. "We talk. You and me. I fix
tea…come."

#

As warm and inviting as the large cottage appeared, Marilyn shivered with a chill of anxiety. Something wasn't right with any of this, but out of all the issues she'd encountered, which one bothered her the most? All of them.

"Sit. Sit. I make tea with honey."

Nonni motioned for her to sit at the table. She studied the old wooden beams that supported the house and rafters. Stone, wood and brick with white plaster made up the interior. The windows were arched with red brick and the plastered walls were thick enough to keep out all sorts of elements. There were no vents for central air, no old radiators for heating, only fireplaces and wood burning stoves to take out the chill.

She knew asking for internet connection to contact her mother via social media or email was useless. If the old woman didn't have electricity, she sure as hell didn't have wireless connection.

"I don't believe in the work of aghiută." She spat on the floor. "The devil, he make man lazy and tame."

Nonni could read her thoughts?

"Yes. Did Draylon not tell you of my gifts? I am strega…a witch."

"I never believed in it—other than following ancient teachings. It was always referred to as a derogatory term."

Nonni looked confused for a moment as the words seemed unfamiliar. "Ah! A bad name." She nodded. "I've been called all things. No one bothers me. I keep to myself."

Placing the pot of tea on the table, she sat in the chair on the end, nearest the kitchen hearth. Marilyn took the initiative to pour the steaming brew into their delicate cups. She smiled. The china appeared out of place in such a rustic setting. But the aroma of sweet rooibos and honey made all of Marilyn's cares vanish.

"Drink. You like." Nonni motioned for her to drink.

They sipped in silence for a few moments, letting the flowery taste of the tea seep into their blood stream and warm them internally. Hints of orange and cinnamon blended with the honey. For the time being, Marilyn didn't have a care. The aches in her muscles dispersed and the warmth of the tea, the aroma of the burning firewood, it all settled into her soul, warming it from the inside. Still, the unknown fear lingered of what was outside that heavy door.

"There is no need to fear. Draylon will protect you with his life."

Accepting the fact Nonni would read her thoughts, the difficult part would be controlling them. "Why? I don't even know him. And since we've been together he's tried to abduct me, we've been chased by vampires and threatened to be made into one. I think I was safer before we met."

"He was sent to protect you at all cost."

"I don't need a bodyguard…or at least I didn't think I needed one. I came to Romania for research. Mr. Vamier offered me the opportunity to be his personal assistant this semester."

Nonni shook her head. "He is not to be trusted. He is bad. He will not lead you to the truth. He is only after what you have."

Marilyn snorted. Like Daniel? Her mother had set her up with a congressman's son. He was always polite around her mother, well-mannered, loving, sweet and attentive. She should have listened to Tina when her friend told her there was something about him she didn't like.

Their relationship was hot and cold to begin. He'd managed to convince her to transfer from Hood College down to Towson to be near him. She did so just to get out from under her mother's thumb. But she'd never seen him in his natural habitat before arriving on campus. He liked to party, skipped classes and expected her to bail him out when he was either too drunk or needed a paper done overnight.

He only showed affection around their friends and family—until their last night together. She never did tell her mother the truth. Marilyn shivered as a chill shot down her spine and disgust curled her lip.

She tried to focus on Nonni and the conversation.

"...he not good for you." Nonni spat at the floor. "You need better. Draylon is a good man. He protect you."

"Why?" Marilyn looked up at Nonni whose small beady eyes glowed with knowledge. "Because it is meant to be."

"Really? I don't think so. I'm not here for a man, Nonni. I'm here to find myself."

Nonni sat back and sighed, nodding in understanding. "There was a woman I knew once, she wanted same thing. She left her home far, far away and came to a strange land to see what it might be like away from home. She fell in love while finding her way—only it wasn't the right way—she'd chosen the wrong way. Not only did it affect her life but those of a whole race of people...and Zmei."

"Z-what?"

Nonni cackled. "Zmei. Ah...you have not heard, and yet you have the very emblem of their kind."

Marilyn thought about her medallion. "The wolf or the serpent?"

The old woman's eyes rounded. "Oh no. So much more than a bălaur or hound! They shift-shapes..."

"They're 'shape-shifters'?" Marilyn corrected in awe.

"Yes...yes. Bălaur is their true shape but not always so. They fly and are much powerful, sometimes turning into fire to slip into a young woman's room, turning *musat*, handsome...oh so handsome, as a man and to seduce her to become his mate."

"They are evil then."

"Eh," Nonni struggled for the right term,

"misunderstood."

"So you are telling me these *Zmei* exist?"

"Once a long time ago. Now, all gone…except one."

Marilyn sat forward, the steam from her cup of tea warming her face. This was like some of the fantastical stories she'd read in her father's papers. Fascinated, she wanted more.

"He lives still. But he is so very old. His home is all but forgotten by time, but it still is a sacred place in the high mountains of the Suhard Massif."

"What happened to them? Why is there only one left?"

Nonni sat back in her chair and closed her eyes. When she opened them there was a far-away look about her.

Anxious to hear more, Marilyn pushed her cup to the side so she wouldn't spill it in her excitement. She loved stories like this. History and folklore went hand in hand. If she had more information about the tales then she'd have a better understanding of the mystical people her father wrote about in his papers.

"A long time ago, back before the Romans came, the Dacian were a warrior race of people. We battled against all foe who dared to cross our rivers. The Danube was a boundary to many tribes from other countries. Our forests, so dark and full of wild and mystical beings, no one dared to enter.

"Every battle we fought was beside our brethren Zmei— the creatures the gods had gifted to our people for protection. In exchange for the Zmei help they requested one young maiden every decade for their token bride. The women were of special birth, prepared and blessed to take on the role when the time came. An honor, a true calling, something the Dacian celebrated."

Nonni got up from her chair. Her head bowed and weary, she shuffled slowly into the kitchen. Pouring golden meal into a large, black pot hanging from an iron rod in the fireplace she stirred in a pitcher of cream.

Don't stop.

"You are hungry. You need to eat. I make mămăligă."

Marilyn wasn't hungry, not for food. She wanted more details. She hated movie sequels because she didn't like to wait to find out the next chapter in the story. And she had no idea what mămăligă was. But Nonni wasn't one to be rushed.

She drank her tea and poured herself another cup. Nonni had only taken a few sips, so she left hers alone. The howling of wind rattled the windowpanes in the kitchen and whistled through the cracks around the door.

"Ah…ală works his magic, too. He's the beast who brings the viscol—winterstorms." She stirred the bubbling pot. "Do you hear his cries? Not to worry, he won't get in."

"But Draylon and the other men are out there. Aren't you worried about them?"

Nonni waved her hand. "They are fine. They go to their watering holes to drink and raise a fuss. They are good boys, though."

Worried, Marilyn didn't want to put up with more guys who partied and drank. She had a feeling it was a male norm though. She'd have to deal with it again, sooner or later.

She watched as Nonni ladled out thick gruel into their bowls and placed sliced bread onto a board. Getting up, she went to help the tiny woman bring the simple fare to the table. Sniffing the bowls, she realized it was corn meal mush. Her nanny, Francis, used to make it.

A jar of honey and maple syrup was placed before her, along with whipped honey butter. Her stomach growled.

"See, you are hungry! Two days sick in bed with nothing but broth—you must eat."

"I've been here two days?"

"Much fever and tired."

Two days? She'd lost so much time and what did her mother think? She must be going out of her mind! The one person who didn't want her to leave was now without a clue where her daughter was. That made two of them. *She* didn't know where she was. She figured she was still in Romania though.

Delving into her sweetened cereal, she cleaned the bowl in little time. Nonni filled it again, her toothless smile happy. Marilyn slathered a thick slice of crusty bread with butter and honey while she waited for Nonni's return to the table.

"So tell me more about the Zmei."

"Oh yes! Where was I?"

"Women were trained to be wives of the Zmei…"

Nodding, Nonni picked up the story. "As I said, very honorable to be chosen as a Zmei mate. Until the young lady who'd left home had been chosen and rebelled. She'd fallen in love with another who was of good birth—but not good. He was false."

"So they married instead?"

"No. She was forced to marry the Zmeu. He was kind and treated her well as all Zmei did. She was the honored one. She loved him and honored her Zmei mate, but she always wondered about her lost love. He promised he'd come for her."

"But he didn't? Did he?"

"Oh yes, he came for her—along with hundreds of men he'd gathered. But it wasn't for her alone…it was for power and glory. His troops rushed into the Zmei fortress and slaughtered every one of them, taking the woman with him as his own. Devastated at seeing such a massacre—on her behalf—she cried for days. When the Dacian tribes found out about the Zmei, they shouted to the gods to curse the evil ones. The gods heard and instead of cursing just the couple—they were so angry that their gift of the precious Zmei had been destroyed, they cursed all the clans."

"Oh no."

"It was terrible. They were no longer to be warriors but hunters, hunters of the night. The Dacian baier of the Zmei and the Wolf was broken—the talisman separated forever by their betrayal. The Dacians would become wolves and live off of the land as beasts of the night. The goddess of fertility—she turned the Dacian—sterp, barren, infertile.

The men who killed the Zmei were to become another entity all together. They were cursed by the sun god, Derzelas, and would die if they were to try to live in his light. The goddess of the hunt cursed them with never finding nourishment in the flesh of beast—only the blood of man. And the goddess of fertility she cursed them severely—they could only create more of their kind by exchange of blood for blood...at the victim's request."

"Wait, you said that there was one Zmeu left though. Where did he go?" Marilyn sat on the edge of the bench, waiting to hear more. If what Nonni told her was real then could the medallion hold some truth? Even folklore and legend held kernels of fact in them.

"So eager you are." Nonni cleared the used dishes. Marilyn went to help her, afraid she'd do something else and not tell her the rest, but the old woman continued, "There is one. Only because of a kind young prophet who went to pray over the desecrated Zmei. He found one, still alive, barely breathing. He'd turned into a human to protect the mate of the Zmei leader, but in doing so, received a nearly fatal wound. The prophet took him to his teacher, the god known as Zamolxis, and worked to heal the last of the Zmei.

The gods looked on the young prophet favorably for his kindness. They blessed him with the ability to one day mate and produce an offspring, when the time was right."

"So this Zmeu is immortal? Was he cursed?"

The wizened woman smiled. "Zmei are immortal to begin with. The Zmeu curses himself. He desires to find a mate who will accept him for what he is."

She felt sorry for the creature. Thousands of years and no real companionship. He was stuck up in a mountain like some mythical Sasquatch, biding his time.

Marilyn couldn't help but think on the whole story. So much folklore and mysticism. Did she believe any of it? She carefully dried the dishes as Nonni washed. The old woman seemed to believe. She was strega. Witches were those who believed in the past, using it to guide them. As she hung up the dishtowel, the door burst open on a gust of wind and men.

"Nonni, get Marilyn packed up. We need to leave, now."

"What's going on, Draylon?" Marilyn went to his side. The other two men were busy packing up what they could find for comfort and security. She remembered them naked the other night. But now they all looked as they were nearly torn to shreds.

"You all bleed. Sit, Nonni take care of you." The old woman hustled around for herbs and dressings.

"There isn't time, Nonni. We need to get you out of here," Therron commanded.

Marilyn noticed blood caked and some dripping from Draylon's head. She went to touch it and he grabbed her hand. "We don't have time. The Vamiers are on their way."

Ren checked a shotgun for ammunition. "They invaded the Wolves Den looking for you. When they saw Draylon, they knew you couldn't be far away."

"I'll get packed." Marilyn scurried to her room and collected her things. The suitcase would be too much of a hassle if they had to walk. She took out the knapsack she'd stowed away for mountain hiking and packed it with essential clothing and supplies. Checking the inner most pocket of her suitcase, she found the medallion. Securing it inside the vintage handkerchief Nonni had wrapped it in, she placed the medallion in the secret zippered pocket where it wouldn't be damaged or lost. All was good.

Dressed in layers and hiking boots she'd brought with her, Marilyn was as ready as she could be. She didn't know how far they would have to travel.

Nonni entered the room, dressed and ready for the twins to take her to safety. "I have something for you…for your journeys." The old woman placed a withered hand on her forehead and whispered words of a blessing or spell.

Nonni smiled up at her when she finished.

"What did you do?"

"I placed a blessing on you to protect you on your journeys," Nonni said.

"I'm going on more than one journey?"

Nonni smiled her toothless grin. "There are many

journeys in one's life…this will be one of the hardest."

Chapter Five

Trying to outrun Vamier's goons was never easy. Draylon needed to get them to the airport in Cluj. If he could get there without any Vamiers tracking him then he was good to go. He'd already called to have his plane fueled and ready. After arguing with Nonni this morning, he'd made a call to Rick. Draylon planned on taking Marilyn to the Dacian compound in the Hoia Forest—it would be the safest place, but Rick didn't agree. He said her well-being would be at stake if he brought her to Dacia.

His next best place was his home in the Austrian Alps. Built into the tallest, most secluded range he'd found over six hundred years ago, it was the closest thing to his birth home, Eskardel near Dacia. The only way in or out though—flying.

Marilyn pulled down the wool scarf she'd borrowed from Nonni. "Is Nonni going to be okay? Wouldn't the Vamiers harm her if they knew she'd have access to me?"

"The guys will take care of her. Ron and Ren won't let anything happen. They have some safe havens," Draylon replied, as they bounced along, hidden amongst the bales of hay and sacks of feed in the farmer's cart.

Draylon admired the fact Marilyn was concerned about Nonni. He wasn't sure how the two would get along. Nonni's odd reaction to her at first worried him, but when Marilyn took ill, the old woman doted on her as if she were a precious child. The old woman was predictable to a fault, and he'd never seen her so wishy-washy about someone she'd just met.

Still, Marilyn appeared to take everything in stride—so far.

A delicate hand came up to feather his hair out of his face. "I wish you'd let me take a look at your wound. Head injuries shouldn't be ignored."

Draylon shied away, not because of any pain. Her touch did things to him he'd rather not think about while trying to get to safety. It had been a dry spell for him the past decade or so and being around her had him thinking irrational thoughts. She didn't need a demon with blue balls right now.

"It'll heal. I've suffered worse."

"Not at my expense, I'm sure."

Damn, she was adorable. Bundled in layers of clothing, woolen scarf, mittens and hat she looked ready for a playful day in the snow. She'd been easy to work with when they had to make a break for it. She managed to pack practical clothing into a knapsack with the bare minimal supplies. She dressed sensible, too, thermals, denims, sweater under her heavy woolen pea coat. Her shoes of choice, hiking boots. Not the usual six-inch heels his former female acquaintances preferred.

He'd thought each one he met would be the one. When it came down to the real deal though, he had to let them go and wipe their memories of any time spent together. It was for the best.

"What are we doing? Do you even have a plan?" Marilyn asked.

"For now, staying out of sight until we get to Cluj. We

may have to walk. Are you up for the trek?"

"I hike the Appalachian Trail with my friends at least once a year. I think so."

Draylon laughed. "Good for you. Haven't done that one yet."

"You're welcome to join us this summer…if you want to…I mean…" She blushed, stammering like a schoolgirl. Her pale, freckled cheeks turned ruddy.

"I will definitely think about it. Thank you for the invitation."

Silence stretched for a moment as he studied her. She still had the awkward, coltishness about her, but the past few days of illness had transformed her a bit. Instead of being a tall, slender reed of a young lady, she'd filled out a bit. Her shoulders were broader, her figure rounder and toned. Even her hair appeared to hold more body and waves. What had Nonni done to her?

"So what do you do when you're not rescuing damsels in distress?"

"Maybe this is what I do." Draylon knew the best thing to do was keep things light and ease her into the transition she would be making.

Marilyn rolled her eyes and sighed. "Great. And here I thought I was special."

He smiled. "I'm the head of a pharmaceutical company."

"In other words, you're a drug dealer?" She backed away from him. "That's just fantastic. I feel so much safer now."

He loved seeing her riled. Something told him she wasn't one to get her dander up much. She had an all accepting side to her that as adorable as it was, sometimes made a person weak. The spark and humor in her eyes, the stand-offishness, Draylon wanted to see how far he could go but didn't want to frighten her. "All legal, I assure you. My company specializes in research and development."

"Sounds like Livedel, the company my mother works for."

"My company is a part of Livedel. We merged many years ago."

"Eskardel Pharmaceuticals?"

"You know of it?"

"Um, yeah…I'm an employee at Livedel. I deal with sales and support for all divisions."

"I thought you were a student of history?"

"I've been an intern since I was sixteen, while going to school. When I came home for semester break, I became a full-time employee. But I was supposed to be on sabbatical while finishing my degree here in Romania. Mom wasn't happy with me leaving, or studying History for that matter. She wants me to take over her position at Livedel some day." She sighed.

"Not something you want to do, I take it?"

"No. I can't see myself behind a desk, giving orders. I'm not strong enough to do that. I guess I never got that gene from my mother."

"Strength is not just hereditary. Sometimes it comes from the issues we face, what hardships we're dealt."

Marilyn shrugged. "I suppose."

An uncomfortable topic for her? He could change it. "So you know Rick Delvante, too."

"Only that I know he owns Livedel. I've never met him. I don't think many people have."

Draylon shook his head. "No, he keeps to himself for the most part. He's the one who sent me to keep you safe. Somehow he knew you were in danger being here in Europe."

"So that's who started all of this?"

He was delighted to know this young woman knew who Rick Delvante was. Not many young ladies he'd known kept up with international business—no matter how influential the business might be.

"We've been friends for awhile. He asked me to look after you and here I am."

"I'll bet Mom had something to do with it. She didn't want me to come to Romania. She all but forbade me to come here. After my father left her and went missing here in Romania, Mr. Delvante kind of took us under his wing in a way."

"Your father's missing? Who was your father?"

"Richard Reddlin. He was a Romanian archeologist. He'd gone on an expedition into the Hoia Forest to do some research and never returned. The authorities never found his remains," she relayed. "I never got to met him. He went missing before I was born. Still, I think my mother hasn't found closure since losing him."

Draylon's jaw tightened. Romanian archeologist, Hoia Forest, too coincidental or too easy putting two and two together? The Hoia Forest was where Dacia was located. If this Richard Reddlin had gotten too close to Dacia, it was a good bet the man was never heard from again. Rick would have some explaining to do when he called his friend later. Too damn coincidental to have been an accident. What had Rick done with Richard Reddlin?

#

Marilyn didn't remember the trip to Nonni's being so far the other night. But then they had driven some of it, well kind of in a demolition derby sort of way. Still, she followed Draylon through the afternoon shadows, taking back roads and occasionally seeing farmers pulling their wagons of goods into town.

It had been a blessing to be able to get off her feet. Marilyn knew she'd have blisters. So when the farmer and his wife came by with his wagon, they'd asked for a ride into Cluj. The farmer had told them he was only going as far as the hospital to get medical treatment for his wife. Had the couple stopped to show charity or had their good fortune been based on Draylon's mind manipulations? At times she sensed his thoughts, or thought she did, and then a dark wall separated her from seeing past the outer edges. She decided not to dwell on it too much. There was no way she was psychic. Still she wanted to know the truth, and he would be the one with answers.

"Why am I being hunted?"

"Right now is not the best time to discuss the issue. But I haven't a clue. What I'm more concerned about is getting you safely out of this country like I should have done from the start."

"Because Vamier wants me? For what purpose? I'm only a history student."

"Maybe there's something you know that he doesn't."

Marilyn shrugged. "My paper's cut and dry on what Dacian history I could find and what I pieced together from my father's old notes. He'd only told me he was fascinated with my theories and thought we should work together."

#

Frozen, tired and hungry, Marilyn couldn't figure out which one she suffered from more. They'd rode into Cluj in relative safety with the older couple. This was their last stop. Draylon insisted on paying them for their troubles.

"We walk from here. It's not that far."

The large wad of cash Draylon pulled out of his tote had Marilyn wondering if he was possibly a drug dealer after all. She'd never seen someone carry so much at once. The jury was still out on what she thought of him. He was sexy—sure, but that didn't necessarily mean she could trust him. Daniel had been clean cut and handsome, but he'd been a major piece of work.

No, Draylon took care of her, protected her from the vampire-like creatures over the past week and had given her shelter, even though it was within a witch's house. Part of her wondered when this bizarre dream would end.

After dealing with the farmer who they'd been traveling with, Draylon shook his hand and shouldered his backpack onto his back. The farmer argued—trying to give Draylon some of the money back. Finally, the man stopped, looked at the money and tucked it into his pocket.

Touching his hat in salute to the farmer, Draylon motioned for her to hurry. Stunned, Marilyn arranged her backpack and secured everything around her for best comfort and ran to catch up to his long strides.

"Why didn't you just do that mind-manipulation with them and leave it at that?" she asked, catching up with him.

"I didn't have to use my mind control, at least not at first. They were willing to take us to Cluj. But when he wouldn't take the money I offered, I finally persuaded him too. His wife's ill and the medical bills are piling up. I think $200 will help out, it equals about 670 Leu right now."

He shook his head. "They are a proud people…I had to do something. He'd refuse it otherwise."

Okay, Draylon's "nice factor" inched up her judgment scale. He took care of people—even those he didn't necessarily know.

"Come. I want to get us out in the open soon. I have a friend who will take us to the airport."

The hike was at least a good five miles. Marilyn followed Draylon through the city streets, taking her along open passages and high traffic areas. He'd informed her that the moroii, or what the Romanian people called "vampires," didn't want the risk of being caught in daylight—should it appear. They kept to hidden doorways and allies. So avoiding those areas were to their advantage.

Pangs of hunger cramped her stomach, and she doubled over as it gurgled.

Draylon stopped to watch her, his brows turned inward. "Are you okay?"

"Yes…I think so. Just hungry—very hungry." She shook her head. "I'm usually not one to suffer. I can go without eating for awhile. But this is painful."

"Did you eat at Nonni's?"

"Yes. I had corn meal mush and bread with honey."

He gave her a puzzled frown and nodded. "Well, we're almost there. I can see if Ballue has something to eat before we continue."

Nodding, Marilyn felt foolish for having to beg food from a stranger, but if it would help, sure.

They arrived at a large, old European façade fronted home nestled among modern day buildings and small apartment complexes. The glass in the doors and windows were old stained glass, making it church-like. The heavy oak and glass doors were decorated with antique knockers. Marilyn watched and waited for them to turn into Marley from Charles Dickens, A Christmas Carol, as Draylon lifted the heavy ring and let it fall. Just as she thought they might morph, the door creaked open and a man dressed in jeans and a black sweater ushered them in, closing the door behind them.

"Ballue." Draylon gestured to Marilyn. "This is Marilyn Reddlin."

The tall blond-haired Adonis, who looked like he would be more comfortable in a magazine shoot, leaned against the dark wall. His eyes had a strange silver gleam to them.

"Marilyn. I've heard a lot about you."

His accent was difficult to place, but it was his smile that instantly had her on guard.

"He's a moroii! Is he one of Vamier's?"

"At one time, perhaps…I managed to find my own way thankfully." Ballue straightened and led them into the darkened hall. "Come. You are safe here for now."

The hall opened up to a grand room of dark mahogany and shelves upon shelves of books lining the walls. A grand fireplace, complete with roaring fire, pulled Marilyn into its warmth. Even with all her layers the bitter cold had soaked into her bones.

"Let me make you something to drink," Ballue said.

"She would prefer something to eat…if you have food."

"I keep a freezer full of meat in case I need it. I took a couple of steaks out last night, thinking I might need them, but my groceries came in on time." He looked at Draylon before turning back to her. "Would a steak suffice?"

The sound of the word 'meat' made her saliva glands activate. She could drool all over the polished hardwood floor. No, but she might faint. The dizziness indicated low sugar levels or running on empty. But that was impossible.

"Let's go into the kitchen while I prepare it for you."

Marilyn trailed behind the two men down a short hallway into a large modern kitchen with old style charm. Nothing was pre-pressed plywood or plastic. Like Nonni's, this place exuded masculine warmth and ruggedness. The wooden beams across the ceiling looked original, the stucco plaster walls with their black iron sconces and simple candles had her thinking more along the lines of medieval castles. Only the sterling silver appliances made for a restaurant gave it away.

"Sit. I'll pour some wine and wait for the grill to heat."

Watching as Ballue took the raw steak out of the refrigerator, her eyes narrowed on his every move. He laid the plate of meat on the counter in front of the bar where she sat. The two guys weren't paying any attention to her, they were catching up on some local news. Marilyn's taste buds went crazy. The hunger deep in her stomach exploded.

Before she knew what she'd done she tore into the slab of raw meat. Juices coated her hands, running like bloody gashes from her fingers. A hand reached out to try to take the meat.

Snarling her lip, she growled in warning not to come any closer.

Within moments the meat was gone, devoured, her hunger satiated for the time being. She licked the bloody juices from her fingers, making sounds of pleasure. When she finished, she looked up to see the two men gawking at her.

What were they staring at? She glanced from them to her plate and back. Bloody traces of what had once been a large piece of raw meat smeared the fine china. She felt sick. She'd never eaten raw meat.

The minute her brain digested the truth, her stomach decided it didn't want to digest anything. Holding her hand to her mouth, she gestured.

"First door on your left—down the hall," Ballue said quickly for her benefit.

Draylon followed on her heels and burst through the door before she could shut him out of the bathroom. Her stomach rolled, emptying everything she'd just eaten and then some. Holding her hair back from her face, Draylon maneuvered to reach for a washcloth. Soaking it in cold water, he tried to place it on her forehead as another bout of pangs struck her.

"Anything I can do, Old Man?"

"Have any ginger on hand? She could do with some ginger tea. Then I think she'll be fine."

"All right. But I don't think tea will solve her problems."

#

Getting Marilyn out of the country wasn't easy. Draylon wouldn't have Ballue expose himself to daylight, but today, the weather was on their side. He needed the help right now, especially with Marilyn passed out from sickness. It was good to have friends in low places. It was rare to find a rogue Vamier, but Ballue was one of the few he could trust.

Moroii were created by other Vamiers. Most were men dying on battlefields over the millennium, wanting to live and being offered a second chance. Technically, the Vamiers weren't doing anything against the contract written by the gods. As soon as they had the okie-dokie from the fatally wounded, they were fair game.

What didn't sit well with Draylon or Rick, was Vamier's treatment of his victim-offspring. They would starve them and only then offer the blood they so desperately needed to survive, like cocaine to an addict—for a price, the price being "loyalty" in exchange for nourishment. They never let their victims learn to care for themselves. Blood banks all over the world were bootleg businesses for Vamier and his top goons in order to supply his kind.

But a few made it through their control, realizing the game for what it was. They would work to fight the addiction, move out under seclusion, always wary of being lured back. Some found their way to the Dacian Compound where they were safe, once investigated. If there was a price on their head from Vamier, then they were usually legitimately in need of sanctuary.

Rick had his own form of working with them. He would give them a chance for a new start and have them work in some capacity for him—depending on their abilities. Most became an underground railroad of sorts for those wishing to leave the Vamier life-style. Ballue was one of them. He also had connections with government and political allies who could work to get diplomatic situations taken care of.

Right now, they didn't have to deal with any paperwork. Even though Marilyn still had her passport on her, it didn't matter. He was taking her to his house in Austria, where she didn't need to clear customs.

"So what's so important about her that has you taking her to Eskardel? You've never taken anyone to Eskardel as long as I've known you," Ballue said.

"Aiden is after her. He wants to tutor her in Dacian

History. She supposedly wrote a paper on Dacian folklore that Aiden found quite fascinating."

"And that's why he has his army of moroii after her?"

"I know. It doesn't add up."

Draylon shuffled that idea around in his head. No, Aiden wouldn't send his troops out on a rampage just because she had an 'A plus' mind on Dacian history…unless she'd come across something that Aiden Vamier didn't want her to, or worse yet, something that Aiden *or* Rick didn't want anyone to know.

He remembered Rick's dire need to see Marilyn safe. He'd never seen the man more tortured or frantic. The man had been less concerned when Romania became communist. Was it because of her connection to Diane Reddlin and Livedel? He couldn't see that being a reason. No, Rick still hadn't calmed down, even knowing she was safe with him. There had to be another reason.

"Is she going to be all right? She doesn't look so good," Ballue asked as he turned in the passenger seat of the BMW he'd let Draylon drive.

"I don't know. I'm not sure what's wrong with her."

"Could she be wolven?"

Draylon stared at his friend. "She happens to be birthed by two mortal humans, one, and two—when was the last time there's been a female wolf in the pack?"

"But did you see the way she devoured the steak?"

"Yes, I saw." Draylon still mulled the issue over in his head. Something about Marilyn didn't add up. He would like to know more about her. The one thing he did know was her mother was a pain in the ass—maybe she ate raw meat, too. Yeah, he could see her chewing on someone's hide. The woman's bite was definitely worse than her bark. One hell of a businesswoman, but damn did she turn people inside out to get things done.

"And that doesn't worry you? Did you see those teeth? I wasn't sure if she was wolf or Vamier. And her eyes turned all cat-like with those tiny slits for pupils."

He'd seen it all. Ballue didn't have to recap the situation. Looking in his review mirror, he was thankful to see their subject of discussion still sound asleep. She'd passed out on the tile floor of the bathroom after twenty straight minutes of heaving up her guts. With her physically exhausted and mentally weakened, he knew they couldn't stay there any longer than necessary. Calling the airport, he made sure his crew was ready to depart as soon as they arrived.

When they pulled up onto the tarmac, the whine of the engine of his personal jet was the only sound, other than the high winds whipping through the valley. Draylon rolled down the window as his personal assistant, Donovan, came forward, holding onto his bowler hat against the heavy breeze.

"Sir, so good to see you. Everything's awaiting your orders."

"Thank you, Donovan. Go prepare the sofa sleeper for our guest. She's not feeling well and needs some rest."

Donovan nodded and went to carry out the task.

"Call me when you get settled. I'll find out what I can about Vamier. If she's as important as you say, he's going to be pretty pissed by now, knowing you have her. I'm just surprised he doesn't have more of his people out looking for her than he does."

"I know. That's worrying me, too." Getting out of the car, Draylon walked around and retrieved one Marilyn Reddlin from the backseat, marveling at how light her body seemed to be. Was it her illness or was she always so tiny? "I'm not sure of anything right now. But if that's why Rick wants her out of country, it's a good bet she's not safe anywhere. He never wanted her to set foot in Europe, much less Romania."

"Fascinating."

Ballue followed behind with their bags, the only personal luggage they had at the moment. Again, Draylon was thankful for Marilyn being a light packer. It made their desperate attempt to flee Romania easier.

Ballue stored the backpacks in the travel closet and turned to Draylon. "Have a safe flight, my friend. Keep me informed when you can."

Draylon grabbed Ballue in a man hug, pounding his fist on his back. "Keep safe. Let me know if you hear anything out there about our situation."

"Will do."

The jet engines whined higher, preparing for take-off. Draylon watched from the window as Ballue made it back to his BMW and drove away. Once the night darkened, the moroii would be out and then, not even Ballue would be safe.

As soon as the plane took off and reached a steady elevation, Draylon tended to Marilyn. Her features were so pale even her freckles had begun to fade. The contrast set her hair ablaze with warmth. He inhaled her scent, the undertones of sweet vanilla and soothing lavender kicked him straight in the groin. Damn. He didn't have time for these ridiculous thoughts. It'd been awhile, but there were other issues to worry about.

Like her health. Yes, he needed to focus his attention on her well-being. Sitting next to her, he lifted her limp torso so he could remove her woolen coat, scarf and hat. He couldn't help but smile, remembering the difficulty he and Ballue had getting her back in her winter weather gear.

Marilyn's senses started to awaken. He could see her mind opening, trying to put everything together and make it through the fog of illness. Only days ago she'd suffered from fevers and now this. She wasn't fully recovered. Had he pressed her too hard before she had a chance to heal?

Her mind may be waking but her body was still

uncooperative. Struggling with removing her outer sweater equaled wrestling gelatin onto a dessert fork, it just wouldn't work. He managed to pull the sweater inside out over her head but the tight collar was secured about her neck. If he pulled any more he feared her head would pop off.

"Would you care for a hand, sir?"

"Yes Donovan, I would." Draylon huffed.

"Young women can be difficult to undress, though I had the opposite experience. My daughters were impossible as tykes—they squirmed, hated wearing dresses with a passion, and preferred running around naked. My wife and I had to chase them down the street one summer's night because they'd taken their bath and went streaking when we tried to put their nightshifts on them."

Occasionally, his friend would talk about his family, but not often. The wounds were too deep. Draylon didn't know the whole story other than a group of moroii, high on induced blood, had broken code and attacked Donovan's family while he was away on business. They'd tried to cover their bloody massacre by setting fire to his house. The fire was extinguished before the evidence could be destroyed.

When Rick heard about the injustice and the man who wanted his revenge, he took Donovan under his wing and showed him what he could do to avenge his family's death. It wasn't about the revenge so much as learning how to take care of the present and help others against the moroii. Draylon learned that even a man in his mortal forties, given the right training and discipline, could kick the shit out of a Vamier...when the need arose. These mortal men were known as Shields. They were invaluable in their day to day activities with the human race.

"So this is the young woman you were sent to protect?" Donovan asked as he sat down across from Draylon. "She doesn't appear to be your average consideration in women."

Donovan knew his type of woman and no, Marilyn didn't fit the image. He nodded, smiling at the sleeping bundle, snoring away beside him. "I guess this one *is* different."

"Not all women are the same. The problem is finding the right one in a lifetime."

"Whose lifetime?" Draylon's mood turned serious again. "Theirs or mine?"

Chapter Six

Waking up in the same place twice lately had become a luxury. Marilyn fought to remember where she was and couldn't. She didn't remember a damn thing about the room she was in or whose bed for that matter.

Lifting her head, she raised up on her elbows. Nope, didn't help matters at all. She looked down at her sleeping clothes. Someone had dressed her in a linen nightgown that looked more like it belonged on a colonial bride than it did on her. The elegant embroidered stitching and simple tied bow was too old fashioned for her likes.

"Good morning, Miss," a cheerful, British laced voice called out as sunlight poured into the room.

Marilyn screamed but she wasn't sure for what purpose. Was it because of the strange man in a bedroom she wasn't familiar with or the sudden bright light threatening to melt her retinas? She buried herself in the thick down comforters.

"Sorry, I didn't mean to startle you." The muffled apology drifted to her as a hand lifted the blankets from her head. "You look like a ragamuffin all tousled and frizzed. Come, I have a nice breakfast all set out on the patio. I'll draw your bath and have fresh clothing for you momentarily."

"Oh dear." He looked aghast. "I'm such a nit! We haven't been formerly introduced. You were under the weather I'm afraid when Draylon brought you onto his jet. I'm Draylon's assistant, Donovan."

Other than seeing a middle aged Brit with a balding head of hair in formal butler garb, she assumed he was an extra on Downton Abbey. He did mention Draylon though, so he must be around here somewhere.

The man held out a thick, spa-like robe for her, but she wasn't awake enough to be sure about anything right now.

"Draylon doesn't have any women staff, just me." Donovan smiled to try to ease her. "It's all right. I had two daughters of my own I had to dress when they were younger. You will not come to harm in this household. If anyone tries, I assure you I will come to your aid."

Marilyn tried not to smile. It would be rude. What could a pencil thin man of his age do to protect her from the kinds of creatures she'd been running from? He didn't look like he could handle a normal attacker much less ones with deadly fangs.

Making her way to the edge of the bed, she noticed how large it was for the first time. Fine damask drapes were tied back to an elegant, antique canopy. Sheets of fine cotton hugged the mattress as jewel toned duvets and matching shams covered the large down filled comforters and pillows that she'd cocooned herself into during the night.

Donovan held out his hand, helping her to stand and slid the heavy robe over her arms and up her shoulders. He was modest and yet precise in his movements. Marilyn couldn't feel safer and yet she didn't even know the man.

"Thank you, Donovan," she whispered, gathering her hair from beneath the collar and letting it fall down her back.

"My pleasure, Miss." He motioned to a small, femininely

padded stool at a mirrored vanity. "Please sit. I will attend to your hair."

She wanted to argue but her brain didn't respond. Was he trying to manipulate her? Lately, she wouldn't put it past anyone she met. She sat as he gathered an ornate hairbrush from the table top.

Her shoulders bunched as he slowly untangled her hair with gentle tugs and small strokes. Soon she relaxed as the man stroked the brush through her tangle free hair. She closed her eyes, luxuriating in the steady massage of the weight of the bristles dragging though the mass she'd had to deal with daily.

Upon opening her eyes she gasped. Had he done that? Her hair, normally a non-descript reddish brown was ablaze in a deep auburn, almost burgundy curtain of shiny waves that framed her face.

She peered closer into the mirror. Her face had changed too from the last time she remembered seeing its reflection. Her skin was porcelain. Her natural freckles across her nose were gone. Her cheekbones appeared defined, the arch of her brow more pronounced, the natural coloring of her lips replaced by a deep blood red permanent tint.

Marilyn stood up, knocking over the chair and backing away from Donovan. "What the hell happened to me? Who did this?"

Donovan looked puzzled, his hands dropping to his sides. "I don't understand, Miss. What seems to be wrong?"

"My hair...my face. It's me but not me."

"You don't appear any differently than when Draylon brought you here a week ago?"

"A week? I've been here a week!" She looked around, trying to find a way out other than the opened French-style doors leading out onto a balcony overlooking...a very steep Alpine valley a good thousand or two feet below.

Hot panic poured through her veins. She could feel it like

boiling water coursing through her. Burning up, on the verge of combustion, she screamed as pain merged into a pleasurable transformation, but the scream only echoed in her head like an animalistic growl.

She dropped to her hands and knees, the sound of fabric ripping around her. Her body seized.

A door opened and she took off as fast as she could. With no thought or knowledge of what she was doing or where she was going, she just ran.

Someone chased her. She could hear footsteps pounding down the hallways behind her. The warm scent of musk had her turning on the runner. She hunkered down, exposing her snarling lip and that damn raspy growl until it erupted into a full out howl that echoed around them in the cavernous hallway.

Draylon stood still, anticipating her next move. She didn't smell fear on him though. *Why the hell would she be able to smell fear?* No, what she sensed were his natural pheromones setting her glands into overdrive.

She growled at him…he growled back, dominantly. Draylon squatted down to her level, patting his inner thigh. Marilyn took a tentative step towards him and another. He held out his hand. She came closer and sniffed. He didn't try to capture her but instead let her come to him. Closer and closer she moved until she placed her nose along his thigh. His hands cupped her face. Stroking her hair, he smiled at her.

"I'll be damned," his voice fell out in a breathless rush. "Rick's not going to believe this."

#

"What do you mean she's a wolf?" Rick Delvante bellowed into the hands free phone, missing his practice shot on the billiard table in his den. The sudden shock of news had him scratching. He threw the cue stick on the table, sending the remaining balls to scatter.

"She's a gorgeous auburn haired bitch."

"Don't call her that, Draylon," Rick instructed. Yeah, that is what they were known as, but they hadn't had a female of their kind in centuries. She didn't deserve what most commoners would consider a derogatory name.

"What do you know about her that you're not telling me, Rick?"

Too much and not enough. That's what he knew about Marilyn Reddlin. For the first time—no second time in his long, long life—he didn't have a fucking clue what to do. He should've known something like this might happen, and yet he didn't want to accept it.

"I think I should bring her up to the Dacian Compound—"

"No," Rick growled at his friend. That's the last thing he needed. *Fuck. Fuck. Fuck.* He wasn't ready for this. "Do you know what the clan would do to her if they got a hold of her?"

"And you're entrusting her to me? What makes me so different?"

"Because I know you are the one man I can trust. I've trusted you for over a millennium, Draylon, and I know you won't let me down now when I need you the most. This is it man. You wanted to know how you could pay me back. Well *this* is it. I need you to protect her with all you have. Guide her through the transition until I let you know what we need to do."

"You better make it quick, Old Man because she's carrying some heavy pheromones that I'm having a tough time with. I'm not a god, Rick."

"No, but you're the next best thing," Rick said. He rubbed his shadow of beard. "Just take care of her, teach her the ways, and for the sake of the gods, whatever you do, don't change around her."

"Which formation?"

"Either—she won't understand. And I don't want her to

find out."

"Well, I have a feeling Marilyn might be more like her mother if we don't get her questions answered in a timely manner."

"Yeah. That's another thing I have to fear. Just keep her safe and let me know how things progress."

Rick hung up before Draylon could ask any more questions. He could field his calls the rest of the day but he knew his buddy—he could either be your best friend for life or turn you into ash if you pissed him off. There were those you wanted to keep as your friend for the rest of eternity, and Draylon was much better on his side as his friend.

#

Draylon had trusted Rick implicitly for more than a millennium. Now a shutter of doubt closed over their once forthright friendship. He'd noticed it deteriorate over the past half century or so. By the 1980's, when Rick set up Livedel in the United States, his trips there had become more frequent and longer. When he'd been questioned he would get defensive. Then the trips stopped as abruptly as they started and Rick settled in Dacia, taking on the duties as leader like he had in the past. But he wasn't the same Rick Draylon had known for centuries.

Perhaps their occupation with their individual companies, Livedel and Eskardel, had taken away their casual time together. Even after the merger of the companies back in the sixties, Draylon had taken more time with pharmaceutical research. He found himself more engrossed in the changes in medicine, especially those that helped during wartime efforts.

Rick's focus, in the last decade of the twentieth century had turned entirely on the running of Livedel. Even from Dacia he'd buried himself in keeping close tabs on the Maryland headquarters and its people. He'd been obsessed.

Draylon wondered if it could have been because of him.

He'd buried himself in the knowledge and in procuring the pharmaceuticals to help out those who'd suffered at the hands of Vamier on the battlefields. The few who'd found their way to a safe transition, like Ballue, needed medical, psychological and environmental health and he was happy to help them.

One of his greatest accomplishments of late, his discoveries to produce medicines and techniques to help soldiers and veterans deal with PTSD. He'd started working with his friend Mike Linder back when they'd found him in Vietnam and the horrible memories he still faced. It never went away, but learning how to deal with the past and move on to the future was a big part of recovery. The difficult part of being immortal—you never forgot and age never changed to let you forget. Had his and Rick's individual fixations on their own companies created the slow moving rift between them? They were still friends but the difference in their unique relationship had definitely changed.

Donovan entered his office, and Draylon looked up from the paperwork he was attempting to catch up on.

"How is she?"

"Sleeping again." Donovan set down the tray with the decanter of wine. He lifted the stopper and poured a glass. "You can't keep her in a drug induced fog forever, Draylon. You of all people should know that. Isn't it you who tells your patients to 'face your fears and move on'?"

"This is different, Donovan." He swirled the wine in his goblet. "I don't think she's been properly prepared for what she's going through, and there is no one who can help her. We haven't had a female shifter since the curse. I don't know where she came from. How do I explain something I don't understand myself?"

"So what do you intend to do in the meantime?"

"My only two options? Keep her human as long as possible and make sure she doesn't change, at least until Rick figures out what to do. Or," Draylon paused, curling his face in frustration.

"Or?"

"Keep Sleeping Beauty asleep as long as I can."

Chapter Seven

Pacing the confines of her rooms, Marilyn felt like a caged animal. She wanted out but had nowhere to go. She'd been given every courtesy by Donovan, yet it seemed like days since she'd seen Draylon. Donovan informed her that he had business to catch up on and for her to rest and relax.

Relax? She couldn't relax. She paced to the open living space decorated in simplistic yet elegantly detailed furniture and fixtures. The Tudor-style windows looked out onto Austrian mountains and sharp jagged cliff edges, a clear sign that she couldn't escape.

"Would you care for a selection of movies or books? Draylon's procured quite a collection over the years."

"No," Marilyn growled. She sighed. Poor Donovan didn't need to take the brunt of her foul mood. "No…thank you, Donovan," she gentled her voice.

He didn't take offense. "A game of backgammon or cribbage perhaps? Or would you prefer a game of chess? I could use a good challenger."

She'd learned how to play chess from Francis, her old nanny. The woman had been a blessing for her and her mother.

Growing up, Marilyn learned so many skills from her, cooking, baking, domestic skills and reading, writing, not to mention chess, rummy and the occasional poker game for spiced gumdrops. Years later, Marilyn taught Tina how to play chess, and at times, when nothing else appealed to them for entertainment, they'd enjoyed a good, strategic game while indulging in gumdrops.

Marilyn shrugged her shoulders. "Sure. I'll play chess."

Setting up the mahogany pedestal board beside the window, flanked by two matching Victorian era gaming chairs, Marilyn went about placing the Italian marble pieces and commenced trying to best Donovan for the next two hours.

"I do believe we are at a stalemate, Miss Marilyn," Donovan noted after a long moment of perusing the pieces they had left.

"It does appear that way. Shall we call it a draw?"

He studied it again, as if he may have missed a crucial move. "I concede. You are a worthy opponent." He let out a breath as he stood and stretched in his formal jacket. "I must attend to my duties and go to the kitchen to make you dinner. What would you like?"

"Steak…rare. And if you have them…gumdrops."

"Tartar it is. I don't know if we have gumdrops, but I'll see." Donovan nodded with a brief smile and left her to go prepare her steak.

Marilyn watched him leave, closing the door behind him as he always did. It would be useless to try the door, he always locked it. But as usual she checked it anyway.

To her amazement and shock, the door clicked open into a large hall or room fit for a king's court. Sparse in décor, the deep cherry inlay floor gleamed from the late afternoon light coming in through the large windows. The ceiling of the room appeared to be at least a good thirty-feet high with gleaming mahogany woodwork, trim and crown molding. Black iron sconces and chandeliers lit up the walls and ceiling with artificial candlelight.

Nibbling her bottom lip, she checked for possible trouble and snuck out into the grand hall, crossing the massive room to the other side where a series of double doors opened into the rest of the grand house. One set was open. It must be where Donovan had gone.

On bare feet, Marilyn tiptoed to the open door and took another peek. A grand wooden staircase led to another upper floor and the lower main floor. She wandered out and looked over into the lower level. A grand foyer with massive black doors must lead to the outdoors.

She would sneak down and map out her escape for later.

At the bottom of the steps, dark wood paneled hallways stretched on for eternity—on both sides of the foyer. She wanted to explore the hall but her main concern right now was the door and her chance for freedom.

Standing in front of the behemoth doors, she realized there was no way in hell she could open them. They had to weigh a ton or more a piece. Perhaps they were on some remote control system but other than an alarm system on the wall she didn't see one. She shrugged, and maneuvering the large door handle of heavy wrought iron, she pulled. The door opened with amazing grace. No squeaking of hinges or groaning of metal. Snow covered open land surrounded by a dark forest of snow powdered fir pines. No grand circular drives or fountains spewing water and colored lights, just empty, pristine grandeur as far as the eye could see. If this was the front of the house and her side of the house encompassed the sheer cliffs and mountain sides, then how did people get up here?

There had to be a way. She'd gotten here—somehow. She couldn't remember. She awoke the other morning and she was already here. Feeling even more trapped than she had up in her suite of rooms, Marilyn wanted answers and she wanted them now. Screw being locked up anymore.

She went in search of the one man who could tell her what she needed to know…Draylon.

#

Ending the conference call with his contact for the hemoglobin clinic in Baltimore, Draylon informed Rick of the latest news on Vamier's dealings with their supply banks. Someone had masterminded an illegal distribution from the Greater Baltimore Blood Bank. Which if history served to repeat itself, meant they were about to recruit a whole new family of vampires in the states.

The only time there was questionable activity within the blood banks Vamier owned, was when things were about to go down. There weren't any battlefields on North American grounds though. No wars, no mass riots, who were they going after that would agree to their conditions?

"Yeah, I'm getting the news on it, too," Rick said when he picked up the line. He connected his computer screen link to Draylon's large monitor up on his office wall. It showed a detailed map of the world and where vampire units amassed at any given time. The more numbers in a unit, the more trouble was about to happen.

"What do you think? Any clue why they're raiding in the United States?"

"The only thing I can possibly think of is a recent outcropping of vampire-wannabes. The media and entertainment industry seem to enjoy romanticizing the whole Gothic scene. Last decade it was vampires being interviewed. This decade, it's sparkling young, moody immortals. We need to be prepared this All Hallows Eve. I'm thinking we need to keep all clans notified of any possible sightings or hearing anything through the networks."

"Do we have anyone in the blood banks we could use to possibly be on look out?" Draylon asked. It was good to have members in areas of importance, but it could also be an issue when Vamier's goons got too close.

"Let me look," Rick paused.

Draylon knew he had sources all over the world. Rick's connections went deep and wide and with a touch of a few keys on his computer, he could tell you where every single contact was at any given moment.

"We have one I think I can leverage," Rick responded.

"What do we have?"

"We have a human counterpart working for the Greater Baltimore Blood Bank. I think I can get them to head the division in Frederick, Maryland."

"Anything they can do?"

"I think so. They have family working for Livedel so it shouldn't be an issue to keep an eye on the dealings there. They've been taking care of the accounts for the whole division for over two years. I'll look into it and let you know." A deep sigh was followed by the sounds of keyboard clicking. "Who do we have in the vicinity of Baltimore-Washington D.C. area that could keep the accountant safe in case things get tricky?"

"You're asking me? You know the clan better than I do—wait, Mike Linder is out in that area. I'll have him posted and give him the low-down on the guy."

"Um...one small problem. Our connection at the blood bank isn't a guy. We are dealing with a Ms. Christina Johnston, Jon and Kay Johnston's daughter."

Draylon's flat screen went blank for a moment as Rick brought up a photo of a young blonde woman. Christina Johnston, bookkeeper for the Greater Baltimore Blood Bank system.

"You want to explain why you happen to have my friend's picture on your monitor?"

Draylon whirled around in his chair to see a pissed off

Marilyn Reddlin standing barefoot in his office doorway. How the hell did she get out of her room?

"Do you want to explain what the hell is going on, or do I start some major shit, asshole!"

"Who is that, Draylon?" Rick's voice echoed over the intercom.

"Marilyn Reddlin," she replied for Draylon. "And who the hell are you to have pictures of my friend?"

"I happen to be Rick Delvante, owner of Livedel and your boss, Miss Reddlin."

"Good to know…because unless you two tell me why you are keeping tabs on Tina and I'm being held captive in this castle prison, I'm going to start some shit with harassment on the job. The EEO will have a three course meal with your ass."

#

"Deal with her, Draylon," Rick commanded and turned off all communications.

Deal with her? What the hell was he supposed to do?

She entered the office all the way, pacing menacingly in front of his large desk, trapping him. He tried to present a nonchalant reaction to her anger. But the heat she emitted had him wishing to sink into her on such a basic level that his dick ached for the first time in years.

Her body had filled out, toned up in a natural state of change. Her denim jeans that had bagged around her recently now hugged her curves and the simple long sleeved t-shirt she wore showed off her breasts to perfection. She was muscle and sinew and strength wrapped up in a deadly shifter. So far she didn't remember ever shifting. Some neurological process kept her knowledge of her change at bay…for now. He hoped to the gods she didn't know just how deadly she could be.

"I'm waiting…"

"What do you want to know first?"

"Everything. Start at the beginning."

"Too much to tell." It was the truth. "But I'll tell you what you need to know…"

"I want all of it. And if I find out you're lying to me, you won't have a prayer mister."

This was a new side to her. She may be just as bad-assed as her mother after all. Could it be her metamorphosis having some effect on her? Maybe she did know how deadly she could be?

"Fine. But you may not like what you hear," Draylon teased to try to lighten the mood.

"Just tell me and stop beating around the bush. Who are you, really?"

"Draylon Conier." She raised an eyebrow to indicate she wanted more information. "I started the pharmaceutical branch to Livedel years ago, back after World War I."

"Bullshit. I happen it know it was started by Marcus Adranitti from Naples. He joined with Mr. Delvante in the late sixties."

"Marcus was my identity back then." Draylon reached into his file drawer, and pulling out a file folder, pushed it towards her on his desk. She looked at him and then at the file. "Go ahead. Read it."

She picked it up tentatively. Opening the file she studied the insides. He already knew what was in there. It was up to her to believe it.

Marilyn sat down heavily in the nearby leather chair. She shook her head. "No. This can't be…this is you? And…look. It's Momma Kay and Papa Jon when they were younger—You know the Johnstons?" she asked.

He could only nod.

"This is all a set up, isn't it? You're holding me hostage— why?"

Draylon raised his hands. "No. It's not what you think. Rick had me track you down and keep you safe. That is the gods' truth. I didn't know you were wanted by Vamier. When I found out, Rick wanted me to keep you someplace safe."

"Safe from Professor Vamier?" she asked. "Is this place safe?"

"The only place safer is the Dacian Compound."

"Where is that?"

"It's in the Hoia Forest area near Cluj-Napoca."

She stood up and threw the file back on his desk. "That just happens to be where my father disappeared nearly twenty-six years ago. Pretty coincidental don't you think?"

He felt the same way but had no answers. When he'd asked Rick about it his friend said he'd look into it.

"I know. I'm trying to see what I can find out about your father's disappearance, but you may not like the news."

"Why?"

"Most people who venture into the Hoia Forest don't return."

"But the Dacian Compound is there. How do they survive?"

"The Dacians survive because they don't let anyone know of their whereabouts. Those that come too close end up...disappearing."

"You mean dead."

"It's the only way our kind can survive."

"And your kind is what, special?" Marilyn snorted sarcastically.

"We're immortal...."

Chapter Eight

Stunned, Marilyn sat. Immortal? As in, never aged, never died…creatures of the night. She looked at the file folder still sitting there on the desk. The picture was him, decades ago, only looking like he did now. Still the same.

"How old are you?"

Draylon smiled and leaned back in his chair. "I was born in what you would consider 750 B.C."

"You're kidding, right?"

"No. I'm afraid not." He laughed. "My land was called Dacia at the time…"

"Before the Roman conquest. You are one of the original clans?"

"There are more of us. It's difficult to explain, but we reside all over the world, separately, keeping our lives private for many centuries, but recently we have committed part of our knowledge and abilities in helping our brethren human counterparts."

"Under the radar, I assume?"

"Yes. You might consider us a 'secret society.' Our confidentiality must remain though. People are not ready to come to terms with what we are."

Marilyn looked away. She understood their needs for

secrecy, but did they have to kill to keep it? She had no doubt her father must have come in contact with them and been "taken care of."

"Would you know if my father was one of those who were killed in order to keep your secrets?"

Draylon sighed. His eyes took on a weary, heart-felt sadness. "There are ways to find out, and I will for your sake, but you must understand our need to remain anonymous."

"I do understand. I just want closure—and don't let my mom know the truth, she'll raise all kinds of hell. As long as I can tell her something, perhaps have his remains so we can have a proper burial, it might help her to finally heal."

"Closure, of course. Again, I will see what I can do."

"Thank you."

"You're welcome." He smiled, his eyes never leaving hers.

It was uncomfortable, his continued stare. So she did what she usually did when encountering such a moment. She crossed her eyes and twisted her lips into a funny face. Draylon cocked his head at her and then laughed—a real gut busting laugh. The first one she'd heard from him.

Her heart beat erratically, making her flush. The deep rumbling from his chest had sparked warmth into her the likes no other man had done. Daniel never made her feel this safe, this free, and she thought she'd known him. This mysterious, immortal man was so out of her league, and yet he was the one to make her want to know him better.

"Do you always make faces when you are in discomfort?" he asked once his laughter settled.

"It tends to break the tension."

"And you are tense? Do I make you uncomfortable?"

Marilyn shrugged. "I guess you could say, I'm leery of you. But truthfully, and I don't know why, I feel good when I'm around you. It shouldn't make any sense at all. You're immortal after all. You can read my mind—"

"Not all the time. You are safe for the most part. For some reason I cannot delve into your mind like I am used to with women. You could say you are unique."

A subtle quiet disrupted them again.

"So. All is good then? I guess I'm free to roam?"

"No."

"No? But why not? I know who you are and there aren't any Vamiers around, right?"

It was absurd. She hadn't done anything wrong, and now that she was out and about things should be fine.

"You need to be kept safe at all times."

"From who?"

Draylon stood up from behind his desk and walked over to where she sat. He hunkered down so that his blue, fathomless eyes were level to hers. His scent intoxicatingly close, her body responded, tingling between her legs. His hand came up and cupped her chin.

"From me."

#

The shock of his touch electrified her, but the heat in his eyes had her heart melting. Closing her eyes she gave into the feel and nuzzled his hand. The need to be petted, caressed had her nearly purring in pleasure. He didn't disappoint.

Draylon stroked her jaw, reaching up under the massive weight of her hair. His fingers tangled into it, pulling ever so slightly. The sting of the nerve endings shot straight to her ultra sensitive nipples. Slithering from the chair she found herself on the floor in front of him, craving more of his touch. His lips traveled along her jaw, leaving his hot breath trailing along her skin.

He nipped her ear and spoke words she didn't understand but sounded so erotic, she didn't need to understand them to know what they might mean. She gasped before his hand

clutched her hair, and he devoured her mouth in one hungry
motion.

It frightened and elated her at the same time. He was
fierce. A low moan turned into a growl. Excitement over
knowing she had this effect on him had her giving back as
good as she got. Rising up onto her knees, she straddled his lap
and took his face between her hands, forcing the kiss back on
him, finding herself more dominating than she'd ever been or
ever thought she could, not after Daniel.

Draylon Conier wasn't Daniel. This man had years of
experience and knew how to touch, taste and set a woman to
find her own easy response. It was the first time she didn't
think. She knew what she needed to do, and he appeared to be
enjoying it.

He tasted of warm spiced ale as she inhaled sandalwood
and his musk. Were these pheromones, those elusive chemical
essences scientists talked about which attracted two people?

Her body shifted as he stood with her still clinging to him.
Wrapping her legs around his hips, not wanting to let go,
Marilyn clutched his hair as he broke the kiss briefly. Sudden
contact with solid surface had her sandwiched between a wall
and his hardness. His animalistic maleness overwhelmed as his
hands roamed her body, pressing her closer, grasping her
tighter.

Struggling for breath, she sucked in a large gulp of air in
excitement as his erection pressed against her lower abdomen.
Tingles of awareness shot through her and instinctively her
hands smoothed down his sides, over the placket of his slacks,
tracing the length and girth of him through the fine Italian
linen.

He broke the kiss and stared at her. It was a hard, fierce
gaze as his eyes changed color and shape. Blue the color of the
hottest part of a flame dominated his irises and turned the
pupils into narrowed slits of black. His lips quirked in an

uncontrolled sneer as a deep throated growl erupted. It didn't frighten her, in fact she became more aroused. The scent took on a stronger fragrance, overpowering, yet it only caused her to hunger for something just out of her reach.

Pushed to the side, Draylon bounded from the office as if hell itself were at his heels. Marilyn followed. What had she done wrong? She chased him through the long wide corridors of his palace fortress. Pieces of men's clothing littered the floor, trailing behind Draylon as he ran. She didn't stop but continued the chase, his scent strong in her senses.

Something dark and wild forced its way into her mind. Various beasts and formations, each one fighting the other until she saw the image of a wolf imprinted in the illuminated recesses coming to life in her brain.

Her clothing joined the cascade of tossed linens in the hallway as she kept a few paces behind Draylon. Busting through the heavy front doors, they both leapt naked down the wide front steps. Marilyn's breath caught in her throat as a kind of weightlessness forced her leap to stretch. Her body contorted mid stride, and she landed on the ground at the foot of the steps on all fours.

Growling sounds alerted her and she turned. A large blue/black furred wolf stood with its haunches squared and its teeth bared. She returned the stance, snarling and growling in reply.

What the hell?

The beast attacked without any warning. She countered and a fierce dominance for control hit her like a fatal blow. Teeth gnashed as canine bodies tumbled into the snow covered field. She yipped as teeth came down into her throat and shook her like a chew toy.

Draylon? Help. Where are you? she screamed in her mind as the wolf pawed at her.

Fight me. Come on, Marilyn. Put me in my place.

W...what? Are you...sweet Jesus! Was it true? Was this great wolf attacking her really Draylon?

I'm going to dominate and tear the hell out of you if you don't counter. You're not ready for this, and I'm in no position to control myself. You have to do something to stop me.

She didn't know how to fight a wolf. Hell, she'd been the laughing stock of her Karate class because she was too clumsy and naïve. She hadn't wanted to hurt anyone. She hadn't been able to fight off Daniel's advances either because she didn't want him mad at her. That's why she'd let him have his way, why she hadn't fought him.

The wolf backed off. He sat back on his haunches, his canine head cocked at her as if trying to understand what she was. Slowly his body morphed back into the naked image of Draylon, sitting modestly in front of her, still studying her.

"You let someone take advantage of you...without wanting him to?"

The truth hadn't hit her until now. She *hadn't* wanted Daniel mad at her. She'd given in to his demands and then... "It was a while ago. It was nothing—"

"Nothing," he echoed. "Is that how you perceive the physical act? Sharing of bodies should not be taken lightly."

She looked down and realized she'd morphed back into her human form, too. "I'm freezing my ass off, literally. Can we talk about this later?" She crossed her arms over her chest, knowing the rest of her was bare, and that her nudity shouldn't matter. She'd exposed herself, laid herself open at a deeper level than nudity could ever go, to someone she wasn't sure she could trust.

Draylon stood. Standing before her he offered her his hand. Tentatively she took it and he helped her to stand.

"Gods breath, Marilyn." He cupped her face, holding it in his large hand. "When I told you to do something to stop me, I meant in a physical way. You managed to do the one thing that would take me down in any form. Not for one moment would I try to dominate you without it being mutual. I don't care how fast, how far we go, I won't go any further than what you are okay with. And never, ever give yourself to a man without feeling the strongest of desires to do so."

She shivered, but not from the cold, alpine winds against her naked skin. Draylon's sultry voice touched her exposed soul. Her heart thudded inside against her breast and she felt the sudden urge to be wrapped in the security of him—nothing more, nothing less.

He shook his head with a sad smile. "Only when you feel you can trust me."

Donovan met them at the base of the stairs, undeterred by their nakedness and handed Draylon large, thick blankets. Wrapping one securely around her first, Draylon kissed her forehead gently as if placing a blessing upon her. Donovan escorted her up the stairs into the warmth of the fortress. She turned to watch as a black wolf darted off into the distance.

#

Draylon ran as if demons were nipping at his paws. His heart ached with every labored breath. He couldn't run fast enough or far enough to get the image of what she hadn't realized she'd portrayed in his mind. She'd not only revealed the thought but the memory of the episode with the bastard she'd been dating.

He had taken her without gaining her permission. He'd taken her virginity without even preparing her for the pleasure it could have given her. She'd been unsure, only wanting to do whatever it was to please him, because she didn't want to lose him.

He saw the smug face of the asshole as he'd taken her innocence, felt the sharp pain of her discomfort and disillusioned disappointment in an act that should have made angels weep, and then the heart wrenching fracture of the relationship, what there was of it, as he railed at her for being a virgin.

The shit-head should've been honored she'd given herself to him. Instead he'd made her feel less than honorable by cursing her out and claiming she'd tried to trap him. He'd left her lying there in her dorm room bed with the stain of embarrassment and the natural stain of her innocence to keep her company as she'd cried herself to sleep.

Her pain, too intense even for him, had every creature within, fighting to get free. He finally let go and morphed into his natural form. The darkness of the tall pines sheltering from every view, he was able to slither among the tree trunks on his short, strong reptilian legs. His spaded tail lashed out taking down small saplings in his path. Hot breath snorted out from his nose and mouth, thawing the winter white all around.

Making his way up out into the tundra, the thinner air was much more to his liking. He looked down from the edge of the mountain crest into the empty snow filled valley below. It was his private valley. No one resided or traversed its boundaries of the two ranges. It had been awhile since he'd felt the need to spread his wings, but if there ever was a day, this was the one.

Taking a leap, Draylon's leathery wings unfurled from his scaly back and he soared down between his private mountains. Screaming, like a giant hawk, reveling in the freedom of flight, he cast off the image of Marilyn's defeat on the wind. And just as the wind carried the image away, he would find a way to wipe every memory of "Asshole Daniel" from her consciousness as well.

#

Rick's instructions to help Marilyn with her transformation were vague. Draylon had helped moroii through their transformation as they shook off their blood addiction, but that was different. Every other wolf he knew was ancient enough to have learned the change eons ago. How did one go about teaching a human to control and enjoy the change? And a woman at that? Not even Therron or Kurren would have any idea how to instruct a female, there weren't any.

Zamolxis really messed them up good. The god had only changed the warrior faction, not the women. Over the first century the Dacian women died off of natural causes, died during child birth with their new breed of children, or left in fear of becoming a wolf mate and dying with child. Now after centuries without female wolves, one showed up out of nowhere.

Draylon rubbed his jaw, knowing that in a few moments he'd have another full day of instruction with Marilyn. The past week she'd begun to accept her new change, and he'd even helped her to find the best way to enjoy the physical aspect of the biological transformation.

"So what are we doing today?" Marilyn came forth, wearing what looked to Draylon like a white linen bed sheet strategically wrapped around her.

"Is that one of the bed sheets?"

"Yes. I've managed to ruin nearly every shirt and pair of slacks I have trying to morph, so I figured something easier to divest while shifting would be a plus. You must go through a ton of clothes."

"Truthfully, I don't transform as much as you think. I'm only doing so for your benefit. The human form is easier to adapt to than my oth…wolf form." Draylon caught himself as he put down the file he'd been reading, hoping she didn't notice his faux pas. He was able to block his thoughts from her more so than she could with him, but she was learning.

No, it wouldn't be a good idea to let her know of his other transformations. He was a shape-shifter because of his race. But she had just begun to accept the fact he was part man and part wolf. Explaining flames, dragons and other fabled entities to her might be a stretch.

Draylon sighed. She had so much to learn, and yet he knew he didn't have the proper materials to teach her. "Let's go for a run, shall we?"

Marilyn shrugged. "Sure."

He'd shown her all there was to running and learning to shift. He'd even taught her how to hunt and forage for shelter, most animal training was based on natural instinct.

He'd learned it was easier to morph if he was already naked. Nudity to him was no big deal, but Marilyn seemed shy still. He tried to be as modest as he could until he could become the creature. She'd wait until he'd morphed before disrobing and making the connection. Draylon loved watching her morph. Today he let her take the lead and watched her throw off her bed sheet dress as she switched positions with her naked, pale beauty into the auburn colored wolf with Gypsy gold eyes.

The recent snow had led to a deeper field for them. Jumping and tossing snow with their snouts at one another was a simple snowball fight. Nipping and lunging like a couple of friendly dogs, they tussled and rolled in the snow, shaking each other off.

Draylon led her on a hunt, chasing after a wild hare bounding through the forest. He knew it was littered with all sorts of wild animals indigenous to the European mountains. It was his land, an animal retreat where human hunting was forbidden.

She needed to learn her place and a female wolf mate had to learn to hunt and care for her young—though she may or may not ever be able to have any. It would be a damn shame. Marilyn would make beautiful children and pups.

He let up on the hunt and had her take over the pursuing. Attacking the large hare, she killed it and started to feast.

Draylon approached and she growled at him. He backed away. He would let her finish and then take what was left.

Good. You are learning. Draylon laughed.

She paused only a moment to acknowledge him and returned to her feast. Eating her fill she stood up, pushing the remaining carcass over towards him and took a stance to protect their surroundings.

The sound of rustling through the trees brought her ears up, and she turned as a pack of female wolves lumbered towards them. Their eyes narrowed in on the carcass he chewed on. But one female in the pack showed interest in him by licking his chops and nuzzling up against him. He growled low in his throat. But that didn't stop her.

Marilyn growled at the alpha pack leader, not liking the other female's advances. Draylon continued to gnaw on the carcass. This wasn't his fight. Marilyn would need to learn the ways of the wolves. The female would either take her growl as a warning and move on or challenge Marilyn to prove herself.

The wolf didn't heed her warning. With her head lowered the alpha growled back, challenging Marilyn to a fight of the fittest.

Sounds of snarling wolves echoed off the trees. Lunging for the nosy female, Marilyn latched onto her throat. The aroma of female musk and blood saturated the area.

Draylon couldn't get a good mental bead on Marilyn. She wasn't in communication. This was all her, all wolf.

Moments later the alpha lay beneath the red wolf, dominated with a bite wound to the side. There was a new alpha now. Marilyn stood, howling her victory over dominating the pack as alpha female.

She too suffered from the fight. Patches of fur were matted with blood—hers or the former alpha, Draylon wasn't sure. Her pheromones were heavy with her musk. She'd marked the territory as hers and watched patiently until the last of the females had gone. Lying down, she licked at her wounds.

He ventured forth. *Marilyn? Are you okay?*

At first there was no response, but then she laid her nose down on her front paws and whined.

What...what happened? Draylon, I'm hurt, I think.

Her body morphed into her human form, revealing a bloody mess.

Draylon crept towards her in a non-threatening way while her body formed. Her auburn hair lay in tatters, blood oozed from various cuts and tears in her thighs, arms and chest. He morphed while kneeling on all fours. Checking on her vitals, she had a strong heartbeat as her adrenaline still raced high, but she could also be going into shock. As an immortal wolf, it would take her hours to heal from the wounds. She could lose too much blood in the meantime. They were a long way from the safety of the house, and he had nothing to use to stop the flow of her precious life essence.

Marilyn, I need you to sleep. Sleeping will help slow the flow of blood.

How bad is it? I'm so weak.

I know.

This wasn't a good lesson, Draylon.

He gave a half laugh. *This wasn't my lesson. You took on an alpha female wolf...and survived.*

No shit? Really? She smiled up at him wearily.

Really. Now sleep. I've got you. He could see the shock trying to settle into her conscious self. He needed to get her home...fast. And there was only one way he knew to do so. Her mental lethargy served two great purposes. One, it slowed down her heart rate so her blood didn't flow as fast and two, she wouldn't have to witness his true form.

Chapter Nine

"Do you think Draylon will let me get in touch with my mother? He has internet connection. It wouldn't be difficult to send her an email just to let her know I'm all right," Marilyn asked as Donovan cleared away her breakfast dishes.

She tried to remember how long she'd been here by calculating days and nights of routine and skills she'd learned. But the days seemed so short she wasn't sure time was a factor. For her time appeared to stop while she'd been here. If Draylon would just allow her access to media or even a calendar or clock, she wouldn't feel so disassociated with the real world.

"I'll see what I can do, miss. He's more concerned about your health. You took a real beating yesterday with that wolf."

Her brain tried to process the afternoon. "I guess." He left her, and she managed to find a pair of jeans that she hadn't shredded yet. Looking through the rest of her belongings, she found her Ravens jersey she usually wore for pajamas. A wrapped bundle fell out, exposing her medallion. She'd somehow forgotten about it and that frightened her. But now, it was safe in her protection.

Odd. The image of the wolf head had more meaning to her now. It was one of the sacred symbols of the ancient Dacian people. Whether it was because of their fierce wolf-like warrior tribes or how they worked as a clan, much like a wolf pack, she didn't know all historical facts on the symbol's true meaning. But she had a deeper education now.

No sense of wearing it, though. She'd never be able to keep it on with all of her morphing and shredding.

Wrapping it up, she placed the medallion back in the security of the zippered pocket. It would be fine until she could get home, whenever that was.

Opening the heavy drapes, Marilyn stared out over the serenity of the snow covered pass. It appeared as if she were on top of the world. The wicked crags and crevices that made up the steep sides weren't inhabitable by man or beast, but they were beautiful.

A floating speck far beyond the first rise of cliffs caught her attention. The creature soared and swooped gracefully with a colossal wingspan. At first she thought it might be a hawk, but even from this distance, she wouldn't be able to see it as clearly as she could this creature. She strained her sight, focusing on the details, but couldn't quite grasp shape or size.

It brought to mind her odd dream last night. She'd been flying, cradled against a large serpentine body. Draylon's voice had drifted in and out of her head telling her to sleep, that she was in shock and needed to close her eyes and rest. She remembered coming to a stop. Her eyes had opened, she noticed a tragic white mar along the reptilian flesh. She traced her hand over the scar, feeling the deep loneliness and ache from the creature, sensing a connection so painfully sharp, only to have Draylon's voice lull her back to sleep.

Donovan knocked and entered upon her greeting. He crossed the room to make her bed.

"Can you tell me what this is?" she asked, motioning to

the window.

"What what is?"

Donovan walked over to the window, and she pointed out to the speck in the distance.

"Possibly a hawk. We have some magnificent winged creatures in this area."

"It's too big to be a hawk at that distance. And the shape is not quite right for a hawk."

"Hard to say, miss. These old eyes aren't what they used to be."

Marilyn sighed. "I wish I had some binoculars."

Donovan went to close the drapes as if part of his job.

"No, it's okay. Leave them open. It's beautiful out there."

He shrugged and went back to fluffing pillows and straightening the covers before leaving the room and shutting the doors.

Marilyn went back to watching the bird-creature, hoping it would come closer, even just a mountain ridge or two this way would be good. She pulled up one of the chairs and watched. She had nothing better to do. Moments later she stood as the creature flew closer, its size drawing her. But the shape was not that of a bird, not unless one had a long tail.

She stared in awe. The raven colored beast soared and dipped on the alpine currents. He opened his wings, the span was twice the length of his body. Dear God! She blinked her eyes to clear her mind. Was that what she thought it was? It wasn't possible.

"Donovan." She ran out of the room, calling his name. "Donovan!"

The halls were empty. "Draylon!" she called out for him in case he was nearby. He had to see this to believe it.

Flinging open every door along her route, she found no one else. Empty rooms, not even any furniture, dominated most of the floor. She ran to Draylon's office but he wasn't there either.

Where was everyone? She'd just seen what she thought to be something out of fables and folklore…and she'd really seen it.

Hurrying down to the main floor, she searched the large chef's kitchen and elaborate dining hall with a table for twenty. The library and study were empty, too.

"Donovan? Draylon?" She ran from room to room, up and down the massive corridors.

The east wing door opened at the far end of the hall, and Draylon stood there in naked glory. His sleek body shining with sweat. Marilyn ran to him.

"What are you doing up? You should be resting."

"Draylon, you'll never guess what I just saw," she squealed. "A dragon! I saw a dragon."

"She's hallucinating, my lord." Donovan came up behind her. "She'd been watching one of the mountain hawks circling in the distance from her bedroom window. I fear she might be suffering from the fever again."

"No, I feel fine," Marilyn tried to argue. "I did see a dragon. He was magnificent with an enormous wingspan, so graceful and perfect soaring out there." She rambled on as Draylon lifted her in his arms and walked with her down the hall where she came from.

"I'm sure he was." He smiled, placating her as a child telling a fantastical tale of imaginary friends to an adult. He kissed her forehead. "You are still running a fever. Let's get you back to bed."

But she felt fine. Why didn't he believe her? She knew what she saw. She looked into Draylon's deep blue eyes, trying to gage what he was saying, feeling. There were so many thoughts and secrets jumbled there in his mind. Her head felt fuzzy, and all she could do was hold on to him. Maybe she was sick.

#

Draylon settled Marilyn into a deep slumber. Lying beside her he touched her hair, brushing it from her face. He placed his fingertips lightly against her temples, imparting his memory loss techniques, erasing the image of her seeing the dragon.

Marilyn's breathing pattern took on that of true sleep, and yet he lay wide awake staring at the canopied ceiling of his bed. What was up with him lately? He'd gone decades, even centuries without his Zmeu form coming out, yet now it demanded to be released. And it didn't even have anything to do with sexual stimulation. He looked at the sweet sleeping form and glared down at his erection. Well, it didn't.

She'd been in a bad way yesterday, and the only way he could get her to safety was by his true form. He wasn't sure he would be able to keep his secret because Marilyn had roused from her slumber several times and he'd had to coax her back to dreamland. When they'd landed and she'd noticed his ancient scar, his body, no…his soul had reacted. Her touch had lit a fire so deep inside of him he felt like an old furnace being brought back to life after centuries without fuel.

Like a man needing a cold shower to shock his system back into control, his restless night had led to a fierce need to emerge and ride the winds. He'd taken a big risk, flying around without a care. He hadn't expected Marilyn to be awake and watching him, though.

Rick needed to hurry up and decide what had to be done. There wasn't much more he could take with Marilyn around him. The constant aching need to be with her drove him insane. He'd had his fair share of female companions over the centuries and could take them or leave them for the most part. Even the ones he'd had a long-term romantic relationship didn't feel as electrifying as what he sensed with Marilyn.

Was it because she was Dacian? There was no doubt. Her

ability to morph into wolf proved that. He had to consider the possibility of the kindred connection. Still, he refused to take the risk of making love with her physically and exposing the truth behind what he was. The danger was too great of having her terrified like the other women had been. His nightmares consisted of the attack on the Zmei and watching the women he'd cared for witness what he was. He would die if he had to view Marilyn's terrorized shock.

She snuggled closer into him, burrowing like a kitten against his chest. Her sleepy sighs and warm breath tickled but in a good way. Holding her like this, he felt at peace.

#

The sound of light snoring roused her from sleep. She'd been lying so relaxed that she hadn't remembered how she got here.

Skin met her hand. It moved beneath her fingers. Marilyn looked up to see Draylon sleeping, his head at an odd angle propped up on the pillows as if he'd fallen asleep in a half lying-half sitting position. He was naked, except for a throw blanket covering his hips.

Leaning up on an elbow she watched him sleep. The shadow of facial hair gave him a dangerous look. But the curve of a smile on his lips and the dark fan of lashes against his angular cheekbones made him appear child-like. Combing her fingers through the neat forest of dark hair on his chest, she trailed it with her eyes all the way down to his manly sculpted "V" where his pelvic bones met.

Never had a man affected her so. As much as she'd wished for Daniel and her to work out, she knew before they'd even had sex that it would never last. She'd offered herself in a last ditch effort to hold onto a sinking ship. She'd wanted to be loved for the sake of love, and yet, she'd had no idea what love was. She'd given herself to the wrong guy for the right reasons, though the reasons were a bit askew now. She only wished she knew back then.

Marilyn didn't want to make the same mistake. There was so much mystery and unknown to Draylon. She couldn't deny that. But what she felt with him, around him, demanded her to open her heart and soul, more than physically. She didn't think it had anything to do with needing to understand the mystery…it just was. The situation freed her and frightened her in a good way. Being with Draylon was like her first time white water rafting, that excitement of the unknown waiting around the bend and when it hit, the thrill and exhilaration took your breath away.

Her fingers drifted over his chest. She didn't want to wake him, she wanted to explore him. Firm muscles, a six-pack she could drink from all day…she smiled, brushing the soft, dark curls. Her smile faded and her brows bunched as she noticed the tail end of a silvery mark across his chest. Separating the furred mat, it trailed across his chest at an angle. It was a huge slash of an old scar, hidden mostly under cover, bisecting his torso nearly in two.

Tracing it, her memory connected to another scar…a recent one. She struggled to remember where she'd seen it. They'd been similar. The rhythm of the chest movement stopped, and she looked up to see Draylon staring down at her. She felt like a child having climbed the cabinets to get a cookie she wasn't supposed to have.

"You're awake," she greeted.

"So are you."

His voice rumbled with sexy sleepiness. Had she woken him up with her touch?

"Where did you get your scar?"

"A battle. A long time ago."

"I thought you were immortal. Wouldn't the scar have disappeared?"

"There are some scars that never go away, Marilyn, even

for immortals."

Sitting up, she continued to trace it. "I like it. It makes you more human."

"I'm not human…"

"I know. You're a dream, a fantasy. One I don't want to wake up from." She lay back down and snuggled into his side once more. She felt comforted, secure, and safe nestled against him like this.

Her memory lit on him saying, *only when you feel you can trust me.*

"I trust you, Draylon."

#

Days of waiting were wearing thin on her. She hadn't seen Draylon since the day he'd lain with her, just sleeping on the bed. It had been more intimate than giving herself to someone. She'd even told him she trusted him. Had that scared him? It wasn't like she'd said she loved him. Most men didn't take to that sentiment in a non-commitment relationship.

Marilyn wasn't sure what kind of relationship she was in, or if they even had one. He ran hot and cold and right now the silence from him froze. She'd been allowed to go running in her wolf form as long as she stayed out of the deep woods. She spent much of her time near the slopes of the high mountain edges waiting and watching for something but not quite sure what. She'd return in the late hours to a light dinner and a game of chess or backgammon with Donovan.

With her limits just about tested, she sat with him drinking a cup of herbal tea. "Why won't he see me?"

"He's been busy with work. Something came up and it's been a pressing issue. He won't leave his office." Donovan shook his head. "I don't think he's slept in days, but then he'll go through times like that when there are major projects due."

"He does know that I am capable of helping. I do have top secret clearance with Livedel. I was an intern until I moved back there permanently in December. Now, I'm a full-time employee."

"I'm sure he knows, miss. Sometimes he just prefers to be alone to work."

"What about getting in touch with my mother? Have you asked him that?"

"I have." He took a careful sip of his tea.

"And?" Marilyn waited for his reply.

"Until Rick gives him the go ahead—"

"Rick! Rick! That's all I hear. I don't care if he is the head of Livedel, what does he have to do with my life? He can't continue to keep me prisoner here. I have no sense of time or even what day it is. And my mother is probably out of her freakin' mind with worry."

"I'm sure Draylon will have answers for you soon." He tried to soothe her ruffled feathers.

"I gave him my trust and this is what I get in return? I want answers, Donovan." She stood up, nearly knocking over their unfinished game of backgammon.

"Where are you going, Marilyn?"

"I'm going to get those answers if I have to break down his damn office door." She seethed.

#

Hanging up from his conference call with an international colleague, Draylon felt the weight of days of fatigue hitting him. He hadn't slept because gods forbid he'd end up dreaming of making love with Marilyn. Trust. She trusted him. He snorted. If she only knew how difficult that one word, that phrase hit him when all he could think about was taking her six ways to heaven and back.

He'd had Donovan keep her at bay, but he wondered if she knew the power she had to push past the man and do whatever she damn well pleased. No, she wouldn't do that. She wasn't that kind of woman. She'd wait until it was time.

When was that? Hell if he knew, he still waited for Rick to inform him. He could understand her frustration—he felt it on this end. Still, there was only so long someone could wait.

His thick mahogany door smashed off of its brass hinges and there stood the object of his greatest fear and greatest desire. Had she changed in the past few days? How long had it been since he'd seen her. She was the image of fire. Her small spark had spread into a glorious riot worthy of a forest fire at its best.

"No more games, Draylon. I want answers…now." Her voice growled with energy and vim. The low tones were deadly soft, contrasting with the wild fire blazing in her golden eyes.

"I can't give you answers I don't know myself." He glanced at the door dangling from one hinge still screwed into the wall.

She stalked him, waiting to pounce. "Well you better make some up then. I've had it. I'm not even where I was supposed to be when I started out…"

"No one ever is," he stated.

Glaring at him she had his full attention. Their eyes locked and he saw everything, the frustration, the anger, the insecurity of not knowing who or what she was—but he also saw the woman she'd become in the past weeks and days.

The weak college girl holding on to old ideals was gone. There wasn't any scrawny, freckled faced geek stumbling along to find her way. In her place, a fierce woman made of the very fire he saw in her had emerged. She would be a flame that no one should smother. She may still be looking for answers but by damn, she had the gumption to get them.

"Damn you are beautiful." He breathed, her face mere inches from his, ready to do battle. "You are standing too fucking close for your own good, Marilyn. You have two seconds to back away or gods help you, I won't be held accountable for my actions."

Draylon didn't know what possessed him to admit his desire for her. He wasn't one to be so open in his needs, but then no woman left him so physically raw. Her rounded eyes reminded him of a wary doe and then her pupil's dilated from their perfect orb shape to long narrow vertical slits filled with liquid fire.

A normal man would flee at such an odd occurrence, but he didn't. Her chest heaved with every breath she took, exhaling heat from parted lips that left moisture across his face. The intensity of the moment went on for an eternity. Her mind opened and all he sensed was how damp she was, the tremors of want rippling through her womb, the ache in her breasts.

One of them growled in a deep, low, seductive whisper that ended in a slithering hiss of need. The other answered in kind. In a flurry of motion, Draylon ended up against the hard edge of his desk with Marilyn's body pressed against him, her leg wrapped around his, holding him captive.

Deft fingers fumbled with the front buttons on his black dress shirt until she seethed in frustration and ripped the shirt the rest of the way down his arms. Those damn eyes of hers glanced up at him, sending a message of things to come. He swallowed hard, taking in the torture of her fingernails trailing red marks along his chest, followed by the tip of her tongue soothing the fiery sting in their wake.

His cock pressed painfully against the front placket of his slacks, growing larger, thicker by the second. As if that wasn't enough the deeper ache of change demanded to be set free. He would let her feel his arousal. Fighting against the tide of change he let his human, baser needs take charge, hopefully counteracting what he didn't want her to see.

Marilyn lowered her leg along with the rest of her body so she was level with his blood engorged shaft. Draylon held his breath, waiting to see what she had in store for him. He closed his eyes. He could hear the clink of his buckle and the raspy hiss of his belt being stripped from its loops in one smooth motion. Her fingers, sure and steady and in full control, unlatched his slacks, releasing the aching part of him to full view. His eyes opened as the cool air touched the heated skin of his cock.

His unusual, fully erect length and girth didn't shock or frighten her as she took him in hand, caressing it from hilt to tip, all the while keeping her eyes fixed on his. The imagery and sensation of sharing what he knew to be her thoughts heightened the whole sensual experience. He'd never had a woman be so bold with him. As ancient as he was, Draylon found himself entering his own virgin territory. He smiled down at her as she explored the length of him. The curiosity behind those eyes and sudden uncertainty of what to do...Draylon gasped, nearly choking as the searing warmth of her mouth engulfed him.

Sweet heavenly gods! Clutching his desk he dug his nails into the under-edge, fighting three urges at once, each one struggling for dominance. He tried spouting ancient Dacian proverbs for control and battle statistics from tribal conflicts. Her hand trailed down his pant leg to tug the material off further, delving in to cup his sac in her other hand.

Marilyn's mouth swallowed him whole. She tongued the smooth underside of his shaft as she sucked and pulled. Her other hand joined in, holding onto the base as she moved up and down, at first a slow but steady pace, making it difficult to stand without the aid of his solid wooden desk. The ache building inside of him made his jaw clench. He had to stop this fantastic torture or face hurting her permanently.

"Marilyn..." he breathed as he twined her glorious mane of hair around his fist. "You must...stop...before...it's too...late."

Fuck! It was too late! Had she assumed his hand in her hair meant for her to go faster, take him deeper? He could feel his balls draw up within her hand. She gave them a playful tug, causing him to look down at her. Those deep gold eyes, laced with fire turned up to gaze at him, his cock circled by those blood red lips of hers, her nostrils flaring as she took in air. He lost control and shoved himself in, to the hilt. He felt the smooth back of her throat and her tongue flattened out along the length of his shaft, curling itself around him as he came in violent bursts, releasing not only years of pent up seed but sexual frustration. He drove into her. Each sight of her swallowing what he gave her only forced him to give her more until he was physically drained.

Exhausted, Draylon leaned back on his elbows, trying like hell to keep himself in check as he pumped his hips one final time. He could feel Marilyn's tongue lick him clean. Her hands came up to his sides, shimmying up his torso like a panther stalking its prey. Those damn eyes of hers held him enthralled. Her hair trailed like feathers across his damp skin.

She balanced, knees on either side of him and reached up, crossing her arms and lifting her t-shirt top over her head. Divesting herself of the bra, she sat there straddling his naked lap, the friction of her jean clad sweetness over his semi-erect cock had him rock hard instantly.

She knew what she was doing, her hips undulating against him, her fingers trailing across his sensitized chest and abs until she pushed him flat against his desk blotter. Down on all fours, her face mere inches from his, she licked his lips.

Draylon could taste the heady mix of their scents—his salty spice she'd partaken of and the sweet hot breath on her tongue. It should've turned him off but the low animalistic growl answered the need in him, and he devoured her mouth like she'd devoured him only moments ago.

Her soft belly pressed against his cock. He had one hand

tangled in her hair as his other found the curve of her breast, petting and stroking until he found the perky tip. He gave it a slight pinch, and she groaned into his mouth. Returning the favor, she reached down and managed to stroke the piece of flesh just under his sac. The shockwaves traveled up his spine to the part of his brain he couldn't control.

All bets were off now—somewhere between the heated kiss and her finger touching such a sensitive area, he managed to kick off the remainder of his clothes. He growled and turned her over on his desk, divesting her of her jeans in one swift yank and tossing them, gods only knew where.

They cleared his desktop, kicking and shoving items out of the way. He held her down and she growled at him. Draylon nuzzled her ear, nipping at it as he maneuvered her onto her knees and pressed her back into a downward position.

Reaching between her thighs, he caressed the tender bridge of flesh. Dampness and her scent coated his finger and he reached beneath her and entered her, testing to see if she was as ready as he was.

She gasped as his finger explored within her. He added another finger, hooking and stretching. She was small, warm and tight. He didn't want to hurt her.

She groaned as he pushed a third digit up into her. Her head went down and she opened for him so he could push in all the way. She wiggled back on his hand, wanting more.

Oh yeah, Draylon...now!

The mental connection was opened. *Oh, trust me. I will.*

His other hand reached around her front to press in and downward on the outer wall of her womb until he could feel his fingers working her from the inside. She rode his hand, her inner muscles tightening around him, the tiny spasms of pre-orgasm hitting her.

That's it, baby. Ride it.

The words spewing from her mouth were lewd and hot.

He would lose it soon if he didn't do something. But he wouldn't mate with her. He couldn't. There was no way he would let himself go that far. He took himself in hand as he worked her to climax.

Her body bucked and rocked, and she tossed back her hair and turned to look over her shoulder at him. Eyes the color of burning embers seared his soul. She opened her mouth to scream and a hiss of sexual need echoed in the room. Rearing back, he lost the control he held onto so tenaciously, and as her inner muscles clenched around his fingers, his hand pushed himself to the limit. Her climax set him off, sending bursts of heat and fire through him. His body shifted between wolf, his true Zmeu form and that of a man losing his fucking mind as he bathed the small of her back with his seed.

#

Draylon waited. Lying against her body as their breathing returned to normal, he had gathered enough function to morph back into his human form. There would be the aftermath of what had just transpired to deal with.

No woman had the mental capacity to withstand his sudden metamorphosis when he was at full sexual peak. The traumatic experience was too much for them once they came down off of their sensual high. It was the main reason he didn't allow himself to get involved with women on a regular basis. The pain of watching someone he'd become attached to go through the horror of knowing what he was…it was too much for him to bear. He'd had to wipe their memories of any contact with him to keep them from becoming mentally unstable.

He wouldn't risk it with Marilyn. Before she could recover her mental capabilities after their arduous act, he slipped into her psyche and demanded she forget all that had happened—since they'd met. No use trying to figure out vampires, witches and the dragon-like creature he'd turned into while having sex with her. Screw Rick and his lack of decisions. She would return home, none the wiser.

Dressing himself, he lifted a naked, semi-conscience Marilyn Reddlin in his arms. Her body lolled like dead weight, but he managed to pull the throw from the chaise lounge in the corner and cover her enough to get things rolling.

Hitting the intercom system with his elbow, he waited for Donovan's voice.

"How may I help you, Draylon?"

"I need you to have the jet prepared for a flight to the United States, immediately. We're taking Miss Reddlin home."

#

Diane Reddlin held up her cell phone in a futile attempt at getting any signal. She should know better, and she did. Spreading the map she'd picked up at the local sporting goods hut near the Hoia Forest on the nearest boulder, she took a look at where she was. Thank God her folks had insisted on her being in Girl Scouts. Her leader had been an avid camper and hiker, teaching the girls survival skills in the forests. Ms. Martz would be pissed with her though. She was out here alone and should never hike without the buddy system.

Her daughter's last triangulated cell phone call had been from Cluj-Napoca, Romania, near the airport. But according to the local polizi, it could be anywhere in a ten mile radius. Not only that, it had been a week since they'd lost contact. Marilyn could be dead. Her daughter had come here to work with Professor Aiden Vamier, but she couldn't get in touch with him. The dean of the university told her there had been no record of Marilyn even checking in for the semester.

That only left one other place she may have ventured, The Hoia Forest. It was the last known location they had on Marilyn's father, Richard.

If her coordinates were correct, she should be making

some sort of headway. But after awhile every odd crooked tree and rocky outcrop looked the same. She took off her yellow bandana and tore it into strips. Tying pieces of the cloth onto the nearest branches would keep her from going in circles.

Taking a swig of her bottled water, she recapped it and placed it back in the netted pocket of her backpack. With a last look at the map and compass she made her decision to go further into the woods. Folding the map, she placed it back in her front pouch along with the compass and sally-forthed, hoping to find some signs of her daughter.

After about a half an hour she'd made it to a barren, circular field. There wasn't a single iota of green growth or snow. The trees around the circle avoided the area at all cost, bending and arching away from the dead spot as if touching it or growing near it would destroy them. Something prickled the back of her neck as if she were being watched. Looking around, there was nobody she could see. The open space between the trees revealed no other vegetation to block or hide any possible attackers.

This had to be the strangest forest she'd ever encountered. No birds, no animals or even small rodent-like creatures flitting about. There wasn't any undergrowth or dead leaves carpeting the floor. Diane had to document this. Reaching for her small digital camera she took a shot. Nothing happened. Trying again, she realized her batteries must be dead.

Taking out her cell phone, she went to take a picture and it too was completely dead. Only a half an hour ago she had full power. She made sure she'd charged her phone the night before along with her rechargeable batteries for her camera and emergency use.

Sighing, Diane looked at her watch—sonofabitch! Her watch had also stopped working at nine forty-five. By the looks of the sun's position, it was nearing midday.

Adjusting the weight of her pack, she stopped from

crossing the open area as a low, menacing growl echoed behind her. Diane wasn't going to move fast anytime soon. She stood rock still and waited. Perhaps whatever made the sound would realize she wasn't a threat and move on. The rustling of weeds and brush and another growl had her lips moving in silent prayer.

Rapid human language followed. Even though Diane was fluent in seven different languages, she wasn't sure what nationality this came from, but it sounded angry. Hopefully it was scolding the animal.

An old crone of a woman, stooped over with age, walked around to face her. Beady black eyes were set into a weathered face etched with deep wrinkles. Gray strands of hair peeked out from her woolen scarf wrapped around her head. She leaned in, peering at Diane as if she needed to be up close to see someone.

The growling commenced and the woman looked down at two large wolves, their mouths snarling, exposing dangerous looking teeth. She tapped the one on his nose, scolding him in her language and then turned on the other one, shaking her walking stick at him. They both sat on their haunches, their tongues lolling out of their mouths.

The old woman yelled at her. Diane backed away, holding up her hands in surrender as the woman before her ranted and raged.

"I'm sorry. I don't speak your language."

The woman stopped, peered at her again, her brows twitching, creasing her weathered face even more. She turned and walked away, the wolves following her.

Stunned, Diane wasn't sure what just happened.

Not wanting to move and upset either the wolves or the old lady, Diane contemplated moving forward. Cautiously taking that step, she wasn't sure how anything was going to go right now, but she wasn't letting her fear keep her from finding

Marilyn. "I'm looking for my daughter. Can you help me?" She spoke slowly, not knowing if the woman even understood her.

The old woman stopped but didn't turn around. She held up her gnarled hand and stretched a bony finger out before hooking it to indicate Diane should follow.

Chapter Ten

Mid-January—Frederick, Maryland

Marilyn didn't understand anything. According to everyone she'd talked to she'd never left Maryland. She'd been deathly ill for a few weeks after Christmas break, unable to go back to work. Nothing proved otherwise.

Her mother was in Europe on business but there was no contact from her. Something was definitely wrong with the whole picture. Her mother never left the state, much less the country.

"I don't know what you're looking for." Tina Johnston sat on the couch with a bowl of ice cream, still wearing her uniform lab coat from the blood bank.

Defeated, Marilyn slumped in her comfy desk chair, gazing distractedly out the window. "I'm not sure either."

Her friend had recently moved in with her until she could find her own place. Having been reassigned from the Baltimore blood bank headquarters to the blood bank here in Frederick, Marilyn didn't remember her moving in and oddly enough, Tina couldn't remember all the details of her move either.

"Do you want to go through your story again? Maybe there's something you left out?"

She knew Tina placated her. What she could remember, or thought she remembered, were nothing but fevered dreams from her illness, according to Dr. Jon Johnston and the rest of the medical team who'd worked on her at Livedel's private medical facility.

"Have you found your phone yet?"

"No. I told you the guy tossed it out the window of the car as we were being chased." She sighed.

"Any luck on tracking down this character?"

"No." She pinched the bridge of her nose. "No clue where to even look." Unless the random dreams she had at night of him were any clue. "I can't even describe him to you. If I was an artist I wouldn't be able to capture—"

"Hey, I hear it's natural to fantasize about a man. Especially after what Daniel put you through. Do you think there's a connection?"

"No, no and no." Pushing away from her desk Marilyn jumped up and paced. Days of agitation and frustration, trying to make sense of her memories and lack thereof had her reaching maximum stress levels. If she didn't get out of the apartment now, she'd go mad, or madder than she was. She needed to run free. "I need to go for a run."

"Why?" Tina looked at her over her spoonful of vanilla bean ice cream. "You don't run."

"Don't tell me what I don't do! Tell me what I am now." She grabbed the framed photo of the two of them at Christmas time off of her desk. "Is this me now?" Marilyn shoved it in her friend's face.

"You were sick. You'd lost so much weight and your iron and vitamin D levels were depleted, Marilyn. You'd let yourself go after the disaster you'd suffered with Daniel. He really did a number on you."

"No…" She shook her head.

Tina was wrong. Everyone was wrong. Nothing was right. Her muscles ached to explode. Jon told her it was residual aches and pains. She doubted him. She doubted everyone…she doubted herself.

"I'm heading out."

"It's after ten o'clock at night."

But Marilyn didn't care. She needed to be wild.

#

Living a few blocks from Baker Park, she figured that would be a good place to run. She didn't care if the park was closed after ten. Surely people still jogged after hours. The lobby of the old Francis Scott Key Hotel where she lived was softly lit. The 1920's décor soothed her most of the time, but not now.

She'd loved the old place and how they'd renovated it into modern apartments. They were in the mod section of town where the theater district met the local downtown cultured restaurants and antique shops. The Carroll Creek Promenade held a flare for cosmopolitan night life and summer time entertainment, but in the middle of winter, the empty streets were filled with nothing more than an array of colonial street lights and the occasional couple returning from a mid-week date night.

Marilyn realized she'd left her apartment without a jacket. She wore her sneakers, jeans and her old Towson University sweatshirt. The digital display at the local bank showed a chilly thirty-seven degrees. She didn't feel it. Maybe she did have a fever still.

Increasing her brisk walk down Court Street towards the city hall, she found even that to be too slow for what she needed. Tina was right. She wasn't a runner. She'd never even been much for sports. She liked to hike the Appalachian Trail or even the smaller trails of Gambrills and Catoctin but running…Nah.

Still her pace increased. Church Street dead ended at Baker Park with the Carillion Bell tower in the distance. The deserted band shell, waiting for summer concert goers stood like an empty clam shell in the middle of an ocean of white snow. The theater seats peeked out of the white blanket like hundreds of rounded, ancient steps leading to nowhere.

The recent day's Nor'easter didn't faze her as much as the fact she didn't feel the cold. In fact the heat inside of her had her ready to combust. Heat which created an odd energy within her had her needing to explode into…into…what? And why?

She ran across the street at Bentz and didn't stop. The wide open grounds lay before her, not a soul in sight. Not a car, not a late night dog walk, nothing. Her sprint turned heated, her body broke a barrier she didn't realize was there. Her arms pumped, matching the rhythm of her legs.

Now she felt it, the oddly familiar change to her body. She ran. Like the natural transition of letting your hair down, the change freed her. The aches and pains were not of illness…but of transformation. And there it was…she ran on four legs, free into the night.

Aha! I'm not crazy.

As much as the idea elated her, she still had no clue in hell what it meant.

How had she been able to do this? Where did the dream end and reality begin? Marilyn wasn't sure if she was still asleep and dreaming all this as Dr. Johnston informed her. No, impossible.

Who'd been lying to her? Did her mother know she was a freak of nature? Maybe her father knew, and that was why he left all those years ago. She ran to the most remote area of Baker Park, down along the frozen pond. She howled in frustration, knowing that someone she'd trusted all of her life must have known about her. Surely, Dr. Johnston knew…did Tina?

As she neared the pond at the far end of Baker Park, she slowed her pace and nosed her way to the edge. Gazing down into the frozen water, the very image she'd dreamed, or thought she'd dreamed, stared back at her, the auburn haired wolf was her.

She had so many questions to muddle through now. All Marilyn knew was someone had better damn well start explaining things. Unfortunately, she wasn't sure who would know—and who could she actually trust to tell her secret to?

#

Heading back to the apartment complex, Marilyn stayed close to the shadows of the back alleys. A dog barked, setting off a chain reaction from other dogs in the area. They sensed her in her canine form. Understanding their growls as actual words, warning each other of her presence, startled her. But then, she was one of them now. Clenching her jaw, she fought the urge to join in on their response—she wasn't keen on alerting her neighbors to her new existence.

Happy to make it back, Marilyn realized she had a problem. How in the hell was she going to get in? The door to the main lobby closed at nights. The only way in was through the back door, and she would have to find some way to key herself in. The small parking area remained empty, no one to let her in. And who would let a wolf inside? Anyone's first instinct would be to call animal control.

Okay, how did one change from wolf back to human form? *Yeah, like there's a manual on transformation, Marilyn.*

She needed to think, and fast. Closing her eyes she focused on the possibilities, trying to remember every shape-shifting, paranormal romance she'd ever read. How had they done it? Wolf to human…wolf to human…how could she morph back?

Imposs...whoa! Marilyn opened her eyes and looked at her body. She was back in her human form. Okay, so all she had to do was think about the change and it would happen? She'd have to test that theory, later. Right now, she just wanted to get inside and tell Tina about her transformation. Tell her she wasn't crazy, that what she remembered as 'dreams' weren't dreams after all.

But first, she had a different problem. She'd keyed in her entry number to unlock the outer door, only to see her reflection in the glass. Umm...naked, and standing in front of the security cameras. Damn! One of the big reasons she'd moved here was for the phenomenal security, and now she would be viewed by the staff in the morning. Great!

Taking a deep breath and setting her shoulders, she had no other option than to fake it. She would walk in, take the stairs up to hide from those who would be in the elevator—no one used the stairs.

The sound of her bare feet slapping the cold linoleum steps echoed in the empty stairwell. She lived on the third floor. Ignoring the rest of the video cameras on each floor, she made her way up to her level. Opening the heavy door to their floor, she prayed for a clean break...no such luck.

The guy from their floor had just gotten done with his late night work out and had evidently taken the stairs. Hoping he didn't see her as he used his towel to wipe sweat off of his face—she was lousy with good fortune tonight—he spied her. They both stopped and stared, him in awe and her like the naked woman caught off guard that she was.

Crossing her arms over her chest, she turned her back to him and walked briskly to her door. It was locked and she'd forgotten to take her key. Knocking, hoping Tina was there to let her in, she looked over her shoulder to see the guy staring at her.

Marilyn felt her lip curl back and her teeth gnashed out a vicious snarl. He backed up and walked away in the direction of his own unit.

The door swung open and Tina stared at her in aghast.

"Um…you're naked."

"Just shut up and let me in before I have security on me," she hissed as Tina moved to the side to let her enter.

"What happened to you? Are you okay? Did someone attack you?"

"No…I'm fine…I…" Marilyn didn't know where to begin. Tina continued to stare at her. She hurried down the hall to her room and found her robe, trying to figure out how to explain the situation to make her friend understand.

That was it. There was no way her friend could understand. She barely understood.

"You what?" Tina stood in her doorway, waiting for her to continue.

Marilyn's shoulders dropped in defeat. As much as she'd always trusted Tina to believe in her, now she wasn't sure if she would. She couldn't blame her if she didn't—Tina would find her certifiably crazy.

Exhaling, Marilyn racked her fingers nervously through her hair. "I'm going to tell you a story, but I need you to have an open mind." Upon saying that, she took off her robe and thought about being a wolf.

Tina's eyes drew wide as she backed away, shaking her head and slammed the bedroom door to separate them.

Yeah…her friend wasn't ready to be open minded, just yet.

#

Being stuck in the apartment while 'recovering,' was not her idea of spending time off of work. Though sitting and drinking cappuccinos while staring out the wintery window wasn't a bad way to spend a snowy morning, it just wasn't her

norm. Dr. Johnston had yet to give her the go-ahead to return
to Livedel. She'd called, wanting to talk to him about the
changes she was going through. He should know something.
He'd been her doctor for awhile. Hadn't he given her
medicines for her aches and pains before leaving—
for…her…trip?

Damn, damn, damn! It came back to her. She knew she'd
been in to see him *before her trip.* She'd kept her files from
her appointments. They were in her medical files on-line.
Nearly spilling her cappuccino, she ran into her room. Opening
her laptop and waiting for it to go through the start up
operations, she began to dress in her work out clothes. Once
she found the paperwork for her appointment back in early
January, she was going to go over to see Tina's dad and start
asking all kinds of questions.

Slipping on her running shoes, she sat down and typed her
password into her medical files at Livedel. Password incorrect.
She typed it in again, only to have the same error message
come up, blocking her from her own files.

She knew her password. It was always the same. She
logged onto her work center at Livedel. Working from home
occasionally, she had full access…password denied…or used
to. Something wasn't right.

Grabbing her cell phone she dialed Tina, forgetting she
hadn't been answering her calls the past few days. After the
fiasco the other night, Tina had gone to stay at her folk's
house. Marilyn didn't blame her. But it was still difficult not
having her friend around for a sounding board.

"Hi."

"Tina?"

"Yeah…it's me."

The odd silence spoke volumes. What could either one say
at a time like this? Marilyn figured she'd just come out and tell
her friend what was going on.

"Um, I have a problem,"

"No shit, really?" her friend replied. "Could it be because…" She paused. "Look Marilyn, I can't talk right now. Can I call you back later?"

"Sure. No problem."

Tina hung up. Marilyn had never felt more alone.

#

Her nightly runs took her further away from home. Marilyn made a point of keeping an extra set of clothing in her car. She'd head up to Gambrills, park in the parking lot and slip into the night unobserved. Memories or maybe just instinct flooded back at times, hunting in the quiet woods of…she wasn't sure where…but there'd been another wolf. She remembered eyes as blue as sapphires in a background of raven colored fur. The urge to howl hit her whenever she thought about the creature. She stifled her need to keep from being detected.

Some nights she'd been able to hunt a bit. The rare wild hare or turkey would have her on the prowl but as she was taught, she kept her hunting clean, eating her fill and burying the remains to keep others from finding it. She'd return hours later to her car, change into her clothes and head home to her empty apartment.

It wasn't the same without Tina there. They'd shared an apartment down in Baltimore until recently when Marilyn had moved up here after the semester ended and her breakup with Daniel. Except for that brief period and now, they hadn't been apart since senior year in high school. Tina's dismissal hurt more than Daniel's did at times, especially since they'd always been so close. They relied on each other. But still, Marilyn couldn't blame her—coming to her own terms with her changes was troubling enough. Explaining them to someone else, impossible. Still, she'd managed to accept her fate, even knowing she didn't understand why.

Noticing her landline phone blinking as she turned on the light in her living room, Marilyn checked her voice mails.

"Hey Mari, it's me Tina. I wanted to touch base with you. Something is wrong and I'm not sure what...I mean other than...well you know. Call me? I'll be up until eleven or so if you want to call tonight."

The clock read ten-twenty-nine. Marilyn dialed her friend's cell phone.

"It's me Tina. What's up?"

"Meet me at Denny's in ten minutes."

"What's going on?" Tina sounded shaken...more so than when she'd seen her morph.

"Ju...just meet me there, please."

"Okay. On my way."

#

Only a few people were sitting in Denny's drinking coffee and having a late night breakfast or dessert. Tina sat toying with her soda and straw. Looking around nervously, she smiled when she saw Marilyn and brushed a stray blonde curl back behind her ear.

"I promise I won't bite," Marilyn teased to break the strained mood.

Seeing Tina's eyes well up with moisture had her instantly regretting her words. But Tina held up her hand and shook her head. "No...it's okay. It's not you."

The waitress came by to take her order as Marilyn slipped into the booth across from her life-long friend. She ordered a hot chocolate, not really hungry after her recent hunt. Waiting for the woman to leave, she leaned forward.

"What's up? You look like you've been through the wringer backwards."

Tina looked down at her hands, clasped together in front of her on the table. They shook. Marilyn placed her hand over them, hoping to calm her friend's fears instead of sickening her by her touch.

"Something awful happened at work tonight," she whispered, her voice quivering in time with her hands.

"Tell me Max didn't do anything to you...I'll rip his heart out!" Marilyn seethed. She'd met Tina's boss at the Greater Baltimore Blood Bank a time or two when he'd been the manager at her other office in Towson. He was a sleaze bag with hands that loved to touch things that didn't belong to him...namely the other female co-workers.

"No. It wasn't Max." She looked around as if to see who might be listening. "It was his supervisor—"

"*He* touched you?"

Tina's brow furrowed and she shook her head. "He...I was finishing up work. It was late and everyone had left...or so I thought." She took a cleansing breath. "As I was taking the trash out to the dumpster, I saw Gerlich, the new supervisor...I saw him...he...oh God!" Tina buried her face in her hands and sobbed.

She'd never seen her friend so hysterical. Tina, the bright light on any rainy day, was a mess. Slipping over into her side of the booth, Marilyn took her friend in her arms to comfort her. The waitress came with the hot cocoa and nodded towards Tina in a gesture asking if she was all right. Marilyn nodded and gave a half smile. The waitress retreated.

She gently patted and stroked Tina's back, trying to get her to settle down. Her sobs stuttered into sighs and she used her napkin to wipe her face. Still, Marilyn waited. What had this Gerlich done to upset Tina so?

"You know how we always thought vampires were so sexy?" Tina asked, starting to laugh in a hysterical hiccup. "Well, they aren't." Tina looked straight at Marilyn. "I swear, I saw this man bite the neck of another man...and then he bit into his own wrist and made him swallow his blood."

Sitting back away from Tina, Marilyn's mind went into a

whirl. Memories of fanged people approaching her and exploding…running away…

"You don't believe me?" Tina asked, her lip snarled. "You of all people?"

"No. It's not that." Marilyn shook her head. "Did he see you?"

"You believe me? You believe that I saw a vampire?"

"Yes, I believe you but that's not important. Did he see you?"

Tina sat back, thinking. "I don't know. I made a gasping sound and he turned in my direction, but he was too far away and it was kind of dark. I was in shadow."

"Vamiers don't have problems with vision," Marilyn said, her voice distant even to her own ears. Vamiers? She knew the name or term…Her head throbbed and her insides turned warm—more than fever it was a raging inferno. "We need to get out of here."

"Why?"

"I need air…" Fishing a twenty out of her purse she laid it down, and leaving her hot cocoa untouched, she pulled Tina behind her and out the door. The frosty air did nothing to cool her down. "Meet me back at the apartment."

"Are you going to be okay?"

"Yes. Go on. Go straight there and lock the door behind you. Don't let anyone in other than me."

#

Running through the woods of Gambrills, Marilyn's heart rate sped. She knew she needed to run but what was going on inside her body didn't feel like it did when she was a wolf. Fleet of foot, her body adapted to every tree, every root, every outcropping of rock. Naked she ran through the woods, waiting for her body to morph into her wolf. She'd accepted her new change over the past week, realizing that her crazy dreams weren't crazy after all and that somehow everything would fit back together.

She continued running and waiting. Concern swelled in her brain when she didn't feel the change. Usually an image or a canine tic of muscular motion drew her into the first signs of transition. This time there was no wolf. The edge of the cliff was only yards away. She knew the area. She'd come up here many times on hikes to look out over the valley. It was a helluva drop with sheer sides straight down. Her mind slammed into her, telling her to stop, but an involuntary force had her going at a dead run. Panic laced through her as her nervous system played havoc, fighting both her voluntary and involuntary nervous system.

Her legs didn't stop, her heart sped up and her brain screeched at her, but instead of a feminine scream the screech of a beast erupted and her body launched itself off of the cliff. Squealing, Marilyn hoped to God this was a dream and she'd wake up. The sound of her voice continued as she fell…and the screech turned back into a scream, throwing her into a semi-conscious state of waking.

She didn't stay asleep long enough to sense the unfurling of magnificent, blood red wings behind her, keeping her aloft.

#

Draylon woke with a start. He wasn't sure what roused him but the phone next to him shrilled like the shrieking call of a Zmeu. Lifting his head off of his desk blotter, he rubbed at his eyes and picked it up.

"Hello?"

"Dray, we have a problem and I need you to see to it ASAP."

He looked at the caller ID. "Rick? What's going on?"

"Who would be the best contact to handle a Vamier situation in the United States?"

"Depends whereabouts."

"We have alerts of a massive blood bank take over in the

Baltimore/Washington D.C. area."

"Isn't Mike Linder on the case?"

"Yes. But I want you there also. There's a possibility we might be dealing with one of Aiden's top henchmen, Gerlich. You know of him?"

"Yeah, I know of him, former Nazi soldier that turned vamp back in 1940. What happened to Trevor? He's usually handling Aiden's deals."

"Reports have it that Trevor is no longer Aiden's number one. Seems there was a falling out when he couldn't capture Marilyn Reddlin and bring her in. Gerlich is now in charge of Aiden's United States operations."

"Sonofabitch. And I trusted Trevor more."

"Exactly what I thought." Rick sighed. "That's not all. There are human lives at stake. Remember me telling you about Christina Johnston? They moved her from the Towson branch to the Frederick branch of the blood bank. Gerlich is up in Frederick, working over the blood storage. She may be in danger if Gerlich gets to her. Not only that, if Gerlich finds out she's friends with Marilyn, both will be in danger."

"Fuck."

"Yeah…I knew sending Marilyn back prematurely was a bad idea. I still don't understand why you didn't wait for my instructions."

"Because I got tired of waiting, Rick. She was in danger here with me. I couldn't hold out without giving in…if you get my drift."

"Yeah, I got your drift and if I hear you talking about 'your drift' where Marilyn Reddlin is concerned, I will personally lop it off. I don't want to hear it…ever! You got that?"

Draylon removed the phone receiver from his ear and looked at it as if Rick had just jumped through it to grab him by the throat. "I've got it. Rick, what is up with you? Ever since this whole fiasco with Marilyn Reddlin came up you've not been yourself."

"What's up with me? Putting up with more shit than I can right now. Oh and to add the proverbial cherry on top, I just found out that my chief financial officer is MIA. She told her staff I asked her to join me for a business conference in Europe. Funny thing about that…no one informed me of any business conference. The last I knew she'd called me to see if I could find her daughter."

"And did you?" Draylon smirked, knowing damn well that Rick hadn't informed Diane Reddlin of anything.

Silence. "It wasn't the right time."

"Nothing is the right time with you anymore, Rick. And it's making some of us edgy. You need to come clean soon or all hell is going to break loose."

"Hell is breaking loose, my friend. Unfortunately it's not in my power to stop it."

#

Why was Rick involving him in all of this right now? Everything had been going well lately. He'd managed to get Marilyn back to the states and was on his way of trying to forget about her. Now, he was going back into the hell he'd just gotten himself out of.

Draylon managed to contact his friend, Mike Linder, a former Navy SEAL, circa Vietnam era. The man had been the leader of his SEAL Team and lost them all in a rescue mission gone bad. On top of that, he'd been turned by one of Aiden's vampires—without permission.

When they'd brought him in to the mobile medical facility he'd been in a bad way. But the post-traumatic stress disorder he suffered made his eternal life a living hell. The man never got over losing every member of his company only to remain alive.

"I'll get over there as soon as I can," Mike said as he

relayed the message from Rick.

"Don't go in there all Rambo on me. Just keep things in check and report to me when I show up. As long as no humans are being harmed, we can deal with it low key."

"Gotcha. Any humans in the equation that I need to keep an eye out for?"

"We have a civilian who might be at risk. The blood bank accountant from Baltimore was recently relocated to the Frederick branch. Her name is Christina Johnston."

Mike snorted over the phone. "Any relation to Doc Johnston?"

"Matter of fact she is. She's Jon and Claire's daughter."

Mike swore. The 'f-bombs' heard around the world via satellite right now would have brought about World War III, if they were fatal.

"Just keep an eye out for her. I don't think she's in any danger right now, so relax." Draylon looked at his watch as his jet took a turbulence bounce, reminding him of flying with Marilyn from Timisoara to Cluj. "Watch out for her friend Marilyn Reddlin, too. You know how women are, if one goes to the ladies room…they all go."

"Marilyn Reddlin? God, don't tell me she's related to Diane 'the bitch' Reddlin."

"One and the same."

"Is there anyone who isn't related to half the humans we know?"

"Right now? No," Draylon said, yawning. "I'll be landing at Frederick's airport around five o'clock tonight your time. Keep me posted on surveillance and I'll meet you there."

"Will do. Catch some zzzs man. You sound like your bleeding from your eyeballs."

"You should see them from my side." He snorted. "Hey thanks man, I appreciate your help in this situation."

"No problem. I've got your six."

Draylon switched off his mobile and let the pilot know he was off cellular connection. He still didn't understand the military lingo Mike would throw at him from time to time. But he knew his 'six' meant he had his back. Good, because his back was getting pretty, damn sore.

Putting his reclining passenger seat back, he tried to relax. He hadn't had a chance to do so in weeks, not since before he'd sent Marilyn back home. He'd worked to erase her memory and those of her closest associates. Tina Johnston had been a bit of a challenge, much like Marilyn had been. But he'd managed to cause her a bit of a memory lapse, hopefully it was enough to convince Marilyn. He was thankful for Nonni having the foresight to instruct him to take Marilyn to his Austrian home, Eskardel. Very few places in the world provided the ability to stop time—the Bermuda Triangle, Easter Island, Stonehenge, Hoia Forest and Eskardel, his home in Austria that he named after his family mountain home.

Time, as mortals knew it, didn't exist in these places and he was able to keep Marilyn from losing time as she knew it and take her home within only days of her original travel schedule. One in which he and Rick took great care in deleting from her past.

#

Marilyn had that damn dream again, the one where she was soaring above the clouds. It wasn't as bad as it could be. She knew she was dreaming. It was the dragon dream. She'd managed to finally leap without screaming herself awake after the fifth time. Now she accepted the fact she was a blood red dragon with an emerald stone in her forehead. It was kind of sexy in a way. Like a piercing of the belly button only about seven feet higher.

She had a wingspan that could encompass the length of the Raven's football field. She found that kind of cool. Her tail had a mind of its own though—taking out trees and half of the ground she traversed. But it made for a great stabilizer. It had taken her a while to figure it out but once she did, flying had a whole new meaning for her.

Her nostrils flared as she picked up a familiar scent. She followed the aroma like a homing beacon, around another ridge that wasn't a familiar Maryland landscape. No, this one looked like steep Alpine slopes of snow and ice. Still, something kicked in her head that she knew where this was. A screech echoed off the rocky terrain. It wasn't her. She'd flown into a flight pattern of another dragon…a black one nearly two feet taller and broader than her own form.

The creature sported a glorious wingspan. A vibrant, electric blue gem settled between fiery red eyes. He stopped in flight, nearly upend on his spaded tale. His head cocked to the side and he screeched at her. She screeched back, not having a clue what either one said.

A chuckle erupted in her dream and a familiar voice in her head spoke.

No way.

I told you there was a dragon, she responded.

The dragon took off but stopped to look back as if to lead them on a chase. Marilyn was game. Sure. This was her dream, she could chase dragons if she wanted to.

He led them to a forested alcove and landed gracefully as if a bird on foot. She hadn't quite mastered her landing skills yet but followed as well as she could. He waddled around, knocking over a few pines and breathing fire on them to break the trunks in half. She joined in the fun and soon had a good size pile of timber. Her flaming breath gave her a whole new meaning to heartburn.

Her raven colored friend set the pile to blaze and walked away a few feet. When he returned, there stood, the man she'd been looking for. He was naked, handsome and the smile on his face, something she'd never witnessed. It was as if he'd never been happy until this moment. Did seeing another dragon make him happy? Maybe in her dream there weren't many dragons.

She found herself shifting and standing before him au natural. She didn't have a care in the world as they stood smiling at each other across the fire.

Welcome to Eskardel, Marilyn.

What is Eskardel?

My home.

Marilyn awoke from her dream…crying with joy.

#

Every day she called in to Livedel to check with the medical office to see if she was able to go back to work and every day she was denied. She still hadn't heard from her mother either. It had been nearly two weeks and still no word. It wasn't like her not to call when she was away, even on business. Maggie, her mother's administrative assistant told her all was well and that she was at a conference with Rick Delvante. As secretive as that man was, she shouldn't worry.

Carrying her weekly bag of groceries, she juggled with the load to unlock her door. But the door swung open without effort.

"Hello?"

"Hello," a dejected voice called from behind her laptop across the apartment.

Tina peeked up over the monitor screen and buried her face in her hands.

"What's going on? What are you doing here so early? Aren't you supposed to be at work?"

Marilyn was proud of her friend for sticking to her guns and returning to work after the frightening incident. But she made Tina promise not to work after hours when the vampire guy might be around.

"I was…until I was suspended." There was shame in her

voice.

"Why?" She had Marilyn's full attention. No one in their right mind would ever have an issue with Tina. She was perfection wrapped up in quality. All of her teachers growing up had loved her. She was "class favorite," "most friendly," "most caring" and would forgive a scorpion if one ever bit her. It just didn't make sense.

"They said my accounting numbers were off. The books don't match the deposits of blood donated." She sighed, fidgeting with her fingernails. Her telltale angst always had her studying her fingernails as if they might be dirty. Dirt didn't touch Tina. It was ashamed to sully such a delicate doll.

"Did they show you the documents?"

She shook her head. "Max just told me I was suspended, and he'd let me know when I could return." She sat down heavily on the bed. "I don't know where I went wrong."

"But you've been handling their accounts so thoroughly for the past two years. Why now?"

Tina shrugged. "I swear I haven't done anything differently. I could do the accounts in my sleep and still come out with everything balanced and in order." She looked to Marilyn. "Maybe it's time for me to move on. Do you think you might be able to get me in on the ground floor at Livedel?"

"Possibly. Update your resume and I'll take it in. I'm not going to promise you anything though. Mom caught a bunch of flack from employees and the board members for taking me on and playing "favorites." She ended up having to take it all the way up to Mr. Delvante himself."

Marilyn unloaded Styrofoam platters of meat from the grocery bag into her refrigerator. "In the meantime though, don't sweat it too much. Maybe they made a mistake and will find out they owe you an apology. Give them a few days to figure things out."

Tina knotted her fingers together. "I'm just so worried. What if they end up firing me? A suspension is the first offense. I can't afford to lose this position. With the economy still struggling and jobs at a minimum, even for an accountant, I don't know what I'd do."

"We'll work it out when we get there. Just take it easy today." She grabbed slices of nearly raw roast beef from the deli bag and devoured it.

"I can't take it easy. I'm supposed to be in Baltimore helping with the annual blood drive this weekend and meeting with the director, Aiden Vamier."

Marilyn stopped chewing immediately. Aiden Vamier? Vamier…why did that name sound so familiar?

She could sense Tina staring at her. "Are you feeling all right?"

No…yes…she wasn't sure. Her temples throbbed as she tried to comprehend what her best friend said. Vamier. Professor Vamier. She *was* supposed to work with him for the semester in Romania. She wasn't crazy. She'd been given the opportunity to study under his tutelage and find out about her medallion.

Her medallion! She remembered having it, wearing it, the heaviness lying on her chest…and then she'd wrapped it around her hand… Marilyn went through the motions as if it were only the night before.

"I was in Nonni's cottage. There were two wolves…no, two naked men who were wolves and then there was Draylon."

Tina tilted her head. "What are you talking about?"

"I was there. I was in Romania. " She went to her jewelry box where she kept her medallion safe when she wasn't wearing it. It wasn't there. Panic laced up her breastbone, the agony making her head hurt all the more. "It's gone."

Her bag. Maybe she'd packed it in her suitcase. No, not her suitcase, her knapsack. Throwing open the closet door she found the bag and opened it. Empty. But she swore this was the bag she'd taken with her when she'd fled Cluj. Frantic and heart sore she sobbed.

"Where is it? Tina I've lost it...oh God, what am I going to do? He entrusted me to keep it safe and now..." Searching the various inner pockets, her fingers lit on an odd piece of linen. She stopped, pulled out the vintage, embroidered handkerchief bundle and sat up on her knees. She shook it out to reveal the medallion, still intact, still safe.

Breathing again she inhaled a faint scent of woodsy smoke. She held the kerchief up to her nose. The fragrance struck a familiar note. Closing her eyes, Marilyn's other senses picked up details of the cottage, the night of her escape from vampires. It wasn't a dream, it had been real.

But just what was it that had been real and why?

Chapter Eleven

Draylon didn't like the situation he'd seen. Gerlich instructed his hoods to load up iced coolers of what could only be the banks supply of blood into the small moving trucks. He'd been sitting in the shadows watching them for two nights now. Rick's assignment didn't leave much to the imagination. He was to keep an eye on Gerlich and report on his findings. But he was not to interfere until they had all the information. He hated being a spy. Let him take out a band of Vamier's vampires and he'd be a happy fuck.

"Anything new?"

His partner and good friend, Mike Linder tried sneaking up on him. He didn't hear the former special-ops agent because of his stealth, but Draylon didn't have any problem picking up scents. It was just one of his many, unusual gifts.

"Nada. Still just packing up trucks full of blood."

"Hell, we don't know that man. Those Styrofoam coolers could be full of picnic supplies. Wouldn't we look stupid if they were?"

"It's a picnic all right, made for every vampire in Vamier's compound." He turned his attention to Mike. "Who did you find out was in charge?"

"Some guy by the name of Maxwell Struthers. He worked with Trevor Lyon before Gerlich took over. I wonder what happened to Trevor to put Gerlich in command?"

"You have to ask?"

The object of their discussion stepped out from inside the building, gave orders to one of his unit leaders and left in his Mercedes, leaving the others to do his dirty deeds.

"Oh I know Aiden took him out in one bite, but why? Trevor had been like a son to him for over two centuries. Hadn't he been one of his recruits from the Crusades?"

"Yeah. He'd been a real sonofabitch back then, too. Gerlich is much younger but moved up in ranks fast for a World War II Nazi soldier."

Trevor had been a major pain in the ass for the better part of the two centuries. But because he and Trevor had been equals in rank under their individual commands for so long, Draylon felt a kindred spirit with him. It bothered him to know he'd been the reason behind Aiden killing him.

But it had been worth it. He still couldn't shake thoughts of her. The month he'd kept her protected had been the most difficult of times, but also the best time he remembered in quite a while. Her intelligence and fun loving nature alone made for a unique experience. He wasn't used to involving himself with such a breed of woman. Most of his dates preferred designer shoes, social functions and seeing how far they could push a man to do their bidding.

What they didn't understand was he wasn't a man to be pushed. Draylon had always focused on finding the one woman who could accept him for what he was. Unfortunately what he was wasn't human. As much as he'd enjoyed Marilyn's company, he wouldn't subject her to having to witness the truth. When her safety from him was no longer an issue, he deemed it necessary to wipe her mind of the memories they'd made and brought her home. The only problem was Rick had sent him right back to where he'd returned her, Frederick, Maryland. Now, there was the chance of seeing her again.

"I still don't know why Rick sent you on this mission," Mike ventured forth. "I'm right here in Frederick and could have handled this job."

And probably better, too. With Mike's Navy SEAL training and stealthy ability, no one was more equipped to go in and spy on Gerlich's business. Draylon preferred to go in and take out his target with guns blazing, so to speak. He excelled at mass killings of vamps when there was a hoard of them attacking.

"I don't know. When Rick assigns me a site, I don't ask questions."

Mike shook his head. "You've got to stop kissing his ass, man."

Draylon looked away from the site to glare at Mike. "He saved my life. I owe him my allegiance. No questions asked."

"We can't go blindly into a situation just on faith. It's your right as a human being to question authority."

"If you remember, Mike…I'm not human."

Mike didn't say anything more.

"Have you managed to locate Christina Johnston?"

"Nope. I checked and she wasn't in today."

A car's headlights split the darkness of the night in the front parking area of the blood bank, canceling the remaining interrogation of his friend. Draylon's senses went on alert. He motioned to Mike who'd already noticed and took inventory of the situation. The lights turned off.

He could make out the shadows of two figures sitting inside the vehicle. Something told him they weren't associated with the goings-on in the back of the building though. They would have pulled up around to the loading docks if they were.

The doors opened on the small two door coup and the distinct chatter of feminine voices echoed in the night. Draylon strained to hear what they were saying.

"You don't have to come with me. I'm just going in to get my bag of cross-stitching I left."

"Tina, it's dark. I'm not letting you go inside a dark building by yourself."

"Fine."

Tina turned and hit the lock button on her key fob, sounding the horn to lock her car doors and alerting some of Gerlich's goons who were busy packing. Shit.

"Shit. Those two women are heading right into a butt load of trouble," Mike echoed his sentiments.

Things were now out of Rick's direct orders not to get involved. He motioned for Mike to head towards the front of the building as he snuck up into the back, hopefully timing his arrival to protect the women from what he knew would be a bad thing.

Draylon had his blade drawn from the inside of his jacket sleeve where he kept it, knowing black-blood would be drawn tonight.

There were five vamps left now that Gerlich was gone from the scene. Draylon counted two at the ramp of the truck, a third on the concrete loading dock but couldn't see the other two. They had to be inside.

Mike made it to the edge of the brick building. He gave the hand signal for "going-in."

Draylon approached the back, keeping to the shadows of the night. Sneaking up on one of the guys on the truck, he quietly slit his throat all the way through to…sonofabitch. Red blood covered the black of his gloves in the lamplight. This wasn't a Vamier vamp, this guy was human. Fuck. He'd have some explaining to do to Rick.

"Hey, what's going on?"

Draylon looked up to see the second guy carrying an ice tote. The guy noticed what happened, seeing his buddy on the ground in a pool of blood. He dropped the tote, withdrew a Glock and shot at him. A mortal man would have died instantly, this time Draylon was thankful he wasn't.

Roundhouse kicking the gun out of his assailant's hands, Draylon was able to knock the guy out without killing him. But where had the third man gone?

Cautiously he closed in on the loading dock, made his way up into the building and looked around. Nothing but storage freezer units and wire cages of office and blood donation supplies. The door to the inner office stood open. This didn't bode well. He hoped Mike had intercepted any issues before anything could get to the two women.

The scene he came up on didn't look as good as he'd wished.

"...sure you came back for your cross-stitch." A middle aged man stood over a blonde haired girl with her back to the wall. The gun he had point-blank at her forehead answered any questions Draylon might have. Still hidden he waited to see if Mike had managed to get a bead on the situation but didn't see his partner. There wasn't much he could see from his angle. Where was the other woman?

"No one 'cross-stitches' anymore, Johnston." The man threw his chin up. "Who are you working for, or are you just trying to get even with me for suspending you?"

"Hey Max." Another guy came down the hallway brandishing an auburn haired woman. "I found another coming out of the ladies room."

Draylon's breath hitched when the abductor turned the struggling form to the front of him as if presenting a prize. But his beefy arm had her in a choke hold and she struggled to breathe.

Marilyn.

The situation just went from bad to worse. What the hell was she doing here?

"Let her go," the blonde squealed.

"You don't have any room to be making demands, Tina," the man addressed as Max commented.

This must be the district manager, Maxwell Struthers. So he was in on it with Gerlich. This didn't follow protocol. Vamier never used humans. Something didn't taste right about any of this. He would add that to his report to Rick—after they got these women out of danger.

Figuring how to proceed with humans involved, and without having the girls get hurt in the process, frustrated him. The man holding Marilyn had her dangling from his arm so she couldn't even get any leverage in her legs. His protective instincts kicked in, and he had to hold them in check before he added more chaos to the situation.

Draylon didn't need to worry.

A throaty growl erupted. At first he didn't know from where. It sounded as if Therron and Kurren were about to attack an unsuspecting trespasser. But it wasn't them. The growl turned into a rabid snarl. Holy Fuck!

Before everyone's eyes, Marilyn thrashed and convulsed in the man's arms. Her body looked as if it were turning inside out until she manifested as an auburn haired wolf and sank her jaws into the man's arm, tearing into flesh and bone.

The whole scene and the shock of seeing the woman turn into an animal set the pace for getting the fucking job done. Draylon and Mike went into action at the same time. Maxwell had taken his eyes off of his blonde captive for a few brief seconds to give her the leverage she needed. Tina took out his knee with a sharp kick. The sound of Maxwell's femur snapping in two had Draylon's senses spasming. With the man down, screaming in pain, the petite, angel faced woman continued to use her killer, denim-short clad legs, to perform the same maneuver on his face. Blood gushed from the man's severely busted nose.

"…and yes, there are still people who cross-stitch," she yelled down at the withering body as she stepped over him and retrieved her sewing bag beneath the desk.

Motionless Draylon stood, waiting for her to notice him. He wasn't about to approach with her adrenaline still rushing. When she turned around with a gasp of shock, he held up his hands in surrender.

She *was* too cute. She reminded him of Shirley Temple who never grew out of her blonde curls. But the look spoke volumes. "Don't piss me off" or the Good Ship Lollypop would be up his ass.

The sound of barking and snarling alerted them to the other issue at hand. Marilyn.

"Draylon," Mike called out from his side of the partitioned wall. "A little help here before this bitch decides to have my balls for her own playthings."

Running to his friend's aid, he found Marilyn standing her ground, teeth bared and hackles up. She wouldn't let Mike move any further.

Tina held her breath.

Draylon focused on her, trying to get into her mind.

She turned towards him and attacked. Instantly transforming, Draylon matched his mate.

Wolf to wolf they stood. He had to show her who was alpha. The wolf attacked, biting him in the throat. A twist of his head and he was able to grab onto her, wherever he could reach, shaking her before tossing her to the side. The skitter of claws trying to find purchase on the slippery tile echoed off the sterile walls. Draylon yelped as she leapt, biting him in the hindquarters. This game was on, she wanted to tangle, he'd tangle.

Rolling and tussling, he tried to get into her head and calm her down. He was used to rough housing with Therron and Kurren but never a female pack member. There weren't any. *Shit.* Fierce and ferocious, she tore at him. He could smell and taste his blood from the various bites and scratches she lavished on his canine form.

Finally he regained the upper hand, tumbling her beneath him. Growling down at her, he bit into the furry underneath of her neck and held on with just enough pressure to let her know he was in command of this situation. He could hear her cursing him to hell and back.

It's okay, Marilyn. I've got you. You'll be fine in a moment. Relax. You are safe.

But was he feeding her a line of crap? Was she safe? He wasn't sure. Draylon realized something troubling. If he'd wiped her memory, how could she be cursing his name and rallying about their time together in Eskardel? The situation just became dicey.

Chapter Twelve

Marilyn relaxed and her body shifted back into normal human conditions—but she was naked, lying beneath a huge black hound. The beast backed up and sat on its haunches staring at her, his head cocked to the side.

Moving away she settled against a cold metal desk, tucking her arms and legs into herself to secure her nudity as much as she could. But her focus was on the dog. Draylon. Whining, it made cautious, non-threatening paces towards her.

Fisting her hand, she reached to him. The furry, black beast sniffed. She unfurled her fingers, and her body relaxed until she noticed the sting of cuts and scrapes on her fingertips. Blood smeared her palm. Small cuts and bite marks dotted her arms and legs. A tiny wound above her navel slowly healed itself before her eyes.

She gasped. "What the hell!"

Panic raced back through her system, sending her blood to churn like a simmering pot of stew. Her facial muscles spasmed with involuntarily tics as her lip curled upward exposing teeth and gum line. Her nose twitched as various scents of hot male, fear, blood and animal musk violated her olfactory senses. She snarled and dropped to all fours, fighting an internal physical demand to morph into something else…but her mind, her body, her soul couldn't sort out the images.

Adrenaline coursed through her as her body contorted while she cried out. Various animalistic sounds echoed in her head, all coming from her.

Arms surrounded her like bands of steel, holding her, forcing her to relax. Marilyn fought to do just that as the rest of her internal images fought for freedom.

Marilyn, relax…breathe…you're fighting the turning and only hurting yourself.

A familiar voice echoed in her head, but she couldn't fathom from where. She tried to focus, only to see her world through a blood red haze of Hell with a dark etching of solid forms interspersed, or worse, watery grays and blacks like a swimmer drowning in a turbulent ocean.

Close your eyes. Slow your breathing. Let your blood slow. Just listen to my voice…it will be over soon. I've got you.

The vice grip around her gentled. Tender hands guided her head to rest against the steady, calming beat of a heart. Marilyn closed her eyes and focused on the sound of the soothing male voice laced with rich European undertones, channeling her fears, drowning out the inner vision terrors.

Within moments she shook but for a different reason. The air conditioning system kicked in. Sitting naked in front of one of the vents, she shivered from the blast of cold touching her heated skin.

"Get me a blanket from the hospitality room." The voice spoke aloud to someone standing behind her. Marilyn didn't want to move from the warm, safe, manly cocoon cradling her. But she did raise her head and open her eyes.

A firm wall of furred chest met her gaze. She pushed away as the dark hairs curling along muscled pecs intrigued her feminine instincts. She needed to see more. A silvery gash of scarred skin ran from his breastbone to his hip. Tracing it lightly with her finger, she noticed gooseflesh emerge on the surface of his skin, too. He shivered.

A blanket's warmth surrounded them and she looked up further to the dark shadow of raspy growth on the man's jaw and chin. His Adam's apple bobbed as the low rumble of "thanks" echoed across her flesh. He lowered his head and their eyes locked. She knew those eyes, that mouth, those lips...

"Draylon," she whispered in reverent awe.

#

She remembered him. Oh, this did not bode well at all. How did she remember his name? He'd wiped her memory of all contact. He'd gone to the extreme, like he always did with the women he had set free over the centuries, wiping their memories, taking care to put them back at the same time and place he'd found them. Well, he had to admit he had taken further steps this time so she wasn't in Romania where he'd found her. She would've been right back in the danger zone.

Draylon glanced over to Mike. He wished he could knock the smug look off of his face. "Shut up, Linder and go get me another blanket," he growled.

"It is you...Draylon? Draylon..." Marilyn appeared to be struggling to remember the rest of his name. He wasn't going to feed it to her.

Staring down into her pale-faced features, he found her more beautiful than he recalled in his dreams. Her hair glowed with the color of the fires that burned in his family's village at night, her lips the color of iron rich blood. But it was her eyes that held him. The elongated pupils were stamped with flames. Those flames turned hotter with her dangerous arousal. A major reason he shouldn't reveal their previous connection.

"Here." Mike tossed another blanket to him. "Cover

yourself."

Scowling at his friend, he put the blanket to the side and adjusted Marilyn's blanket around her in her confused state of shock. Gently he moved her off of his lap and grabbed the blanket before standing to his full height.

Tucking the blanket around his hips, Draylon decided covering the lower half of his body would be better than trying and failing to cover everything. He sensed the heated gaze and twitched at the feminine pheromones seeping into his soul, radiating from the auburn haired creature standing so close to him. He had to get away from her, yet find a way to protect her at the same time.

"Come on. We need to get out of here and some place safe." Draylon held out his hand to help Marilyn gain her footing. She'd swaddled herself in the blanket but sat staring at him. He tried to reassure her telepathically but she'd blocked him. Damn. "It's okay. I'm not going to bite you...again." Okay, so he had bitten her a few moments ago.

She took his hand and stood with regal grace. Her head tilted up as if trying to prove that everything that just happened to her was fine. Or maybe she tried to reassure her friend who remained in a quiet stance of uncertainty.

"My house is far enough away and secluded. Security is optimal," Mike offered.

"Lead us there. I'll drive their car." Mike turned to the stunned blonde, asking for her keys.

"We're not going anywhere with you." Tina backed away. "We're going home."

"It's not safe, Christina," Mike said. "Gerlich might very well know where you live and come hunting for you and Marilyn." He shook his head. "We can't let that happen. We need to protect you."

"Who are you two? And what happened to Marilyn?" She sat down from the shock weaning itself out of her system. "I don't understand. I just came for my cross-stitch." She looked up. "Am I having a nightmare?"

"We'll explain everything when we get you two to safety."

"It's okay, Tina." Marilyn stepped forward. There was an air of reassurance about her stance and her gestures. "I know Draylon. They're right. We need to move to safety."

She knew him? Oh hell, he hoped to the gods she didn't. Just how much did she remember?

"What do we do with the bodies lying about?" Tina looked around at the littered floor where their attackers lay unconscious.

"They'll wake up sooner or later—I would prefer later—after we've left," Draylon replied. "When they do, they won't remember anything."

At least he hoped so. If Marilyn was any indication, his average of wiping memories was kind of shitty lately.

Winding around the tunneled trees into the Catoctin Mountain range, it would take a keen sense of direction to ever follow Mike Linder to his lair. Marilyn Reddlin hadn't uttered a word since they'd left Frederick. Glancing over at her profile occasionally, Draylon checked to see if she was still awake. She was. It was late. The clock on the dash glared a teal blue twelve forty-five.

He sighed. He couldn't get inside her head. She'd blocked him…just like she had weeks ago when they first met. He smiled, internally remembering her sass when he'd tried to command her to leave Romania.

"What?" she asked.

"Nothing. Why?" Draylon looked at her briefly before turning his sight back on Mike's taillights guiding him through the forest drive.

"What's so funny?"

Funny? Nothing was funny. He'd been reminiscing about their first meeting...aww shit!

"Oh so turn-about is not fair game?" She turned in her seat, as much as the safety belt would allow and laid into him verbally. "You mean to tell me it's okay for you to try to mess with my head, but I'm not supposed to be able to read yours? That's some bullshit, mister."

"Let's just say it isn't normal. It's unnerving," he replied.

"Yeah, ya think?" she snorted in displeasure.

Okay. Touchè. He would have to be careful what he thought now. Especially since...

"Especially since, what? You're not going to finish the thought? Does it have something to do with me? If it does I need to know. I need to know what the hell's wrong with me, with you, with everything that's starting to flood into my head now. I remember having gone to Romania. It wasn't a dream...none of it...it was real, wasn't it?"

"Marilyn, calm down. I can explain everything when we get to Mike's, just let me get us there in one piece."

They took the county road to a gravel one leading further into the darkened forest. Mike braked and put his left blinker on to indicate they were turning. But there was no road. Mike's Dodge Ram had no problems with the dry rutted, two tire track dirt path meandering through more dense forest. But Tina's low riding, two-door coupe bounced along in a bone jarring dance among loose rock, bits of remaining foliage and low bed streams. Yeah, Vamier's goons would have their fangs knocked loose trying to get into this place.

Marilyn crossed her arms over her chest as her breasts bounced beneath the top edge of the blanket. Without any foundation support she would no doubt be exposed. It wouldn't bother him in the least.

The silent but deadly glare she sent him reminded him to curb his thoughts. How did one do that? He'd never had to. No one could read his thoughts…except her.

Thankfully they pulled up to a dark clearing where a simple styled log cabin stood beside a large garage separated from the cabin by a breezeway. The one story structure's length belied its plainness. Two rough hewn Adirondack chairs and a bench table were all that adorned the full, wrap-around porch. Two railroad lamps lit the sides of the door, but that was all the décor Mike had on the outside. It blended into the surrounding area and unless you knew what to look for, it was fairly well camouflaged into the night.

A door opened in the garage, lighting the night with its florescent ambiance. Mike drove into the building, and the floor of the garage lowered like an elevator shaft. A few moments later the floor came back up with Mike waving him inside. Draylon drove in and silently they too were lowered into the underground garage where Tina stood biting at a fingernail.

Draylon opened his door and maneuvered out of the tiny coupe. Marilyn did the same and went to her friend and hugged her.

"Nice place," Draylon complemented his friend. He'd never seen Mike's home but knew of some of the upgrades he'd installed as Mike built it over the years.

"Thanks."

Draylon looked around the massive room. The lift lowered vehicles below ground level and rose back up to camouflage the vehicles and make it look ordinary. But he knew it was nothing ordinary at all. Nothing about their kind could be in order to survive in a mortal world.

"The building materials I used are radar and satellite free, undetectable from the outside, if you were wondering."

Nodding, looking around, Draylon knew he would follow protocol. Mike followed orders, plain and simple. Six vehicles took up most of the garage area, a Hummer, a '68 Corvette, his

Dodge Ram truck, a Dodge Charger and two motorcycles, a
BMW touring bike and a Ducati 1098s.

Impressive. But he preferred sleek and pricy to Mike's
power and speed. It wasn't that Draylon didn't like to race, he
would just rather drive in style and comfort. The timing and
age difference between them could make for their differences
in taste.

Mike nodded towards the girls over in the corner talking
low. How Draylon wished he could sense Marilyn's thoughts.
Were they plotting an escape? Figuring out ways to neuter
them? The gods only knew what went through women's heads
sometimes. Yeah, they needed to get them to understand the
situation and see reason before they got the wrong impression
and tried something that would endanger everyone.

"Shall we, ladies?" Mike motioned them to follow as he
led the way into his domain.

The underground level of the house was a cavernous rock
and timber foundation dug into the side of the mountain. Sheer
glass panels from floor to ceiling took in the grandeur of the
valley below. They could see all the way to the city of
Frederick with its twinkling of lights.

"I know what you're thinking Draylon, but the glass is
one way only and tinted to protect the interior from the
sunlight. I can see out but no one can see in. I designed a
camouflage pattern for the exterior."

Mike's job as a secret government contractor working on
behalf of Livedel gave him the freedom to experiment. He
designed shelters, mobile Army support structures and
weapons used in the Iraq and Afghanistan Wars. Just as
Draylon had developed pharmaceuticals over the past century
and a half for not only the Delvante clans and defecting
vampires from Vamier's clans, but also the United States
Government and their Allies, Mike did the same with his
company.

"Wow! It's so beautiful. " Tina stared out into the night. "You mean no one can see in at all?"

"Nope. Not even if they were standing on the narrow ledge out there." He motioned to the half foot of stone edging the glass was secured to. "I'm also a big believer of green energy. I've harnessed the sun's energy through various solar panels on my roof and have propane only for emergency."

Tina smiled up at his friend, admiring him for his environmental concerns. She wasn't always easy to read either, but moments like this, her mind was completely lax.

Draylon didn't miss the longing in his friend's eyes as they lingered just a little too long on the petite woman. His smile was short lived as he realized it could never be. Mike wouldn't allow it, not with someone as wholesome as Tina Johnston. But then she was a bit of a spitfire if her martial arts training back at the blood bank had proved anything.

"So, are we going to stand here discussing décor or are you going to tell us what the hell's going on and why we're here?"

Marilyn wasn't one to be forgotten. Straight-forwardness had crept into her personality since they'd first met. Any mild-mannered traits being replaced by Alpha female—this with the change shouldn't be a surprise. Eventually, the only thing to curb her dominance would be an Alpha male mate.

Draylon looked to Mike. Tina joined Marilyn in the power play, now that her curiosity of the scenery had been satisfied. Mike raised an eyebrow, crossing his muscled arms over his chest and gave a slight nod.

"Shall we sit?" Draylon suggested, trying to take the edge off of the thickness in the room. No one moved. "O…kay. We'll stand."

He wasn't sure where to start. Some things were difficult to explain. "How much do you remember of the past, Marilyn?" He figured if he had a starting point he could jump in from there.

She thought for a moment. He could see the pain and the turmoil of trying to remember bits and pieces of the past month or so. He just prayed to the gods she hadn't kept in mind *all* of the incidents they'd shared.

"I'm having difficulties in some areas, but I keep seeing flashes of scenarios that I'm not sure are dreams or real so please let me know which are which," Marilyn revealed.

Draylon nodded.

"I remember chocolate cake in a restaurant…you were sitting at the table across from me." She closed her eyes, deciphering the past. "You were in a leather duster jacket…wings…no—that doesn't make sense." Her brow furrowed and she shook her head. "There were blond groupies…that attacked. A car chase, an accident…you decapitating them."

So she did remember, but it was all in scattered moments and pieces. She struggled to put the puzzle together and make sense.

"Then we were in a house with an old woman…Nannie…Connie…Nonni! Her name was Nonni."

She stared at him, her mind opening. He could easily slip in right now and try blocking further thoughts, but it wouldn't help the situation. She looked down, remembering.

"…have you ever had tea with a witch…" she mumbled and looked back up at him. "You asked me that. I remember. And then two wolves who turned into men…naked men. A cart full of hay, we were traveling to a city where your friend fed me, and I got violently ill. And then a house, a large Tudor style mansion in the mountains, but it was more like a prison…"

Okay that was enough. If she tried to consider more of the situation, things could get dicey. With great stealth, Draylon meandered into her thoughts without her knowing and blocked the rest, hoping it would work this time.

After a moment he cautiously asked, "What else do you remember?"

She struggled but gave up and shook her head. "Waking up in my bedroom apartment."

Marilyn let out a deep exhale of breath and sat down, exhausted, in the soft leather conventional sofa. Finding memories could be taxing. "Did any of that actually happen? You were in most of the scenes I recalled."

"Yes…they happened." Draylon stated.

"But what about her? She turned into a wolf." Tina spoke up. "What is that all about?"

He looked to Mike for support, but his friend only grinned at him. This was all on him. Taking a deep breath, he decided to dive in and test the waters. The worst thing they could do would be to laugh at him and think he was a loon.

"Romania is a mystical land…always has been, even when we were known as Dacia, before the Romans conquered. Our people were all powerful. Other tribes and clans refused to cross the Danube into the dark forests of Dacia because of our magical supremacy above all others. Our prophet, Zamolxis led us into battles, terrorizing our foe. We were unstoppable, we were his immortal warriors."

"I've read about Dacian history. It's my main thesis," Marilyn replied. "I want to know the other stuff."

"In order to understand the other stuff you must understand our past," Draylon demanded. "Our present and future is all based on our past. We are immortal warriors. Our kind does not die the same as humans. We still live in our world of Dacia and yet have to live among the mortals as well."

"Why?" Tina asked sitting next to her friend, taking her hand in hers to soothe.

A light aura glowed from her, passing into Marilyn's

hand. Draylon could see it plainly. He turned to Mike who didn't appear to notice. Draylon shook his head to clear his vision. Perhaps *he* was exhausted and hallucinated. When he looked back the light was gone.

Chapter Thirteen

"Why?" Tina repeated.

Marilyn could see the confusion and wariness in the man. The same she'd experienced only moments ago—and now felt a refreshing calm. God bless, Tina. She always had the ability to calm her when things seemed too much to take.

"We have learned it is easier to adapt to the mortal world than stay secluded in our own. Over the centuries we nearly annihilated our own kind by fighting among ourselves for dominance, too many alphas and not enough betas tend to lead to self-destruction of a species. We found ways to adapt and live within the norm, but we still must be very careful."

"Because of your immortality," Marilyn said.

"Yes. Every few decades we must 're-invent' ourselves, move to a new location and start over in society. We don't age so people would become suspicious as time goes by."

"So what are you actually?" Tina asked. "Are you a vampire?"

"No, he's not," Mike spoke up. "But I am."

Tina gasped and placed a hand to her throat.

"I'm not going to bite you. Even if I did, I would never let you remember me doing so," Mike soothed. "And I take less than normal lab work-ups for a physical, so it doesn't affect you physically."

"Still…a vampire?" Tina whispered.

"It's a long story. One I don't like to get into." Mike shook his head.

"So is he a Vamier vampire?" Marilyn questioned Draylon. She remembered the gang attacking in the airport, trying to bite her, as bits of memory began to tie in with the situation they were discussing.

"Originally, yes. But we were able to get to him in time and help him to adapt to a better way of life. Others are not so lucky."

"Who's Vamier?" Tina asked. "Wait. Isn't that the name of the professor you were going to work with for the semester or something?" Her brows knitted with confusion. "Vamier— he wouldn't be the owner of the Greater Baltimore Blood Bank, too, would he?"

"He does own the Baltimore blood bank and various others around the world," Draylon stated.

"Yes. Yes it was. Professor Aiden Vamier from Cluj-Napoca, Romania." Marilyn's recollection kicked in again. "Wait. He also owns the Greater Baltimore Blood Bank?" She looked from Draylon to Tina and back. "He's a vampire and you were warning me away from him."

"He wanted you. Not to work with but to capture," Draylon explained. "We still are not sure why."

"I did a paper on Dacian history and folklore. He was intrigued by it and sent for me to work with him. I was honored. He's the foremost expert on pre-Romanian history in the world."

"No doubt." Draylon scoffed. "He was there. Trust me, he could give you blow-by-blow accounts of what happened in the late B.C. of our country. But what you wouldn't get is the truth. You'd get his version of history."

"So what is the truth? There is very little beyond the Roman conquest…"

"Marilyn." Draylon sat down next to her in his blanket wrapped, half-naked body. It was difficult not to peruse the toned structure of his chest and abs, but the nasty silver streak of scar tissue always drew her interest. There was a story there. "You must understand, our history is much more than folklore and mythology. We are the ones who the myths and stories were told of. The villagers feared us for a reason. Their stories of boogie-men and evil spirits were handed down because of us. We are the true Dacians. We were the ones the Romans could not conquer. But we had destroyed ourselves before the Romans could."

Marilyn shook her head. "I'm not following you."

"You know of our prophet, Zamolxis the Great. He is more than a prophet, he is our god. He was sent to us by the god of the sun and moon to mold us into a great people. He asked for the gods to create creatures to help the Dacia in battle against their neighboring foes. Those creatures were known as Zmei.

"Folklore made them into evil shape-shifting creatures that turned into flame to creep into women's bed chambers and seduce them as a mortal man in their sleep. They stole women to take them as their own. The stories became so elaborate that history told them as dragons stealing the damsel in distress…"

"…and the handsome prince slays the dragon and rescues the lovely maiden. Yes a typical fairy tale troupe. But that is not what a Zmeu is?" She looked to Draylon for more answers.

"No. They ar…were shape-shifters. Most held a distinguished character depending on their paternal DNA, but all had their true form and that of a human. Animal forms in both land and flight usually were their secondary characteristics.

"The only problem with the race was they were all males. There were no female Zmei to breed with. Every ten years an honored warrior's daughter was selected to be betrothed to one of the Zmei. She was taken away to be prepared for her wedding day by the other females and the goddess Zamora, who looked upon the Zmei as her coveted pets. The women considered it a great honor…until one day when one of the intended brides refused to wed because she was in love with another."

"What happened?" Tina asked, enthralled with the story.

Marilyn had heard this story before, somewhere. "The woman wed the Zmeu against her wishes. After awhile she began to fall in love with her mate, only to have her previous lover gather an army of men and storm their home, destroying the Zmei. All died, except one." Her monotone speech sounded recorded, even to her own ears.

Silence followed. Draylon stared at her, keeping her mesmerized within his gaze. For a moment she thought she could actually envision the horror of the poor Zmei as flames danced in his eyes and screams of terror both human and beast echoed in her head. Gasping, she snapped out of the trance.

"How sad." Tina sighed.

"Angered, Bendis, the moon goddess, asked all the gods to do something about the atrocity. The sun god, Derzelas took away the light of day from the clan who destroyed the Zmei. They had to live in the dark of night. Bendis demanded they suffer by not hunting her wild beasts. They would have to learn to live off the blood of their fellow man. Sanziana, goddess of fertility, took away their ability to breed by sexual procreation. The only way to create more of their kind was through changing humans—but they had to have permission.

"The story didn't stop there. The young Zmeu bride wept over the slaughter of her new family. But her former lover captured her and forced her to wed him. She despised him,

seeing how he really was. He wasn't the one to love, and
besides, he had even a darker side now. Full with child, she
managed to run away one night to the sanctuary of her father's
home village. But she wasn't welcomed. Her family and
clansmen shunned her because of her part in her betrayal. So
she took refuge in Zamolxis' home where she was cared for
until her child was born, and Zamolxis took her and her child
to the safety of a neighboring land."

"So where do the wolves fit in?" Marilyn asked.

"They were always there. They were Zamolxis' immortal
warriors, the ones who'd shunned the young woman," Draylon
continued and shook his head. "Unfortunately, Zamolxis was
upset that they wouldn't give her a chance to redeem herself or
explain how she'd accepted the Zmei as her family. It wasn't
her fault…" Draylon didn't sound pleased, as if he didn't agree
with the woman's innocence. "So he had his immortal warriors
live the life as their battle mascot, the wolf. Clans fought for
dominance. Alpha against alpha, they shifted into wolves
when battles were necessary. It was these battles against clans
that caused the rift in strength, making the Romans able to
conquer."

Marilyn took it from there. "Many of the Dacia became
Roman slaves. Women were used as concubines. The ways of
the Dacian people was destroyed."

Nodding, Draylon continued, "Our numbers began to die
out as some of our remaining clan left to find freedom. Those
with life mates were lucky. The younger breed, not so much.
Women were scarce. After awhile the clan had to share mates,
but the interbreeding took its toll and produced weak pups or
infertility among them. There are now less than a hundred
males in the Delvante clan…the only remaining true Dacian
clan left…and no females."

"…until now," Marilyn muttered.

"At first that is why I thought Rick wanted me to keep you

safe. You would be in danger from the male population struggling to reproduce. It wouldn't be fun. You would be used as a breeding mare, nothing else. But it's more than that. Vamier wants you and is stopping at nothing to get to you. I had to send you back here to safety."

"Could he want her because she's the link to his enemy's survival?" Tina asked.

Draylon looked to Mike who shrugged casually.

"It's a possibility, Dray."

Rubbing his shadowy growth on his chin, Draylon appeared to ponder the thought. "It is probable, but no, I think there is something more they're after…I just don't know what. And Rick's not saying."

#

Marilyn couldn't sleep, her mind raced with everything that had happened tonight and with what she could remember from before. Tina and she had been given guest rooms in the massive underground retreat connected by a Jack and Jill bathroom. They'd discussed the situation they were in and decided perhaps it was best to stay safely hidden for awhile.

But that was mostly Tina's decision. Marilyn knew after what they'd encountered at the blood bank tonight Tina didn't trust being exposed. Marilyn didn't like confinement, but she would stay for her friend's sake, until they could figure out what else they could do. It wasn't that she didn't feel safe here…she did. But she struggled with what Mike and Draylon were capable of doing. A vampire and a shape-shifter wolf? Not a very secure scenario. She chuckled to herself. She was one to talk.

Frustrated to be wide awake, she got out of the comfy bed and tiptoed down the hall, wearing a men's button down dress shirt and a pair of boxers that Mike had let her borrow to sleep in. The pitch black didn't hinder her. Her vision was so much sharper than she remembered. But that wasn't all that was heightened. Breathing in the musky scent of dominant male, Marilyn followed her nose through the labyrinth halls and into the main room where they'd been most of the night. The signature spice pricked a memory. It hit her with the force of a solid punch to her chest. Catching her breath, she leaned up against the wall as the haze cleared from her mind, and she viewed the image of her…her and Draylon…on a desk…

Oh my God. She clasped her hand over her mouth to keep from gasping aloud. Had she…did she? No, that wasn't her. She shook her head. After her horrible failure with Daniel, there was no way she'd be bold enough. How could the image be her…doing *that*!

Needing to sit and clear her head of the disturbingly intimate thought, she made her way into the dark room and sat down heavily in the large over-stuffed leather chair. The musky scent enveloped her. She inhaled the aroma like a lovers embrace, curling up into a contented ball in the chair. Staring out into the night, mesmerized by the twinkling of lights making up the silhouette of Frederick fifteen minutes away, Marilyn jumped as a huge black shadow passed in front of the window.

Coming out of her seat she ran to the window, pressing her face against the glass to see what it was. All was calm. What she could see. The flat panel of window didn't give anymore view along the peripheral sides of the walls so whatever it was could be long gone or just on the other side of her vision. She waited to see if it might reappear. Minutes ticked by.

"You should be in bed."

Marilyn squealed at the deep, whispered tenor behind her. A figure moved forth from the dark shadows of the cavernous room, its eyes blazing with an unearthly glow, but it might have only been a trick of her mind, a reflection off of the glass—oh my…he was naked.

Draylon stood there in front of her in all of his natural glory. Her voice got stuck somewhere between her aching need and her salivating mouth. She stared at him as if she were enthralled in animated time.

"Are you typical of all Dacians?"

Draylon walked towards her, and her breath stopped in her lungs. All man and muscle mixed with a natural grace in his step and posturing. She looked up for fear of staring at…wow…yeah. Her thoughts went crazy as she involuntarily looked down. The word, *magnificent* came to mind. He smiled. A genuine smile. It was in the quirk of his lips, the relaxed line of his jaw, but more importantly, it was in his eyes.

"No, I'm not typical…and thank you."

The sexiness of his softly spoken words had her pressing her thighs together for fear she would make a puddle on the floor. She tried to figure out what he was replying to, forgetting he could probably read her mind. Mentally slapping a hand to her forehead, she cleared her throat. "You're welcome."

Only a few inches separated them. Heat and the familiar musk radiated from his body. A sheen of sweat covered him, and she craved the thought of washing his body as they both stood naked beneath a shower spray.

"What are you doing up?" He growled low in his throat as he moved even closer. His thigh brushed hers along with his erect cock.

Marilyn's gaze traveled quickly to take a peek at his rock hard length. She licked her lips nervously. "I could ask you the same thing."

Her brain couldn't think in terms other than sexual. The tension building in her set about a chain reaction of sensations throughout her body. Baser needs and animalistic mating rituals played out, some her own thoughts, some she swore were implanted images, along with the one of them on his desk. Her hands came up to flatten on his chest. Whether it was defensive or just her desire to touch him, she couldn't fathom.

"Did we actually do…that? Is that a true memory or something I dreamed?"

The heated look in his eyes, the way his manhood stood rigid and ready, bobbing against the thin material of her shirt, had her heart in a panic flight within her chest.

"I can neither confirm nor deny," he whispered against her ear, the sensitive skin of her throat.

"Would…would…it kill me, if I knew?" she stammered, hoping she could remain standing before oozing into a puddle of sexually frustrated goo on the floor.

"There is a good chance it could." His lips nipped her earlobe with such delicate force she nearly swooned. She'd never fainted from desperation before. The tip of Draylon's tongue ran a light trail along the corded tendon of her neck from the base of her ear to her collar bone. She mewed like a kitten.

His hands roamed up her hips clad in satin boxers and beneath the hem of the shirt, bunching the material as it rose, exposing her heated flesh to the coolness of the room. She shivered but definitely not from the cold.

Wide, strong hands encircled her torso, traveling from hip to rib, using his thumbs to skim over her abdomen and the skin just beneath the band of the boxers as his lips explored the curves and plains of her throat, collar bone, the racing throb of her pulse which matched the ache in her sex.

I can smell your heat…your want. It's driving me mad.

Her mind, fully opened, allowed his thoughts in. *You're driving me mad.*

There was something to be said for being able to communicate like this. He didn't have to stop the ecstasy of his mouth on her skin. She gasped. His thumbs brushed over her erect nipples just light enough to possibly be accidental until she felt them again.

Oh, it's no accident, Marilyn. Trust me, I know exactly what I'm doing.

Tender pain shot straight to her pussy as Draylon pinched her nipples. Covering her mouth with his own, he swallowed her cries of pleasure. Shivers trailed along her nerves as masculine hands worked down her body to the band of the boxer shorts. Within seconds they were around her ankles.

Lost. She was lost in his heat, his scent, the overwhelming urge to take him and be taken by him, anywhere, anyway…anytime. Right now would be fantastic. Kicking off the satin boxers, she wrapped her leg up around his hips, pushing her mons directly against his rigid length. He lifted her up onto his hips, and she wrapped her other leg around him as she melted into his kiss.

Solid wall pressed against her back as the kiss deepened, became hotter. Marilyn thought she heard a low, menacing growl from deep in his throat and it only heightened her sexual tension. Her fingers dug into his scalp, clutching at him to be closer. She wanted him inside of her. She wanted him to fuck her into a mind-blowing orgasm until she felt his hot seed…

The growl deepened, and he held her in place with his hips alone as he rendered the shirt from her body. Buttons skittered like marbles hitting the floor. Chest to breast they meshed. Searing heat spread over her torso as Draylon's mouth captured a breast, suckling like a greedy babe. The muscles in her cunt spasmed at the intensity of the pleasure his mouth released on her.

Images of creatures fighting within her for dominance had her struggling against the wonderful torment of Draylon and her self-imposed demons. She opened her eyes to keep the images at bay, giving herself directly to the pleasure of his touch. Tossing her head to the side, she noticed she was up against the large panel of windows looking out over Frederick. A thrill of voyeurism scuttled along sensual nerves, thinking how erotic it would be if the world could see what she was experiencing. How exciting it would be for others to see how hot Draylon was making her. He bit her nipple. She cried out, nearly coming.

Damn you. She heard him growl in her head.

Fuck me.

Had she just begged? He stopped, letting her breast pop out of his mouth. The cool air touched on the wet areola, and she shivered from the sensation. Gasping, she looked into his eyes and swore flames licked deep in the dark irises. His breath came out ragged and deep. His chest heaving, covered in sweat. A tic in his tightened jaw had her eyes widening. But he wasn't angry. She could sense his tightly bound restraint as he rode the edge of a very sharp sword. Still holding her, his nostrils flared and he reared back.

Marilyn cried out as he lifted her higher from his waist. His hands came up under her thighs and placed them around his neck, leaving her weight on his broad shoulders and up against the glass, even higher. He spread her thighs and dove into her heat, his mouth plundering, laving, tasting every inch of skin and fold. His tongue flicked across her clitoris before drawing it between his lips, and she nearly came right then.

Hanging onto his head for dear life, she fought a lethal change within her. She writhed and bucked against his torturous onslaught, fighting whatever was dominating her inner soul. He spread her vaginal walls with his fingers, making way for his tongue to plunder as deep as he could.

Come for me, Marilyn. I want to see you lose control. I want to taste your sweetness coating my tongue.

Draylon's voice growled deeply within her mind as he continued to drive her into madness. He plunged two fingers inside of her, finding her g-spot within moments. Her body

couldn't take anymore. Screaming silently along with the
fighting creatures within her, all of their animalistic sounds
merged into one inside of her head.

Muscles throbbed and released, sending shock wave after
shock wave of pleasure flowing through her, drenching her
thighs, Draylon's chin and mouth with her juices. But he
wasn't finished. He continued the sweet torture, feasting on
her like a ravenous bear seeking out all the honey from a hive.

Echoes of spasms continued until she was sobbing from
the intensity.

Please, make love to me, Draylon.

He stopped, lowering her gently to the floor. Marilyn had
to lean on him for support. Exhausted, her body drained of
energy, she looked up into dark eyes filled with a deep sadness
and regret. He shook his head.

Was he going to bolt? He looked like he might at any
moment. Was she pushing him? Her body wanted them to join
intimately…but something even more primitive ached with the
need. She wanted to crumple into a heap on the floor and
throw a temper-tantrum at his denial.

Instead of walking away, Draylon picked her up, her
tattered shirt hanging off of her shoulders and carried her back
down the hall where her bedroom awaited. Excited, she bit her
lip. Maybe he'd changed his mind. Kicking open the door to
her room, he crossed to her bed and gently laid her among the
tangled covers.

Marilyn waited breathlessly for him to join her. She could
see his beautifully erect penis still as hard, if not harder, than it
had been. She reached out to touch it, brushing her fingers
against its heat as he bent over her. He closed his eyes, the tic
in his jaw activated as his lips firmed into a thin line of
concentration.

Pulling the tangled sheet up, he covered her semi-
nakedness and placed a gentle kiss to her lips before turning

away and leaving her empty and aching. Tears flowed from the corners of her eyes down to pool in her hair as the door closed heavily behind him. Why wouldn't he make love to her? What had she done?

#

Draylon didn't know what was killing him more, the need to find sexual release or feeling the gut wrenching madness of her frustration. How could he tell her she hadn't done anything wrong without her asking too many questions he didn't want to answer?

The trek to his room hurt like hell. All he'd wanted was to spread his wings a bit tonight to release the stress of meeting up with the unforgettable Marilyn Reddlin. He wasn't ready to have to deal with her again. She did things to him that were better left undone. But seeing her in the oversized shirt, her hair down around her like a nymph…those lips, the surprise in her eyes at seeing him naked…he couldn't resist.

It had been almost a decade since he'd dealt with the sexual tension a woman put him through. But he didn't remember it being so intense. It had taken all of his will power not to bury himself within Marilyn's warmth and let nature take over. But he didn't want to see her fear and horror when he went too far…and he would, there was no mistaking the fact he would go too far with her. The pain of having to wipe her memory again and forget about her would be too great.

Lying on his bed, willing his erection to go away didn't help matters. The image of Marilyn against the window, her pale breasts glowing in the shadows of night, the gleam of fire flaring in her eyes, the sheen of moisture covering her skin…fuck.

Placing his arm over his eyes, he took pleasure in his own hands, imagining it as her stroking him like she had that day in his office. He tightened his grip, pretending it was her sweet, hot mouth. He could see her clear as day in his mind's eye.

Her hair loose over her face, the movement of her hand, her head as it dipped and sucked had him hotter than the fires of Hell.

Growling, he could sense the other creatures within him emerge, their randy mating rituals ready for the real thing as much as his human side. But then he witnessed other creatures in the picture—mates. Each of his shifting characters had an equal just beyond his vision, waiting in the shadows…and then he saw Marilyn lying on her bed where he'd left her. Her tears had dried and the torn shirt lay open to his gaze. She smiled up at him as her hands roamed her naked flesh.

Sweet gods! She touched her nipples, pinching them until they were perky points of pink perfection. Her body writhed among the satin sheets tangled about her. Her hand trailed further along her svelte form, stopping at her mons, trailing through her trimmed nest of hair to part her nether lips. The healthy pink petals opened to his view, the shimmer of her dew sparkled in the night like fresh clear water to a thirsty man.

He'd drank from her fountain earlier, the heady perfume of her essence still intoxicatingly familiar in his memory. Draylon arched into his hand, feeling the energy crescendo within him. He pumped faster as he viewed the image in his head.

With her knees bent, Marilyn lifted her hips, opening herself up to his view. Her fingers trailed over her open lips, her middle finger tapping at the swollen pink bud of her clit. She continued to rub and tap, driving him past the brink of madness. Draylon's breath came out in hot spurts of flame as he continued to stroke his turgid flesh.

When she penetrated her vagina with her finger, rising up to meet her personal thrust, Draylon knew he wouldn't be able to hold on much longer. Fire seared through his groin to his testicles, watching her pleasure herself. She added a finger and found her own point of no return.

Throwing her head back, she cried out his name as she continued to stroke and drive herself beyond the limits to her own sexual endurance. Hearing his name torn from the ravaged depths of her pleasure points, he lost his control and groaned out his own release, thrashing about in his sweat slicked linens and pumping his seed over his fist in tortured agony of release.

When he finally opened his eyes, the exhausted efforts made it difficult to breathe much less move. He lay there spent, gazing into the darkness surrounding him only to see blazing red eyes staring back. Those eyes calmed the man in him but aroused the Zmeu…but he was too weak, too tired to comprehend what it could possibly mean.

Chapter Fourteen

"What do you mean you still haven't heard from Mom?" Marilyn held up a finger as Tina asked what was going on. She was talking to Maggie, her mother's personal assistant on the phone. "She never went on the business trip? Where did she go then?"

"I'm sorry Marilyn," Maggie said. "Your mother left me strict instructions to tell everyone it was a business trip."

"So where is she, really?"

It took a moment but Maggie sighed. "She went to look for you."

Marilyn couldn't believe what bullshit Maggie had fed her. The people she trusted most had lied to her.

"Did she leave any messages? When was the last time she called?" Listening patiently but dying inside with the revealing of her mother's disappearance on her account, fear threatened to choke her to death. "Cluj-Napoca…yeah, I know…okay."

"Should I contact Mr. Delvante?"

Pacing, Marilyn noticed Tina biting her lip, waiting to hear the latest news. "No. I don't want Rick Delvante to know unless it's the last resort. I'm not sure I trust him right now.

I'm not sure I trust anyone." She sighed. "Just keep things under wraps until I can locate her. I'll stay in touch," she promised Maggie.

"What's going on?" Tina asked when Marilyn clicked off her cell phone.

"My mother's missing. She went to search for me in Romania when we lost contact. She hasn't returned."

Tina covered her mouth and shook her head in denial. Her big blue eyes welled up with tears. "Your father and now your mother…"

"She's not dead. She's missing," Marilyn announced heatedly.

Already a wreck, Marilyn hadn't slept much last night. Thoughts of Draylon, what he'd done to her in the living room, the dream she'd had about him after…watching him, feeling his pleasure as if he were right there inside of her…gave a whole new meaning to waking up in a sweat.

Tina had come in and woken her up, hoping they might be able to sneak away, but they had no clue how to get their car out of the hidden garage. In their morning exploration they did find the secret passage leading up to the main house, a simple model home façade to cover up the actual sanctuary beneath. Quite an ingenious idea for a man.

"What are you going to do?"

The only thing she knew…she needed to find her mother. She logged into her bank account and knew she would need to get into her trust fund in order to make another trip. The only problem was she couldn't get into it without her mother's co-signature.

"Do you want me to go with you?"

"No. I don't want to put you in jeopardy too. I have an idea of where she might be, and if what Draylon told me is the truth, I'll be heading into the lion's den without any protection."

"You're going back to see Aiden Vamier." Tina assumed. "Are you sure you want to do this?"

"I don't have a choice. He has my mother…"

"You don't know if he has her or not. It could be a trap."

"It's a risk I'll have to take."

"How are you going to get there?"

Tina knew her financial status as well as anyone. There was only one way she knew to get where she needed to go. She'd turn herself in to Gerlich to take her to Vamier.

#

"When did she leave?"

Tina curled up in a ball on the couch as Draylon interrogated her with the vengeance of a mad man.

"A…about two hours ago," she replied.

"She's had a good head start, Draylon. They probably have her in custody already." Mike sighed.

Draylon was a bundle of nerves and frustration. Marilyn Reddlin would be the death of him. He'd either go out by combusting in a sexually frustrated ball of flames or die by killing her himself and having Rick take him out in retaliation.

"You going to call the old man and put him on the alert?"

"Fuck no. Are you nuts?" Draylon had back up plans on various levels. Nonni and the cubs were always a good plan when he didn't want to directly involve Rick. Nonni didn't like Rick all that much and the feeling was mutual. "I'm calling on Nonni, Ren and Ron to see if they can give me a hand."

"What do you need me to do in the meantime?" Mike asked his friend.

Draylon looked to Tina, still cowering on the sofa. "Take her back to their apartment. If Marilyn is there, tie her up, sit on her, drug her…I don't care, anything to keep her from heading into trouble."

"If she's not there?"

"Have Tina pack a suitcase and get back here. I don't trust

Gerlich and his men. Tina's already in trouble with them, I
don't want her involved any more than she already is.
Hopefully you can keep her safe here long enough until things
boil over and Gerlich moves on his way."

"You can't keep me here like some prisoner." Tina
jumped from her seat and tried to stand up to Draylon, but he
stalked her and backed her into the broad form of his friend
Mike.

Mike gentled her with a hand on her shoulder. "It's okay.
You won't be a prisoner but Draylon's right, you won't be safe
with Gerlich around. Something tells me you're involved with
the Vamiers too, and it isn't necessarily connected with
Marilyn."

"So what's your next move, Dray?" Mike asked.

"Not quite sure. My instincts tell me she's being set up,
that this is all a trap."

"And?"

"I'm praying to the gods that for once, my instincts are
wrong."

#

Upon leaving the façade house, Marilyn started to run, and
as she ran, the animal instincts in her took over and she
became the wild wolf once again. Keeping to the outskirts of
Frederick as long as possible before heading in, she stopped at
a friend's house where everyone came and went of their own
accord. The house was empty and she was able to slip in and
find a change of clothes, leaving a note to let Heather know
she'd borrowed a dress before heading to her and Tina's
apartment in town.

Still, she kept out of site. She had things to do before
turning herself in to Gerlich. Marilyn just hoped he would be
at the blood bank. She didn't want to run the risk of having
Draylon try to rescue her or talk her out of finding her mother.
She was no longer afraid to take a chance. Her mother's life

depended on her being strong. She needed to do this.

The apartment hadn't changed since leaving to find Tina's cross-stitch. They'd planned to watch a movie, eat popcorn and chill. The air popcorn machine still sat out on the counter, ready for use, the container of popcorn, popcorn oil and bowls were all there. A bottle of moscato d'asti sat chilling in a bucket of what had been ice but now was a pail of tepid water. Had it all been just yesterday? Not even twenty-four hours and now life as she knew it, or remembered had been totally rebuilt into a fantasy of immortality and shape-shifting. She uncorked the bottle and took a healthy swig, hoping it would either calm her nerves or give her strength.

Her room, her sanctuary, held the answer. She needed the medallion. Opening her lingerie drawer, she pulled out a wooden box where she kept her precious artifact. This simple half piece to an ancient puzzle was the reason behind everything happening to her these past few months. But what did it all mean? And would she know what to do with it when and if the time came?

She ran her fingers over the embossed design. The wolf's head, a sacred Dacian symbol. She wondered if this might be more than just a symbolic artifact. What had her father known about the Dacians? Did he lose his life because of this? Had he encountered the paranormal clan she had and suffered the consequences? Did Aiden Vamier get to him before he could turn something so valuable into the proper authorities? So many questions now with no real answers.

Was there an underlying mystery to his disappearance in Romania? To have her most recent events center around the very area her father was last seen was too much of a coincidence. She wanted answers, and she would get them no matter how she had to do it.

With her goals in mind and determination strong, she threw together her backpack of enough clothes and gear to see her through for awhile. Thinking about her changing and shifting she added a few more items. What to do with her medallion? Placing the necklace around her neck, she decided she would keep it on her. No other place would be safe.

Ready as she could ever be, Marilyn gave herself to the dangers of the unknown.

#

Waking up with two huge dogs laying on the bed with her, Diane Reddlin tried to move without jarring them. She was trapped beneath the covers, their bodies too heavy to lift the secure blankets.

She opted to wiggle her way out of the formed area around her. Hunching her knees up to her chest, she swung her body around and made a soft landing to the wooden floor. Thank God for years of yoga and Pilates. At forty-nine, she considered herself pretty flexible for an old broad.

The men's large button down shirt she wore draped to her knees. She remembered coming here with Ren and Ron, realizing that they weren't going to take her home or let her go. She hadn't been happy but they hadn't hurt her…yet.

Walking out into the larger part of the wooden lodge-house the two men shared, she went in search of her backpack. The aroma of fresh brewed coffee had her off her true course in an instant. The open concept house allowed her to view the huge, sunk in living area with over-stuffed leather and suede furniture and the chef's kitchen with an open sitting breakfast bar.

The coffee maker gurgled its last remains of water through the reservoir. The rich, dark brew steamed as she went in search of a large coffee mug.

Heavy wooden cabinets dominated the kitchen, accented with stainless steel, industrial appliances. At least she knew how to work them, having the same brand at home in her kitchen. She would worry about breakfast after she poured some coffee into her system.

Opening the cabinets she found heavy stoneware and beer steins, pilsner glasses and heavy-duty pots and pans, nothing dainty or delicate in this kitchen. This was a man's kitchen. She found the cabinet full of mugs the size of milk pitchers.

Shrugging, she poured her mug three-quarters of the way full, and then searched in the side by side French door style refrigerator for some milk or cream. The appliance was filled with glass bottles of whole milk, cheese, meats and beer. She poured milk into her coffee and searched next for the sweetener. She liked the pink packets but could only find actual sugar. It would have to do.

The morning sun coming in through the large windows and glass doors had her basking in the warmth, staring out at the pristine view of what could only be described as paradise. Lush green grass carpeted the valley before her, edged with dense pine forests climbing up the sides of snow topped mountains.

"Beautiful."

Startled by the husky male voice behind her, Diane jerked, sloshing coffee over her mug. Ron stood before her in a pair of baggy grey sweatpants. Nothing more, nothing less. His dark hair had hints of silver that did nothing but enhance his features. This was all man, though he appeared to be several years younger than her. But from the charming smile and heated look in his eyes, age didn't matter at the moment.

"Even more so in my shirt. I've never seen it look so good, especially with you back-lit by the sun coming through the windows."

Diane blushed and retreated away from the light. She couldn't be taken in by his smooth talk and his disarming good looks. She had a purpose here. She needed to find her daughter and get home.

"We need to talk," she said, sitting down at the rough-hewed kitchen table.

Ron cocked his brow and went to fill a mug with coffee…and sugar. He smiled as she watched him dump in three spoonfuls of the sweetness, stirred and approached her on those feet that were some of the sexiest feet she'd ever seen. It made her wonder about the old adage, "a man and the size of his feet."

He sat down across from her and leaned over the table to capture a lock of her hair. "I like my coffee like I like my women…hot and sweet."

She tugged her hair back out of his hand, and gathering it up self-consciously, flung it over her shoulder so he couldn't get it anymore.

"Well good to know—I'm neither. Don't try to sweet talk me. I want answers." She wasn't the CFO of Livedel for nothing. Her backbone and grit got her into her position. A sexy, younger man who made her insides tingle just listening to his voice wasn't going to sway her.

"To what questions?" He leaned back but maintained a mocking smile.

"Where in the hell are we and why did you bring me here?"

"This is our house and you are our guest," he said simply.

"I got that. I'm looking deeper, so cut the crap."

Ron sobered and crossed his arms over his chest, which didn't help her situation at all. His pectoral muscles bulged against the muscles in his arms. She wasn't a woman who found herself attracted to a man with chest hair, but she wanted to run her fingers through his.

"Fine. You want the truth. I'll give it to you, but it won't make any difference to your circumstance if that's what you're after."

"Just humor me. I'm an old woman."

He eyed her up and down. "There's nothing old about

you, Diane."

There was that sexy voice again, but this time, it sounded sincere.

"Thank you. But please, just give me the facts."

"Very well." He closed his eyes in distress and opened them, squinting at her. "How much do you want to know?"

"Everything."

He slowly let out a breath, nodding. "Your daughter is safe. Marilyn is with Draylon Conier in Austria, being protected from those who might wish to harm her. Ren and I met your daughter when Draylon brought her to Nonni's in Cluj-Napoca a few weeks ago. She'd taken ill but recovered only to have the Vamiers after her. Draylon managed to get her to safety though."

"Vamiers? Who are they?"

"What I'm about to tell you might be difficult for you to understand. You're asking me to tell you everything, so I will, but it's going to take faith for you to believe in what I'm saying."

She waved him on. "Just tell me. Who are the Vamiers and why are they after Marilyn?"

"We are immortal. There are two clans of ancient Dacian warriors who were under our great prophet, Zamolxis when the Romans came and finally conquered our lands. Zamolxis took us into his care, away from the rest of the world into his 'underground,' which is not an underground at all but what most scientists would consider a rip in the fabric of reality.

"These rips are found in few select areas on Earth, one being the Hoia Forest." He paused sipping his coffee, methodically placing the mug back down before continuing. "As I said, there are two immortal clans, the Vamiers and the Delvantes. We're the only ones of our true people remaining."

"Immortal, as in lives forever?" Diane shook her head in disbelief.

"Exactly. We live here the majority of our lives but also blend in with our human brethren. We can come and go from Dacia as we please."

"So the Vamiers live here too?"

"No." Therron shook his head. "They were shunned by the great god himself. They were sent out to seek their own fortune and fate, yet they're always looking for a way to conquer the Delvante clan and re-enter Dacia."

"And this isn't good?" Diane drawled, narrowing her gaze at him.

It was a moment or two before Ron continued. "The Vamiers were the creatures in which so much Romanian folklore is based on, the great vampires, or as they are known here in Dacia, strigoi or moroii. They still exist, hunting the battle grounds of time for those who wish to live forever."

"They suck blood?"

"They only take those who wish to become one of them or those who are dying and asking to live. A long time ago they thirsted on livestock, which brought about the horror stories. But the gods made it so they couldn't feast on them anymore. So some rogues started feasting on unwilling humans and that is when Rick Delvante set up a program in order to hunt down and kill those who didn't abide by the laws the Dacian gods had given them. We still hunt down those who stray."

Was this guy for real? Immortal? Vampires? Rips in reality? Diane stood up from the table and backed away. "Wait? Did you say, Rick Delvante? As in the CEO of Livedel?"

Ron smiled. "The very same."

Her boss, the one she'd worked with for over twenty-five years was…"Is he immortal, too?"

Ron only nodded.

Diane sat back in her chair. Shock, defeat, confusion, it all warred within her. She'd never met the man, and yet he'd taken her in and made her what she was. Why? Was it because of her expertise in the business or something else? Had he known about Richard's disappearance here in the Hoia Forest? Is that why she'd been 'Rick's pet' as office rumors had once stated? Had Rick felt guilty about Richard's death and catered to her? And now, her daughter was under the protection of someone to avoid a group of vampires located just outside this…this *portal*…was it all connected somehow?

"I don't know what kind of shit you're trying to pull on me, but this is sad," she said, shaking her head.

"You asked for everything…I gave it to you. It's up to you on how you wish to deal with it," Ron stated, taking another sip of coffee.

Diane didn't know what to think, but she wasn't going to stay here any longer than necessary. Not with a psycho-delusional man who could make her weak with just a glance. It was said that the mass murderer, Ted Bundy had the same effect on women and look what happened to them.

She shook her head, not sure why but backed away and headed for the hallway to the bedroom, so she could locate her clothes and get the hell out of here.

As she turned to enter the bedroom she stopped in her tracks.

The other dog on the bed woke. Stretching out to full length, it morphed into Ron's twin brother, Ren.

Okay, so maybe she was the psycho-delusional one. There was no way a dog just turned into a man.

Chapter Fifteen

Sitting in front of Aiden Vamier, Marilyn wasn't sure what to expect. Here was the man who had started it all for her. Professor Vamier, the foremost authority on Dacian history. He looked nothing like a professor.

The two days she'd been in Gerlich's custody, she'd been treated kindly and with utmost respect. He'd flown her in a private jet from Frederick to Cluj, making stops only to refuel. But she hadn't been tied up or drugged like she thought she'd be.

No, when Marilyn had turned herself in at the blood bank, Gerlich had treated her as if she were royalty and was delighted to take her to Aiden. She hadn't expected that either. Maybe they were just fattening her up for the kill.

"So what is it that I may do for you, Miss Reddlin?" Aiden sat on the corner of his desk.

The room was early Baroque. Walls of bookshelves made up the interior design of the two floor office. The musty smell of old books and older money permeated the dark room and yet it held an elegance about it, like the man confronting her.

"You know what I want."

His brows twitched. "Indeed, I do not. You came to me. Though I must say I was clearly miffed when you didn't show up as expected for our semester of instruction. I found your paper quite fascinating and wished to discuss it more in length." He threw a charming smile at her. "It's not every day I come across a young student who shares in my love of my early people."

If it wasn't for the knowledge she had on him already, Marilyn would have a difficult time finding fault with the man. He was debonair and smooth with classic blond European features that could be mistaken for a gorgeous soccer star or model for GQ.

"Yes well, truthfully I'd been looking forward to working with you, also. That is until your vampires decided to use me for their main course."

"They wouldn't have taken much. We only need a bit to tide us over. I had sent them out to escort you safely here. But Draylon appeared to have other plans."

She didn't want to egg him on. Something about him couldn't be trusted, and the less he knew for certain, the better.

"Let's dispense with the bullshit, Mr. Vamier. I want to know what you've done with my mother."

"I beg your pardon? Your mother?" He crossed his arms over his chest. "What has led you to believe that I have your mother?"

"She came looking for me when I was in Romania. She knew I would be working with you this semester. As far as she knew, I was still here and under your care."

"And you haven't been in touch with her since?"

Marilyn remembered how Draylon confiscated her phone upon their escape from the airport and how he'd tossed it out the window of their car as they were being chased. "I misplaced my phone and wasn't able to contact her while I was in Romania."

"I see. And because I'm your last known destination she would have looked to me, assuming I had knowledge of *your* whereabouts."

"Yes."

"And how long has your mother been missing?"

"About a month."

"My dear, I can assure you that I have not been in contact with your mother, or anyone's mother for that matter. What is your mother's name?"

"Diane Reddlin."

He mulled the name over in his head. "Why does that name sound familiar? Diane Reddlin…Diane Reddlin…"

Gerlich, who stood silently nearby as if waiting for his "boss" to issue him a decree to breathe, stepped forward. "She's the chief financial officer of Livedel, my lord."

"Really."

Marilyn held her laugh at the shocked expression on his face.

"I have heard much about your mother. Is it true that she likes to eat the male genitalia of the men she deals with? Rumor has it she has them served up on a silver platter every morning when she is breaking her fast."

Aiden appeared almost innocent and naïve in his knowledge of the euphuism. "It's just a saying but yes, she is a dominating presence in the board room. Nine times out of ten, my mother gets what she's after. She refuses to let anyone bully her, and she has a penchant for getting her way in very strategic, sometimes aggressive ways. It's why she's so good at what she does. It's her strength."

"I see." Aiden smiled. "She sounds like a woman after my own heart. I wish I could meet her."

"So you don't know where she is? She hasn't contacted you at all?"

"No. I'm afraid I haven't had the pleasure." He slid off the corner of his desk and walked towards her.

He was tall and slender. Damn, did he have to be so sexy? It would have been difficult to work in his presence if he'd been a normal, Joe-Schmoe professor. She wondered idly if he would be the type of guy who'd have an affair with a student.

His lips quirked in a smile, making his blue eyes twinkle devilishly. Could he read her mind? If he was immortal there was the possibility.

"I do have connections within Romania in which I can try to locate your mother for you, but it might take me a few days." He looked to Gerlich. "See what you can find out on Ms. Diane Reddlin through our connections."

"Right away, my lord." Gerlich snapped his heels together and turned, marching out the door to do Aiden's bidding.

"While we wait to hear, I offer my home to you, Miss Reddlin. You will not be harmed or harassed. In fact, I would like very much to have the chance we never had to discuss your paper in length and perhaps share our knowledge."

Marilyn didn't know what to expect or accept. This all sounded much too easy, too casual. What was that saying— keep your friends close and your enemies closer? Right now though, she still didn't know which was which. She would have to tread lightly and keep her guard up.

"That sounds like a wonderful offer, Professor Vamier. I would like that, thank you."

"Good. Good. I'll have a suite prepared for you right away." He walked to his desk and made contact with his staff to have a room prepared for a "special guest." "I assume you know of my nocturnal habits by now, so I will not burden you with the details. I do have to abide by my habits for survival."

"Of course." Marilyn nodded. "I can adjust my schedule to work around yours for a few hours each night if not more."

"I appreciate your flexibility." Aiden's brow furrowed. "I must admit I was not prepared for a woman like you, Miss

Reddlin. You're very accommodating, but I sense a wilder creature beneath your personal façade. I do not mean that in a negative way, actually, I find it quite refreshing and unique. You will definitely keep me on my toes for the next few days."

"I'm glad you see things that way, professor." She hoped to keep him on his toes as much as she needed to be on hers. If that were a mutual acceptance, then neither one had anything to fear from the other. With any luck, all would work out well.

"You have traveled far these past few days, and I would like for you to settle in before I ask you to join me." He peered at his expensive Cartier watch. "It's early morning here in Cluj. Perhaps a rest to set you on schedule after a morning meal might be on order. My staff is at your disposal. They can prepare you a menu of your choosing and have it sent to your suite."

"Thank you. That would be wonderful."

Now she only hoped she wouldn't be drugged and left for a potential vampire meal in the meantime.

#

Aiden wondered if his dear brother knew that his CFO was MIA. Not that he gave a shit, but if his brother was going through serious difficulties then he'd love to lord it over him. Not only that, but it would cause chaos in the Delvante clan and make it easier for Aiden to send his people out on their missions without having to deal with Rick's "avengers" in the way.

"Rick Delvante please," Aiden said into the phone to the receptionist at the Dacian compound. "No, you may not ask who is calling. But if he needs to know, just tell him his long lost brother." Aiden studied his well manicured fingers as he waited. Would Rick pick up?

"What do you want, Aiden?"

"Ah, so you did pick up."

"It's better to know than to wonder where you are

concerned," Rick said.

"Yes well, I will have you know that this has nothing to do with me, but I thought you might be interested…"

"Get on with it. What's so important that you would deem it worthy to tell me?"

Aiden didn't care for his brother's short-handed tone. They might share their father's blood, but Rick had been the bastard child. "Did you know your Chief Financial Officer is missing?"

"Diane?" There was a momentary shock to Rick's voice. "What do you mean, missing?"

"She's been out searching for her daughter for nearly a month."

"And how do you know this?"

Aiden didn't question Rick's thoughts. More than once had he tried to get to him on various levels using tactics of cunning and conning. It was a favorite pastime for him. But this time, for some reason, he had the upper hand.

"I know this because her daughter told me."

"Marilyn?"

"Yes. She's quite beautiful, witty, intelligent…a true delight." Aiden toyed to get another rise out of Rick.

"Where is she? Leave her alone."

"She is perfectly safe, dear brother—why so protective? What do you have for these simple human beings anyway? I never understood your fascination. They are born, live maybe a century if they are unlucky enough, and die. They're inferior to our kind, like cattle to humans—good for food but not much more."

"Where. Is. Marilyn?"

Intrigued by his enemy's curiosity he decided to play along. "She's with me. We had originally planned to meet and work together over a month ago, but it seems she was detoured by your beastly lackey. Really Rick, why are you trying to keep her away from me? We were only going to discuss her research project on Dacian folklore and antiquities. I found her thesis quite remarkable for an American university history student."

There was silence for awhile on the other end of the line. "What do you want, Aiden?"

"Want? Why nothing, dear brother. I was only concerned for the welfare of your CFO and trying to help her daughter locate her. I thought perhaps you knew of her whereabouts."

"I'll look into it on my end. In the meantime…"

"…yes?"

"I'll have one of my men come for Marilyn and take her somewhere safe."

"Like you did last time? Oh, I don't think so. I think I'm going to enjoy Miss Reddlin's company for awhile. I've been lonely without female companionship. We shall have a time talking history and literature, discussing worldly topics for a good thirty or forty years at least, unless she decides to become my beloved."

"When hell freezes over, Aiden. You will not harm a single hair on her head, and there will not be a drop of her blood shed to feed your gnarly hide." Rick's voice was so level, so calm, but the underlying tone of panic was definitely there.

"Did I say anything about harming her? Not a word. I intend to take very good care of her. I've never been so enthralled with a woman of auburn hair."

"You're a sick bastard, Aiden. I swear if any harm befalls her I will have your ass nailed to my wall as a trophy."

Aiden laughed. Oh, this was too much fun! He'd found a weak link in his brother's holier than thou armor. "Just make sure when you do that my ass faces up…so you can kiss it whenever the mood strikes."

He hung up the phone receiver because he loved having

the last word. Now, on to some real fun.

#

Nonni tilled her garden, pushing her mule hard to get the plow edge to cut into the frozen ground. It was still early spring but it wouldn't be long before she could plant a new harvest. She wished her boys were here to do this labor, but they were busy elsewhere.

Looking up at the murky gray sky she muttered, "I hope you know what you are doing. I am only your humble daughter."

A large, long black car pulled up outside of her fence line. Her old eyes peered at the ominous automobile. "I was only joking, father. I am not ready for death to take me."

The driver's door opened and a man wearing a black suit and cap got out, walked around to the passenger's side and ushered out a familiar looking man...one she hadn't seen face to face in many years, but she still knew him. He hadn't changed at all, except for his modern attire.

Tying the reigns around the yoke of the plow, she patted her old mule and walked to meet the man.

"Nonni." He nodded at her.

"I know who you are. I believe you go by the name, Rick Delvante now." She narrowed her gaze at him. "What do you want? Make it quick, I have work to do."

"I need your help."

"Oh, ho-ho! You need my help now, do ye?" She spit on the ground and waved him off. "I have no need for you—"

"Nonni, please. I'm begging you..."

"Begging? Begging? The great Delvante begs for my help? Wouldn't Zamolxis be proud...begging, indeed." She walked away, back to her work.

"It's not me I'm asking for—it's Marilyn Reddlin."

Nonni stopped and turned. Glancing up at the sky she gave a prayer. "What is wrong with her?"

"Aiden has her. He's keeping her prisoner and gods only know what else." He sighed, raking a nervous hand through his neatly kept hair.

"Why has she gone back to him? I thought Draylon protects her?"

"She somehow managed to turn herself over to Aiden."

"Why would she do such a foolish thing?"

"She was looking for her mother, Diane Reddlin, my chief financial officer. Aiden called to inform me that Marilyn came to him, looking for her after she'd been missing for nearly a month."

Nonni hung her head. "She is not missing. She is with Therron and Kurren."

"Where?"

"She went looking for Marilyn in the Hoia Forest, the last place her husband was when they lost touch with him years ago. She thought Marilyn might have gone in search of his remains."

The tic in Rick's jaw didn't bode well. But he had no room to be angry with her. This was all his fault. "Where is she now?" The deadly calm of his question didn't even linger on the air. The air wanted no part of his wrath.

"She is safe with Therron and Kurren. I told you that—"

"Where!" His voice raised in tenor, a vein popped out of his forehead.

Nonni swallowed hard, her hand went to her chest and a cold wave of nausea settled over her. "She is in Dacia."

If the man had the power of the gods, the earth would be trembling and quaking beneath her slippered feet. His silence spoke volumes.

"What is it you wish me to do?" Perhaps she could soothe his anger by placating his wishes.

"Send one of your wolves to fetch Marilyn Reddlin from Aiden's domicile before it's too late for her."

"As you wish, my lord." She bowed her old head. He may not have the power of the gods, but Rick Delvante had more power than she did right now. She didn't want him to use it on her. Now would not be good...too much to do and so little time.

Chapter Sixteen

Draylon wasn't letting Kurren go into Vamier's compound alone. Marilyn was his responsibility and already he'd let Rick down by losing her—twice. He met Ren on the outskirts of the Hoia Forest, ready to take on Aiden to get to Marilyn.

"How did Rick sound?" Draylon asked the wolf pup as they made their way to the border of Vamier's property.

"I don't know. He went to Nonni for help. She only told me that this was a 'do not fail' order."

"Rick went to Nonni?"

Shit. That didn't sound good at all. Rick and Nonni had an understanding. Centuries ago Rick had wanted the woman killed for what she did to the Dacians. But Zamolxis was merciful. Nonni was spared along with her unborn child, but she was banished from Dacia. Rick still thought to this day that it was she who led the Roman Empire into Dacia as her way of getting even for being forced out of her homeland. Why Nonni had come back, no one knew. All she'd say was, "it is the will of the gods."

Just one more reason Marilyn Reddlin might be more than

Rick let on. He wouldn't go to all this trouble, especially calling on Nonni, for anyone—not even him.

"Yep." Ren held up his hands. "Hey, don't look at me. I wasn't there. Though it would have been interesting to see. You think those two were lovers at one time?"

"No. They definitely were not lovers."

"What do you know about her? You were around back then."

"I was unconscious from my injuries during the Zmei massacre. All I was told was she'd been a young pregnant woman seeking shelter from an abusive relationship."

"And?"

"There's more to it, I'm sure, but all I know is Rick banished her from Dacia for doing something evil."

"Well, she is a witch. But I can't see Rick having an issue with witchcraft—unless she tried to usurp power from him and the gods."

Draylon shrugged. "I don't know. And Rick isn't saying. I can tell you this, never ask. You'll regret it."

"Good to know."

They made their way to a good starting point, checking out their game plan. "I've never had to infiltrate Vamier's actual home. This may be tricky," Draylon whispered.

"Where do we start?"

"Damned if I know." He thought about his situation for a few minutes. Could he get a mental picture of where Marilyn might be? Trying to connect with her, he came up empty. She wasn't receptive right now. Double damn.

"I want you to go in through the side entrance. I'm heading around back. If you get to Marilyn before me, get her the hell out of there. I don't care how, just do it."

"What about you? Where do you want to meet?"

"We'll meet back here in say an hour and a half. Wait for me no more than ten minutes if you can. If not just book it back to Dacia, to Rick's place."

"You want me to take her there? But…"

"I don't care. I'll deal with the legality of the issues later. Right now, that will be the safest place for her, away from Vamier."

#

Three days later Marilyn still hadn't heard anything about her mother's whereabouts. It was disheartening to say the least. Each night she'd ask Aiden, as she was told to call him, and he'd sadly tell her he still hadn't received any word from his connections.

In the meantime, he'd been nothing but kind to her. It was difficult to believe that this man could be the enemy Draylon had warned her about. They'd spent their nights discussing ancient Dacian lore and history but instead of the Zmei being benevolent beings helping them in battle, they'd been deceiving, hideous beasts bent on stealing the Dacians' women, destroying their lands and only seeking more power to take over Dacia. He painted quite the ugly picture of them, and Marilyn had doubts about what she'd been taught in the past. History, unfortunately was based on varying perceptions.

Taking tea with Aiden as they discussed, he'd given her free reign to question everything. "No offense, but I'd been under the impression that you were the one to overthrow the Zmei by destroying them because you were in love with the maiden who'd been promised to them."

Aiden snorted. "We were to have been married and the damn beast turned into flame, snuck into her bedchambers, seduced her and carried her away with him to his lair. If that is being promised then I had other ideas of what that meant." He put down his delicate china cup. "No, it had been a hideous plan of attack. Sariana was kidnapped and raped by those bastards. I gathered my closest allies, and we attacked the Zmei cavern to rescue her. We were met with opposition, but we fought gallantly, slaughtering every one of them. We made sure that no other woman would be used for their purpose, ever again."

"All except the one...right?"

"I beg your pardon? What do you mean, 'all except one'?"

Had she let an unknown secret out of the bag? She swallowed her tea and tried to play it off. "I'd heard rumors that one survived, nursed back to health by Zamolxis and a young prophet."

Aiden's blue eyes narrowed into slits, his angular jaw forming more ridges. "And where did you read this?"

"I...um...I'm not sure where I read it. Perhaps in one of the books I picked up on-line on the religions of Eastern Europe or something."

He templed his fingers under his chin. "Fascinating. I thought I'd read every book there was on our history. Or written them," he teased. "You'll have to find this book. I'd love to read more on this theory."

The studious curiosity in his eyes and face had Marilyn sweating and edgy. Had she revealed too much? Had he not known? Was the last Zmeu a secret from his world?

"So tell me, Marilyn, what was it about our history that intrigued you enough to want to make it your major thesis?"

"I suppose my father. He immigrated to the United States from Romania when he was in his early twenties. He was an archeologist and collector of rare Dacian antiquities. His love for the history and pre-history of his country seeped into the fascinating papers he wrote. I started reading them when I was sixteen."

"Hmmm. What was your father's name, I may have worked with him on some projects."

"Richard Reddlin." Marilyn took a sip of her tea. "He died before I was born. Or at least that is what the reports said. The last report was he went on an expedition into the Hoia Forest.

So truthfully, I don't know."

"I'm sorry to hear that." Aiden paused. "Richard Reddlin...Richard Reddlin...no, the name doesn't sound familiar, and I thought I knew every scholar on our history. After all, I am the Director of Romanian History."

Marilyn smiled uneasily. She felt like an idiot. He didn't know her father? But her father had been such a well-known Dacian historian. That is what he'd done on his trips to Romania—work on sites and lecture about the past...surely Aiden would've heard of him?

Gerlich came in, silently motioning to Aiden.

"Excuse me, Marilyn, but something has just come up. Would you give me a moment?" He rose from his chair and followed Gerlich out of the study, leaving her alone to her own thoughts. Nothing made sense anymore. Self-consciously she touched the medallion she wore just under her blouse. That was real. It had to be. It was the only *real* thing she had of her father's memory, if it was from him. She questioned that now, too.

The side door burst open and she gave a startled gasp. A dark-haired, six foot something man stood there. He looked familiar, but she couldn't put her finger on where they'd met.

"Thank God you are okay." He gasped. "Come on, I need to get you out of here, now!"

"Who are you? What are you talking about?"

"I'm Kurren. We met at Nonni's a few weeks ago...we don't have much time, come on."

She shook her head. "I'm not going anywhere with you..."

"We have your mother. She's safe with my brother Therron," he explained. "Draylon and I were sent to rescue you. This is a dangerous place for you." He glanced around. "I don't have all day to discuss this. Just come on."

"You have my mother? She's safe?"

Kurren nodded briskly.

"Where's Draylon?"

He looked at his watch. "We are to meet him at a rendezvous point in ten minutes. But we need to hurry before Aiden comes back."

Unsure what to do, Marilyn nibbled her lip. Okay, she'd go, but only because she was to meet up with Draylon. She didn't know this guy, even though he seemed familiar.

She followed Kurren out through a side hallway made of rock that appeared to meander through the ancient mansion like a labyrinth maze. As they moved they came upon various dead end walls.

"Did you not leave a trail of bread crumbs or a spool of thread behind you on your way in?"

"Didn't think about it at the time. It took me long enough to find you as it was."

They finally made their way into a larger more modern hallway. "This way." He pulled her along.

Their escape route was cut short as a pack of blond, anorexic looking groupies stepped into their path.

"Shit," Kurren said under his breath as he flipped his arm and shot a nasty looking blade out of the sleeve of his jacket. "Stay behind me."

The first attacked in a flying leap with fangs bared and razor sharp claws emerging from the fingers. Kurren managed to slice its head off.

Marilyn placed a hand to her mouth to keep from gagging at the site and smell before the decapitated head and body turned to ash before their eyes.

One down, a dozen more to go. They were definitely out numbered, and she had nothing on her. Two more went at Kurren and one came at her. With nothing to fight with, she held out her hand. When her assailant's chest came in contact with her palm, the creature turned to dust within seconds.

Shocked, Marilyn wasn't sure what happened. So when another pounced to take its buddy's place and the same thing happened, she knew it had to be something she did. Kurren noticed her ability and gave her an odd stare as another attacked him. He casually sliced its throat, too.

When they had a clear path littered with piles of ashy remains, he pulled her onward. Still coming to terms with what she could do, she tried to speak, but her conversation was interrupted by another band of the blond brotherhood. Again, they managed to defeat them within moments and moved on.

"What the hell is with you?" Kurren gasped as they headed for the main entry foyer.

"I don't know. I was going to ask you."

"And you think I would know anything? I'm like a mushroom, kept in the dark and fed shit."

Another group of Vamier's friends met them at the door, blocking their path. Looking at each other they nodded. They had this down now.

"I've got this," Marilyn said with a cocky nod of her head.

As each one came at her they disintegrated on cue. All except one. He towered over her, an equal to Kurren in height, but scrawnier in build. He laughed, baring those hideous snaggle toothed fangs. She tried touching him again, and he only pushed her backwards as her hand remained in the center of his chest.

"Kurren…I don't think it's going to work on Giganto here."

Kurren was a step ahead of her and removed the giant vampire's head with one swift motion.

"You could have done that to start with," Marilyn grouched.

He shrugged. "You said you had this. You were doing fine."

"Come on. Let's get out of here and go meet up with

Draylon."

Luckily, they didn't encounter anymore of Aiden's friends and family as they made their way to the wooded outskirts of Vamier's fortress.

Crouching down out of sight of possible cameras or sensors, they waited for Draylon to meet up with them.

"What time did he say he'd be here?"

"Five minutes ago. We gave ourselves an extra ten minutes just in case we encountered difficulties."

They waited in silence as the minute hand ticked by. There was no sound, no movement in the rustling of the shrubs and scrub trees around them.

"How many minutes now?" Marilyn asked.

Kurren sighed. "He should've been here by now." He looked around. "We need to go."

"No." She seethed. "We'll wait a few more minutes."

"Draylon said…"

"I don't care. I say we stay just a few more." She narrowed her eyes on Kurren and tried to relax. "Please…just a few more minutes."

Kurren studied her for a moment. "Okay. But only a few. It's not going to take long for Aiden to figure out you're missing and have every one of his fiends out here combing these woods."

They waited, and waited. Where the hell was Draylon? Was he okay? Had he gotten captured? Was he still looking for her?

The sound of alarms and commands being yelled into the night broke out.

"Shit! Damn it. I told you we needed to leave."

"But Draylon…"

"He can take care of himself. We need to get you out of here, now!"

Chapter Seventeen

Draylon woke up chained to a chair with anchor chains. Someone knew of his strength. It would take him awhile to break free from these. His head hurt and he felt groggy.

"So what do you know about Marilyn Reddlin? What is so important that Rick has you keeping track of her safety every damn minute?"

He knew the voice. Aiden Vamier.

"Where…where is she?" Draylon asked. His words sounded slurred to him. He'd been drugged.

"Your friend has her now, but not for long. We're combing the area for them as we speak. Now tell me about Marilyn Reddlin."

"I don't know…what you are talking about." Draylon gasped wearily, trying his damnedest to stay awake, alert.

A fist came out of his peripheral vision and punched him so hard his head snapped sharply to the left.

"I don't want him unconscious, Gerlich, I need him to answer questions," Aiden reprimanded.

"Now I'm going to ask you again, Draylon…what is so important about Marilyn Reddlin that Rick would send his favorite pet *Zmeu* to keep her safe?"

Shit. How did Aiden find out about him? Only a very few people knew his true identity, and he found it difficult to believe Nonni or Rick would have revealed it, not to Aiden.

"Yes, I figured it out. Miss Reddlin informed me that she'd heard that one Zmeu had made it out of the desecration. That Zamolxis' young prophet had nursed him back to health. My brother, having been the prophet…and you, always at his beck and call, I just put two and two together and came up with you.

"All these centuries and I never knew. There you were, hiding in plain sight. And yet, you never came to seek vengeance on me."

"Zamolxis forbid me from doing so. He said it would only make you a martyr for your own people."

"Whatever. It's all past history now. But what has me so perplexed is this Marilyn Reddlin. I know you know something about her…"

"If I did, do you think I'd tell you?" Draylon spat on the ground near Aiden's Italian loafer clad feet.

Aiden sighed. "I really don't have time for you or this…I can find out on my own." He turned to Gerlich. "Take him away. Put him somewhere out of my hair."

Draylon wasn't worried. There weren't many places he couldn't get out of.

Gerlich dragged him down the corridor by the chain around his neck. Draylon fought for every breath. If he could just get enough energy and mental capacity he could shift into his original form and fuck up Gerlich's world to hell and back.

But whatever he'd been drugged with was something even he couldn't fight through. They stopped and Gerlich hung his chain up against a rock wall, leaving Draylon's feet barely touching the ground. Draylon refused to struggle. It would only cause him to lose his footing and hang himself.

But that wasn't the plan, either. Gerlich removed a disk in the floor the size of a manhole cover and pushed it to the side. Taking the heavy chain from the wall, he fed it down into the hole in the rock floor.

Draylon felt the pull of gravity as the chain dropped rapidly into the darkness below. He tried to fight for a grasp on something, but there was nothing for him to hold onto. He screamed as he fell into the dark hole ending up in the bottom of a torturous, medieval chamber known as an oubliette.

He could hear Gerlich laughing above from the narrow rim. Okay, so this could be the *one* place he couldn't get out of.

#

The trip to Dacia wasn't what she expected. It wasn't a town or a village, it wasn't even on the map. They made their way into the Hoia Forest by Kurren's Jeep 4x4 until they came upon a circular clearing with strange curved trees standing sentry around it. No other vegetation grew.

Kurren stopped the Jeep and got out. Coming around the passenger side he helped her down from the seat.

"What is this place? I'm getting a weird vibe…"

"This is the portal to Dacia."

"What do you mean by *portal*?" Marilyn followed Kurren, taking his hand as he led her across the empty patch of earth.

Tingling sensation coursed through her like a live energy fluctuation. Nausea threatened her stomach and her head throbbed from terrible pressure, worse than any migraine she'd ever experienced.

"You'll be okay in a minute."

Kurren continued to walk on until they reached the other side of the forest. Either her vision was playing tricks on her, or they were walking through a mist and into another world. The trees were thicker here, more dense than they'd been a few moments ago.

Pulling her through the mist towards him, Kurren led her to the edge of a cliff. A huge expanse of land as far and wide as the eye could see met her in a twinkling of lights.

Kurren waved his hand, encompassing the view before her. "Welcome to Dacia."

"What actually is Dacia?"

"Dacia is a portal in time and space. Zamolxis created this utopia for his loyal followers. We are allowed to come and go, merge and join the mortal world but here, this is our sanctuary. Those mortals who've traversed through its portal usually find themselves unable to return or deeply mentally incapacitated."

"What about me? Will I be able to return?"

Kurren turned to her but the silent, uncertain look he gave her wasn't hopeful.

"I don't really know. You are different. Draylon told me you've come to realize you are a shifter. That means you are probably, somehow one of us."

"But you don't know how." Marilyn already knew that. There was so much she needed to know, so many uncertainties. All in a fraction of time her life had been swept into a cataclysm of the unknown that not even the immortals knew what to do about.

"I'm hoping that once Rick meets you, he'll be able to give us a better understanding of what you are and your purpose among us."

"You're taking me to Rick Delvante's?"

"Draylon insisted it was the safest place for you. But it's quite a journey, even from here. We'll head to our house where you can recover for a few days."

"Something tells me I'm not safe anywhere," Marilyn mumbled.

"You may be right. But I'll do everything in my power to try to protect you."

"Thank you, Kurren."

#

Rick Delvante still didn't have any information as to Diane Reddlin's whereabouts. He'd contacted every embassy, train station, airport and underground connection he knew in Europe, and the last known address had been a hotel in Cluj. But no one had seen her in weeks. She'd left some of her luggage and hadn't returned but didn't leave a message or any indication of where she might have headed off to.

He'd been searching every avenue he had out in the real world but came up empty. Weary and frustrated, he sat behind his desk trying to figure out what to do next. Looking at his watch, he wondered if Draylon had any luck getting Marilyn out of Aiden's house. He usually called when he'd accomplished a task.

Damn. Was it really three o'clock in the morning? Draylon had left at nine. Something wasn't right. His phone rang. Thank the gods!

"Draylon, where are you? Did you find her?" He spoke rapidly into the phone.

"I don't know where your Zmeu pet is, dearest brother. But you will suffer for sending your buffoons into my domain and killing half of my staff!"

"Aiden, what are you talking about?"

"You sent in your wolf pack to steal the girl and annihilate my people. I have piles of ash everywhere from my corridors to my main entrance."

Rick sat back and pinched the bridge of his nose. This didn't bode well. Neither clan was allowed to kill the other inside of their personal space. Vamier wasn't allowed to kill inside of Dacia and Delvante was not allowed to kill inside of Vamier territory. Still, there was the stipulation of Marilyn in play.

"What about Marilyn? Where is she?"

"Not so fast...I want to know what your fascination is

with her."

"None of your damn business."

"I'm making it my business. She knows too much about Dacian history, making things a bit uncomfortable. No human should have the kind of knowledge she does. Oh and you can thank her for letting me know that one of the Zmei did survive after all. All these years and he was right under my nose. You were clever in keeping him hidden, brother. I would have killed him sooner had I known."

"What do you mean, killed him sooner? Where's Draylon? What have you done with him?"

"I left him to rot in his own lonely grave. He could have died quickly with the rest of his beastly family instead…but thanks to you, he'll die broken and alone…and a most lengthy death."

"You sonofabitch!"

"No, you are the son of the bitch."

Frustrated, Rick hung up on Aiden's sadistic laughter. Teeth clenched tightly, it was the only thing keeping his form from emerging. Fighting the urge to run, Rick calmed enough to try to think things through. The only thoughts were those of how he should've killed his brother years ago when he had the chance.

#

Kurren led her through the forests of Dacia. An untouched paradise compared to the real world. For all its natural beauty, it could have been the Eden the Bible spoke of. There were clean, clear streams and wild, natural habitats for many woodland creatures.

"We are never without food and share to provide for our brethren animals. We take only enough to sustain, not for sport," Kurren explained as a herd of deer scampered off across the open valley. "Our people learned long ago when we nearly annihilated our entire food source that we needed to find alternatives."

"Humans could learn a great deal from the Dacians."

"We have a few who are part of the World Conservation Program with the United Nations, but it doesn't mean we are heard." He turned to her as they continued walking. "How are you feeling now?"

"Better. The queasiness has subsided."

"It gets easier the more you do it. It's the time portal. It messes with the natural equilibrium in the inner ear canal."

"So are there other Dacians who prefer the mortal world to Dacia?"

"Those who do need to come home to Dacia every few years to live. Then they must go to a new destination because…"

"…they never age. It would cause people to wonder."

"Exactly."

"What about Draylon? He can live in the real world for quite awhile it seems."

"No. He travels a bit when needed but his home in the Austrian Alps is much like Dacia. It's a time portal in which all time, as mortals know it, stands still. His confidante, Donovan stays there most of the time."

"Donovan?" Marilyn remembered the name. An image of an older man dressed in coat and tails…in a mountain fortress. "Eskardel!"

"What?"

"Eskardel…what's it mean?" She asked.

"Eskardel was the home of the ancient Zmei, a cavern deep inside the Carpathian Mountains in which they lived. It was a sacred place and only the most honored of the Dacia clans were allowed entrance. Rumor has it if a Zmeu were to seduce a young woman and take her to Eskardel, it was only because she was his true mate."

Marilyn's mind conjured up the dreams she'd been

having. "What were Zmei?"

"They were shape-shifters…"

"I know that. But what was their true form?"

Kurren's brow wrinkled. "Balour. What you would call dragons."

"Dragons with gem stones in their foreheads?"

"Some say, yes. It was supposed to be a third eye…the eye of the gods." Kurren smiled. "Why do you ask?"

She smiled back and shrugged as they continued their trek. But Marilyn knew. Her dreams were finally beginning to make sense and the funny thing about it…she was okay with them.

#

"This is your house?" Marilyn gasped as they came upon the huge A-framed log house.

"Well, Therron—or Ron and I share it. We kind of have our own wing."

"It's absolutely beautiful."

"Thank you." They walked up onto the wrap around deck and walked in through the Dutch doors. "Ron, we have company. Make sure you're decent," he called out.

"We're in here, Ren," Ron yelled back.

Marilyn followed Kerren through the mud room to the huge kitchen and into the massive sunk-in living room.

"Marilyn!"

"Mom?" Marilyn ran to her mother who embraced her in a hug and then stood back to look at her, holding her face, touching her hair.

"You look fabulous! What did you do? Where have you been? I've been so worried…"

"I'm fine Mom. I came looking for you—"

"No time. No time for all this…pshaw!"

They both turned to see Nonni sitting in her chair, waving her crooked cane at them.

"Sit," she ordered. "Much to do and little time."

They all sat down, Marilyn holding her mother's hand, their fingers clasped. It was odd to see her mother in a man's flannel top and sweatpants. Her hair was down, the natural face of her mother, sans cosmetics, glowed. This wasn't the same woman she'd known all of her life. Where was the tailored business suit, the severe knot of hair at the base of her head and power red lipstick that made Diane Reddlin the business demon she'd been known for?

"All is going as the gods have foreseen," Nonni stated.

"Then the gods must like crazy—you have no idea what I've been through." Marilyn snorted.

Nonni whacked her upside the head with her cane.

"Owww! What was that for?"

"You are impertinent. The gods chose the time, the place and the way for things to be followed." The old lady glared at her. "You have the medallion still?"

Marilyn touched her shirt, feeling the bronze piece on the silver chain securely around her neck. She nodded.

"That is good. It is your talisman. Your destiny."

"What medallion are you talking about?" Diane asked.

Marilyn took it out from beneath her collar.

Both men sat closer to look and said a few choice curse words.

"Where did you get that?" her mother asked.

"For my twenty-first birthday, I was sent a package, no return address, but there was a letter inside. The sender was a friend of my father's and this was a special Dacian artifact he'd found and would want me to have. I was told to keep it a secret because there were those who shouldn't know of its whereabouts."

"What is it?" Diane looked around the room.

"It's half of the Dacian code. The gods gave it to the Dacians as a token of unity among the Dacians and the Zmei.

They were considered to be immortal warrior brethren. A
circle of peace and continuity among the two clans," Ron
explained breathlessly.

"The code was broken by Zamolxis when Vamier
desecrated the original Eskardel, 'Home of the Zmei.' The
broken medallion symbolized what the Dacians call, "The
Great Divide" when the Dacian clan was split in two," Ren
continued.

"It happened over a thousand years ago, back before your
Christ was born," Nonni countered. "The gods foretold of a
time when the two pieces would be united and a new order
would begin…that time has come."

"No." Ren stood up. "It was also foretold that if the two
pieces were ever joined the world as we know it would end!"

Nonni shrugged. "Our world ends every once in awhile.
We just don't know it."

"Can you be so lackadaisical in your belief of the gods
that you'd take a chance on an apocalyptic turn of events?"

"The gods have spoken." Nonni glared at Ren. "That is
the way. That is all you need to know."

"Where do I fit in?" Marilyn asked. So she held the
medallion, what did it mean?

Nonni sat forward, leaned on her cane and stared at her.
"You are the new world. You are the medallion…and you are
the mother of a new generation of Dacia."

Silence engulfed the room. The icy chill drifting through
her blood stream had nothing to do with the evil eye Nonni
was watching her with—but with the power of her statement.

"You know it to be so." Nonni sat back as if she'd done
nothing more than to reveal a secret family recipe and not a
pre-ordained millennium old foretelling of the gods.

#

"Mr. Delvante." His assistant, Kassidy MacDonald came
in. "Therron is here to see you."

Rick stopped writing the memo he was working on. That's all he needed, the head of the Dacian Alpha Board to deal with. As if he didn't have enough on his plate.

Rick wiped the fatigue from his face. "Fine. What's he want?"

"Rick."

The voice registered and he pinched the bridge of his nose. "What is it, Ron?"

"Oh my God!"

The feminine voice was not something he expected to hear, and he threw his head up to see the one woman he definitely didn't want to see. It had been years, a little over twenty-five to be exact.

"Diane," he said calmly. He figured someone needed to be the composed one here, might as well be him. It sure in hell wasn't her, not with the look in her eyes.

"You sonofabitch! You bastard!"

Yeah, he could deal with the names, had for centuries. One more person wouldn't matter. And if he ever deserved the names, she would be the one he'd accept them from.

Ron held her back by her forearms as she tried to come at him. She probably wanted to tear him apart, reach in to his chest and rip his heart out. Yep, and she had every right to.

"So...the mighty Rick Delvante is defeated." Nonni stepped forward from behind the couple.

"Come to gloat, Old Lady?"

"No. I come to see you get filleted like the slippery eel you are. It's time a woman puts you in your place."

"Is that why you kidnapped her and brought her here? So you could watch her gut me?" Rick tsked. "I thought you'd have better things to do like brew up some 'bat-wing' surprise or turn men into toads."

"Bah! Men are toads—they don't need a woman to turn them into one." Nonni threw her hands up. "I not kidnap her.

She comes to Dacia on her own, looking for her daughter."

Rick looked to Diane. Her eyes spit venom, hatred and the worst thing he could ever see…hurt. Closing his eyes he sighed.

"Everyone leave. I want to talk to Diane alone," he said calmly.

"Good. It is time." Nonni turned to leave. "Therron, come."

Standing his ground, Ron refused to move.

Rick had counted on him as a trusted sentry over the years, even made him leader of the Alpha Board. But strain on their differences of opinions at times in the changes of democracy over the centuries had caused their friendship to weaken. There was always respect on both parts, though. Their differences were nothing new. Ron was there protecting Diane. Rick could see the determination in his eyes and an awareness of a connection he should be jealous over. Diane was his wife—technically they never divorced. But twenty-five years of abandonment would make her single in the eyes of the court.

"I'm not going anywhere." Ron crossed his arms over his chest in defiance, glaring at Rick. The protective stance Ron took as his body overlapped Diane's gave Rick pause. He didn't want to think about what that might mean. And he didn't want to get into a pissing fight over territory. Diane was no longer his territory. He'd given her up a quarter century ago.

"Fine. Stay then. But I refuse to have two women nagging on me."

"I go." Nonni said. "But you hurt her…"

"He won't have the chance, Nonni," Ron spoke out with deadly calm. "It's all good."

By the time Nonni left, Diane looked as if she might pass out. She hadn't said a thing, moved a muscle or twitched. Was she in shock?

He stood up and walked around his desk to face her. "Are you all right?"

She nodded slightly.

"Can I get you some water?"

She nodded again.

Going to his water pitcher, he poured her a glass and handed it to her. Within seconds he was drenched and standing in the center of glass shards where she had thrown the glass to the floor.

Taking out his linen handkerchief, he mopped his face. "I'll let you have that one, Diane."

"How dare you!"

He cocked his head. "Depends on what the issue is—"

"Don't play cocky with me…Richard Reddlin, Rick Delvante…whoever the hell you are. "You knew Marilyn was safe. All this time you knew where she was, and yet you made me believe you had no idea." She walked around him, sizing him up for the kill. "You are a bastard!"

Ron took a step back. His eyes widened on Rick.

Rick sighed. "I can explain—"

"Can you? Can you explain telling the world you've been missing for twenty-five years? Can you tell your widow how you just decided to leave because she was pregnant with your child?"

"You were unfaithful. I'm Dacian for Christ's sake. We can't breed."

"Well then how in the hell do you want me to explain our daughter?"

Ron stepped forward, staring at Rick. "For the love of the gods! Marilyn is your daughter?" He thought for a moment. "This all is starting to make sense now—"

"Ron…don't," Rick warned in a pleading tone.

"She's part Dacian. That's why she can shift into a wolf!"

"What?" Diane gasped.

"When we met her, she was dealing with the change. Kurren and I noticed she was in heat."

"Ron, stop…you don't understand…"

"She is one of us because…" Ron sat down on the nearby leather sofa, shaking his head, "…because you are the chosen prophet, the one chosen by the gods to produce the heir to Dacia. That's why Nonni sent her the medallion."

"Wait! Marilyn has the medallion? Which half?"

"The head of the wolf…"

"Does Aiden know she has it?"

"I don't know, why?" Ron asked.

"Because if he does all hell is about to break loose, and Marilyn is right in the thick of it."

Diane stood toe to toe with him. He towered over her by nearly a foot, but he knew she could take a man down in a heartbeat. "I don't know what is going on but if our daughter is in trouble, you've got some major explaining to do, and you better tell me everything or so help me God I *will* have your testicles on a silver platter!"

Chapter Eighteen

Nonni told her and Kurren to wait here. But Marilyn didn't know for how long. As spacious as the log house was, it wasn't enough and claustrophobia settled in. She knew she needed to run but why?

Usually there was a reason. Well, it could be because they had yet to hear from Draylon. She'd checked with Ren every fifteen minutes to see if anyone had heard about his whereabouts. He'd tried to calm her down, saying it wasn't unusual for them to go their separate ways after a raid, especially with Dacia involved. It wasn't good for all involved to come back to their native origin at the same time. They usually dissipated and regrouped a few days later.

Still, something didn't sit right. Her nerves were on edge. Just because she'd found her mother didn't mean things were back to normal. Draylon could take care of himself, after all, he'd taken care of her, rescued her from all the evil things that had happened to her in the past month, two months, weeks…hell, however long they'd known each other. These rips in time were screwing with her too much to know what day it was much less month.

"Why don't you go lie down?" Ren suggested. "You look exhausted. You've been through the wringer and it won't do anyone any good if you pass out."

He was right. She'd been on overload for so long she couldn't remember when she'd had a good sleep. "You'll wake me up the minute you hear anything about Draylon?"

"Yes. Now go—get some sleep. You'll be safe here."

"Thanks Ren…for everything."

"No sweat, sweetheart." He winked.

If she ever had a brother, Ren would be it. He was protective and sometimes a pain in the ass, but she liked him anyway. As handsome as the brothers were, she didn't feel the attraction she had with Draylon. Her thoughts turned to him, and she started to worry all over again.

#

Sleep eluded her, but her mind drifted in and out of consciousness. Prior dreams mixed in with her recent reality, making for a hodge-podge of weird emotions and new ideas. She wondered if Doc Johnston might have anything to sort out her thought patterns.

Marilyn kicked off her covers finding the material overwhelming, burdensome and frustrating. She lay there looking up at the dark ceiling, willing her body to relax. But it was more than a muscular thing, her heart beat felt all wrong, skipping beats and racing out of control. Stress and anxiety had to be getting the best of her. She needed to run.

Marilyn.

The simple word echoed in her brain. Had someone called her?

Marilyn…are you…are you safe?

Draylon? Draylon, where are you? she called out in her head.

Not sure. It's dark and small…I can't see anything. Are you okay? Does Ren have you? Did he get you to Rick's?

I'm fine. She focused on him, where he might be. She hadn't realized she could do this, but the dream she'd had that night at Mike's house proved they did have a mental connection of sorts, when either one was open to it…or too weak to block…

He was weak. She could feel pain, his pain. His body lay on a hard, cold ground but closed in, tightly closed in. She inhaled only to find her ribs ache with each breath she took. It was his breaths she felt, his ribs aching. But his mind wasn't functioning. It was drowsy, cloudy and had trouble comprehending function. He moved only to have pain shoot through her hip and thigh—was his leg broken? Why wasn't he healing?

Draylon? Try to show me your last memories? What do you remember?

No! You need to stay safe. Stay with Rick…he'll protect you and keep you safe.

Damn it! Listen to me, I'm fine. Let me send help. I need to know where you might be.

No. It's not worth it. Besides, I think I'm being used as bait. Aiden wants you…he wants to know why you are so special. I know why you are special—because you are one hell of a woman, Marilyn. If I could, I would love you forever.

I'm holding you to that, Draylon. She could feel her eyes misting. But the longer she talked to him the more she could see into his psyche. There were details of images in his memory she studied as she mentally talked with him, keeping him alive. *You* can *love me forever.*

No, I can't. Even if I was out of this hell hole, I could never love you the way you need to be loved. There are things about me that would scare the living hell out of you. I could never trust myself not to terrify you. I'm what nightmares are made of. Just ask any folk historian.

She'd got it. The image of him being shoved into a deep

hole…by Gerlich.

Hold on, Draylon. I'm coming.

You better be referring to the sexual release, Marilyn because if not—I'm going to kick your ass

Kiss my ass? You promise? Don't threaten me with a good time, Draylon, I'll hold you to that.

No I said 'kick your ass'—

But she'd already cut off connection by blocking her thoughts and actions from him. She had all the information she needed to track him down. Now she just had to break into Aiden's fortress and get him out safely.

Slipping out of bed, she tied her sneakers and made her way towards the door.

Ren stopped her. "Where do you think you're going?"

"I'm going back to Vamier's."

"What? Like hell you are."

"Draylon's being held captive somewhere in the fortress. He's injured and close to dying. I won't be responsible. If Aiden wants me, he's going to get me…and all that I am."

"Marilyn, don't do this. If what Nonni says is true, you are the key to everything in the Dacian curse. If he has you, it could mean the start of the apocalypse," Ren warned.

"Maybe that is what I was meant for. Maybe it's up to me to bring about a new world."

"You don't understand the powers behind the curse," he stormed.

"Then it's time I learned."

#

She didn't have a damn clue what she was doing. Going off half-cocked was not her at all. She'd been taught to plan everything down to the minute detail before approaching a situation. But she needed Draylon. They were connected on a level so intense that neither one could survive if the other didn't. He was her destiny. She knew this was the right path.

Marilyn tried to weigh the pros and cons in her head, but her heart over-ruled. She'd never had such a strong connection with a man or any human being for that matter. She was no longer a true human, she was part wolf—and other things she wasn't quite sure about, but she sensed them within her.

"I don't like this, Marilyn," Kurren said as he followed her through the early Dacian dawn.

"It's not for you to like. It's for me to do." She stopped and he barreled into her. Toe to toe they stood. "Did you ever get the sense of rightness and know you had to follow through with it?"

"For us it's constant. We call it instinct."

"Well, this is a first time for me. Since my trip here to Romania, I've had a lot of firsts. But I've never had the connection I have with Draylon with any other man."

"It's the telepathy. Somehow you two are connected mentally." He agreed.

"No…it's something deeper. Something so basic and raw it's as if we are two parts of a whole." She started walking again, moving branches out of the way. "If I'm to be here in Dacia for the rest of my life, I can't imagine being here without him."

"Still, you're willing to go in there, knowing it might be a trap and sacrifice yourself?"

"That's what Draylon did. He's forbidding me to come save him to keep me safe." She stopped again. "But you need to let go and believe in something greater than your sacrifice. If your love drives you to sacrifice yourself—how can you enjoy sharing an eternity of immortality with the one you're meant to share it with?"

Ren looked at her with a touch of confusion. He wasn't following her train of thought. Truthfully, she wasn't sure she followed it herself. She shook her head and moved on. Yes, she knew what she was doing, she needed to stay positive.

"Well if you insist on going back to Vamier's then let me get you some weapons and a crew to go with you."

"No. I have all the support I need, right here." She patted her chest, feeling the security of her medallion. She hugged Ren. "Keep my mom safe for me." With that she ran on ahead of him, losing herself in the woods towards Cluj.

She still didn't know what the hell she was doing, but some inner peace had her believing this to be the right direction, her direction.

#

Draylon had given up hope. He lay in his prison-grave weary and in pain. He'd tried morphing into all of his creatures. Nothing worked, not even his mightiest creature, his true Zmei form. It had no room to morph. So he lay here trying to save his energy and heal from the wounds suffered at Gerlich's hands. But whatever drug they'd given him interfered with his normal healing rate. His inability to breathe deeply suggested he might have suffered some broken ribs. He knew he had a broken leg but what was worse was his broken spirit.

Draylon, can you hear me?

Marilyn. His head lifted from his arms where he sat. Where had she gotten the ability to communicate with him like this? He wasn't going to answer. She'd pissed him off by closing off her telepathy from him when he told her to stay away.

So you're pissed at me? Why? You want to play the hero? Fine, let's see you do it. She sighed. *Why do men have to be such pains in the asses? Wasn't it you who told me I needed to make my own choices and decisions? You were the one to tell me not to be afraid of taking a stand.*

I was referring to other's control over you.

Ah, so you are there.

The imp had conned him into revealing himself. Shit. He

set his jaw and narrowed his thoughts onto her. He could see her running through the woods on all fours. She'd morphed into a bobcat?

Yeah, about that—damnedest thing happened. I started running and then I felt the change coming on, but my mind conjured up this form. You didn't tell me Dacians can shift into more than one form. Kind of cool if you ask me.

They can't. Dacians are wolves or human, nothing more.

Well then I must be special, like Nonni said.

What?

Nonni told me she'd sent me the wolf half of the Dacian medallion for my twenty-first birthday because I was chosen by the gods. Right now, I've got to get to you. How are you holding up?

Dacian medallion? Wolf half? The only medallion he knew of was the—oh hell no.

Marilyn! What are you doing? He didn't have to ask. He could see from her vision Vamier's fortress before her as she lurked beneath the overgrowth of the forest. *You are the Chosen One. If Vamier finds out, your life is over.*

Nope. That is where you are wrong, Draylon. I've finally figured it out...I'm only the Chosen One if we are together.

#

The outside of the fortress was up lit with massive searchlights giving it more of a menacing effect. Were they still on the lookout for her? Marilyn made her way through a side entrance, keeping to the shadows. She had to admit she felt vulnerable in her naked state, the only security she had was in her medallion.

She made her way through the various corridors hoping to find some insight into Draylon's whereabouts. Instead she at least found some bed linens that she fashioned into a simple sarong-style dress to keep her from feeling exposed. There had to be an easier solution to all this changing and ending up without any clothes. Or maybe she just needed to embrace being naked.

"Ah, you are back." A voice with a slight German tone startled her from behind as she rounded a corner to see if it was all clear. She guessed not. "Aiden will be so pleased."

Gerlich stood, leaning against the wall, looking smug and self-satisfied. It was too bad his smarminess interfered with his good looks. Calming her racing heart down, she smiled.

"Yes, well, it's only temporary. I seem to have forgotten a few things." She could play the game, too.

"I like your dress. Did you make it?"

"Yes, matter of fact I did, recently."

He only nodded.

"So I'm assuming you're going to take me to Aiden," she said.

"I thought about it but no." He studied his neat manicure. "I decided there are certain privileges to having rank. You see, I've been climbing this 'chain of command' to get where I want to be. It's all about leverage and having the insight to use it at the apropos time."

"So you're blackmailing, Aiden Vamier?" Marilyn cocked her brow at him and shook her head. "Not a real smart thing to do if you ask me."

"He seems to think you're rather important. He sent his best troops out to hunt you down more than once, and rumor has it, none of the young vamps can touch you without dying a quick death. I wonder why?"

"Beats the hell out of me." It baffled her, too. And by the way he leered at her, Gerlich looked eager to see if he was immune to her touch. "Care to see for yourself?"

Gerlich laughed. The creep even had a rich sounding laugh that could turn a woman on. Damn shame.

"I like you, Miss Reddlin. You have spirit and sass. There is no fear in you."

Damn. Good thing he couldn't read her mind. Her insides were beginning to take on a fight or flight adrenaline rush as he stalked closer.

He stood within her private space. She could see the minute details in the smoothness of his pale features, the prominent shape of his Adam's apple, the short hairs framing his forehead. Scrawny, pale and charming—did he sparkle, too?

Gerlich caressed her face with his palm, his thumb tracing back and forth across her mouth. Her lips twitched and her nose wrinkled but not in involuntary pleasure. His touch set off something lurking deep inside of her. She stared into his eyes and saw an image of the torture Draylon had endured at his hands.

"Where is he?" she questioned in a low tenor.

"Who?" he replied innocently.

"What did you do to Draylon?"

"I put him out of his centuries of misery. It's kind of refreshing to know I am the one who did away with Rick Delvante's famous pet. And now, I feel the need to make even a bigger deal over removing his new one."

His mouth came down as if to kiss her only he went for her throat at last minute, latching on with his razor sharp fangs.

Marilyn went wild. Fear exchanged places with anger. Anger turned into energy, energy that streamed through her veins and every biological system she could fathom. She saw the wolf, witnessed the bobcat form cross her internal vision but what came next was magnificent and frightening. The creature she'd been recently in her dreams. She accepted it, coming to realize what she was all about. She was a Zmeu!

Gerlich hung on, drawing on her life blood even as her body grew and morphed. Scales the color of garnet replaced skin, her hands elongated into thin, finger-like claws curling under in deadly looking sickles. Her shoulders pressed against the wide width of the corridors and took up the height of the chapel-styled rafters.

Plucking Gerlich off of her, she flicked him down the length of the hallway like a piece of lint. Now she was the stalker. She picked him up, shook him awake, no doubt addling his brain if he had any ounce of mortality.

"Where is Draylon?" Her human voice bellowed off the walls in a guttural bass.

"Fuck! What the hell…" He squirmed like a worm on a hook.

She turned, taking out the walls on her way and threw him down back the way they came. The momentum and acrobatic spins he took were definitely more like bowling but instead of pins falling, the roof fell in as the stone walls and plaster ceiling caved in around them, burying Gerlich.

He still hadn't complied, and she couldn't get a good bead on Draylon. Short of tearing down the fortress, she needed him to confess.

Unearthing her nemesis from the rubble and tucking him under her wing, Marilyn went on a rampage through the thousand year old fortress. Nothing stood in her way. She could get used to this.

Dawn had broken and she unearthed vampires who'd only recently called it a night to avoid the power of the sun god. She exposed them to the old god. The echo of hisses and screams as the smell of burning flesh filled the morning air only intensified her hunt.

Looking back the way she'd come, Marilyn realized she'd destroyed one whole wing of the ancient fortress without any sight of Draylon. She lifted her wing, exposing her cargo to say hello to Derzelas, the sun god. He might be able to help her out.

Gerlich screamed like a girl as sunlight streamed over him before she blocked the light with her body.

"You have one last chance to tell me before I fry you like the worm you are—Where is Draylon?"

He coughed from the burning in his lungs. "Beneath the dungeon in the north wing…the oubliette…"

Lumbering through the courtyards, her tail slammed into everything within its path as she made her way to the north wing, Gerlich hanging on for dear life.

With the strength of a massive bulldozer she ransacked the wing, exposing more victims to their sunlit fate. She didn't care. Her only thoughts were on Draylon.

"There!" Gerlich gasped out as he pointed to the iron disc on the stone floor. "He's in there."

Picking up the heavy cover as if it was a mere dime, she flung it, taking off the head of one of the nearby statues. The hole in the ground was much too small though. She bent her head down to peek one massive eyeball into the dark pit but couldn't see anything at all. Frustrated, she clawed at the ground. Rocks and earth flew in every which direction as her angry breath came out in steaming dew.

She'd managed to dig out the large clearing, no longer the shape of a narrow necked vase but that of a huge bowl. Draylon lay naked, curled up among tattered remains of clothing. Marilyn had never seen him so vulnerable. She nudged him with her snout. But there was no response. She tried to get to him mentally, to no avail.

Was she too late? Impossible, he was immortal.

A cacophony of sounds alerted her to the presence of others. Vehicles in various modes surrounded her and the rubble. A man stepped out of a black stretch limo with a slow grace as he stared up at her in awe.

"M…m…Marilyn? What the hell…"

He looked around as his crew of white lab coat physicians stepped in to see to Draylon's prone form. Her instincts kicked in, wanting to protect Draylon from anyone's touch but hers.

The rumble of motorcycles pulled onto the scene. Kurren and Therron took off their helmets and stood back mesmerized, and her mother stood, gawking in paralyzed fear. Therron turned to help a passenger in Kurren's sidecar, a hunched over form hitting at him as if she didn't want his help. But he helped her remove her helmet and Nonni stood there like she expected the whole thing.

But her mother only stared up at her, not having a clue who or what she was.

"What's going on here?" Nonni patted her mother reassuringly.

Diane walked over to Rick. "Is this who I think it is?"

"Depends on who you think it is. The red scales and green gem in her forehead is a dead ringer to me." Rick sighed.

"Marilyn!" Diane screamed upon realizing the truth.

Chapter Nineteen

Marilyn sat in the isolated clinic room awaiting Rick Delvante's arrival. After shifting back into her human form, she'd been poked and prodded by a team of specialists who she would have thought were more vampire for all the blood they'd taken from her.

She wanted to see Draylon or at least know of his condition. He'd been so still when she'd found him. Even after the team was finally able to move him, they wouldn't let her near. They had every right to protect him. She was a monster. How did you explain to someone you've fallen in love with that you're a freak of nature? Shifting into a wolf was one thing—a fire breathing dragon? Well, not many people would understand that.

Her mother had not taken it well. She'd passed out in Ron's arms. But she'd given birth to her. Wouldn't she be aware of her condition? Wasn't it in her DNA? Someone had to have known something about her biological make-up?

She shivered. The thick spa robe they'd given her after her examination was warm enough in the chilly room, but it wasn't the cold she felt. The energy and uncertainty flowing through her had her shaking. Was she in shock?

Nah. People shift into weird creatures all the time. They also fell in love with werewolves and get attacked by vampires. Why in God's name would she be in shock?

Her teeth clattered together, and she huddled into a ball on the narrow examination bed. She wanted to run. She wanted to stay. Closing her eyes tightly against all the wild energy inside of her, she forced her body to try to calm itself, remembering lessons from her Tai-Chi and Karate classes in relaxation.

Visions of her creatures played havoc on her mind, each one trying to dominate the other. Her body twitched and quaked with each snarl, growl or screech.

The door flew open and so did her eyes. Rick Delvante strolled in along with a team of white lab coat specialists who'd been with her earlier.

"Marilyn?" He looked up at the doctors. "What's wrong with her?"

"We don't know. She's showing signs of fatigue, but her adrenaline levels are off the chart. Here are her most recent vital signs." The doctor handed him a chart. He looked it over and nodded before handing it back.

"Give us a few minutes, please." Rick sighed.

The medical team nodded and left the room. Marilyn didn't feel like talking, thinking or socializing right now. But she didn't struggle as Rick picked her up in his arms and adjusted her so she could curl into his chest.

He took her out another door. One she hadn't seen behind her. It led into a neutral painted hallway with white trim. Wonderful aromas of essence oils filled the air. Within moments she was lowered gently onto a chaise lounge and wrapped in a warm blanket. Light classical music drifted around her.

"I hate white sterile rooms. But they needed it for the examination," he said as he pulled up a plush winged-back chair beside her and perched on the edge of the seat, his hands folded together as if settling in to discuss serious issues.

"What…what is wrong with me?" Marilyn found the voice to speak.

"I was about to ask you the same question, but I know exactly what's wrong with you now." He smiled reassuringly. "I should have known. I should have trusted your mother when she told me…but I guess I just didn't want to believe it for myself."

"I don't know what you are talking about?"

"Your mother told me she was pregnant after we'd married. She said it was mine. I should have believed her."

"Wait? But you're Rick Delvante…my father was Richard Reddlin?

"I used Richard Reddlin as my alter ego. I met your mother for the first time when she was being interviewed for her first position at Livedel. I fell head over heels the instant I saw her through the two-way glass. So I followed her after she left, met her on the Metro Red Line and sat next to her.

"I followed her home—"

"You stalked my mother?"

"No…wait, let me finish." Rick sat back in the chair. "Well…actually, maybe I did." He amended.

"The Red Line?… Red line…oh God, tell me you didn't…" Marilyn threw her arm over her eyes in exasperation as what Rick said finally sank in. "Red Line…Reddlin…really?"

"She had me off guard. I didn't know what to do. I sat down next to her on the train. We talked about history and found out we shared a love for it. It had been her second major, and I told her I was an archeologist who was working for the Smithsonian. I came up with the name Richard and struggled to find a last name. I looked up to see the 'Redline' Map and…well…it just sort of happened."

Rolling over onto her back, Marilyn stared up at the twinkling fiber-optic lights in the ceiling that looked like millions of stars shining down on her. She threw her arm over her forehead taking in the news of finding her sire. Who and what was he? If she was this shape-shifting creature she couldn't be human, which meant neither was he.

"What am I?" she asked.

"I'm not sure." He grimaced.

"Great." Sarcasm dripped like honey from her mouth. "In the meantime my insides are going crazy, my head is overloaded with morphing creatures…"

"What creatures do you see?"

"Of course there is the wolf, an auburn haired wolf if that makes sense."

"When you morph it's usually in your true colors. You have your mother's natural auburn hair. So you've experienced your wolf?"

"Yes. And a bobcat…and of course the dragon…God! Was that really me?" She exhaled in distress.

"It was you. But I can't tell you why."

"Well if you can't, you better find someone who can because I'm going bat-shit crazy."

"Now that you mention it, there just might be someone who can help you. She knows a lot about 'bat-shit.'"

#

Nonni walked in and sat down across from her. Rick…Richard…her father, had left them alone. It was probably for the best. She had a feeling Nonni knew a hell of a lot more than even Rick Delvante. And Marilyn wanted all the answers now.

"So you have come full circle." Nonni gave a toothless grin.

"What's that supposed to mean?"

"Do you not understand what you are?" She scoffed.

"I'm Zmei…but how?"

"The gods foretold—"

"Cut the crap with 'the gods foretold.' I've had it up to my gills, feathers, fur…whatever I possess with stories of the gods. Just give it to me straight."

"You mock?"

"Damn right I mock. This is the twenty-first century. If there is a curse let me have it, if the gods are going to strike me down, let them. I'm tired of the folklore and fables. This is real life now, so just tell me the facts. I think I've put up with enough bullshit to be given the facts without all the fiction."

"Well, you've definitely moved on from being the meek little mouse I knew. It's about time. If you don't want the nonsense, I won't give it to you." Nonni sighed.

"Zamolxis told us there would come a time when the DNA of the Zmei would once again merge with that of the Dacians. That time has come."

"I'm both parts?"

"Yes. But there is more to your chemical make-up…and I am the cause of it."

Marilyn's eyes widened, and her head dipped to study the wrinkled old woman. "How so?"

"I carried the blood of the last ruling Zmeu," she said boldly. "I was known as Sariana. I was chosen to be given in marriage to the Zmei, but I'd already betrayed my people by falling in love with another. Still, I wasn't given a choice and was forced to wed the son of a Zmei leader."

"Aiden Vamier, he was the one you'd fallen in love with."

"It was a long time ago."

"Heck, if he looked anything like he does now—not a bad choice. But really? He's evil incarnate."

"He wasn't then, not at first." She sighed. "I didn't see him again for nearly two years. In that time I had fallen in love with Drakon."

"Drakon? Let me guess, Draylon's brother?"

"No. Drakon was the future Zmei leader, Draylon only good friend and warrior." Nonni sat forward and glared at her. "So you know Draylon is Zmei?"

Marilyn shrugged. "It came to me in a dream."

"Yes. I fell in love with Drakon. I was pregnant when Aiden and his warriors came and attacked. Drakon tried to save me. I watched as Aiden personally killed him. I ran, but Draylon ordered me to stay with him, and he morphed into his human form to help me escape. One of Aiden's warriors saw him with me and sliced him across his chest. I thought he was dead until I saw him at Zamolxis' hut being nursed back to health by Rick."

"But Rick didn't want anything to do with you. He felt you were the cause of the Great Divide."

"I was banished from Dacia. To this day Rick believes I'm the one who led the Romans here to conquer us."

"Were you?"

"No. The Dacians created their own demise. The clans were in an upheaval with no leader, no order and learning to adapt to their new image. It was a time easy enough for the Romans to come in and take over. Only a few managed to escape under the leadership of the young prophet and that is when Zamolxis created this haven for them in the time rip."

"What happened to you and the baby? Did you manage to escape?"

"I did. I found my way into what is now Bulgaria. I learned to accept their ways and settled in raising my child. From then on, the generations of Zmei blood line depleted but with the right combination and timing they would combine again."

It all made sense now. "My mother, she's the missing blood line and my father, Rick…he's the Dacian link."

Nonni nodded. "You are the offspring of the true clans."

Marilyn breathed heavily. She couldn't deny the story, the scientific or the paranormal. She'd witnessed both. But what were the odds that her parents would have met at the right time and place?

"The goddess of fate has much to do with timing. Do not discount the power or her knowledge. She controls every step we make," Nonni informed.

There was more that Marilyn could see in Nonni but couldn't put her finger on it. "I hope you don't mind me saying so, Nonni, but I sense you are not all that you appear to be."

The old woman looked up at her, the twinkle in her eye belying her true age. "You are wise beyond your years, Marilyn my dear."

Marilyn couldn't help but fight back a grin. "Just how powerful are *you*?"

Nonni looked around conspiratorially and leaned forward. "Stick around and you'll find out." She winked. "Now go off with you. Do what you need to do."

"Seriously?"

"Without this step that you make—none of anything else will matter. You are the key to what happens next."

#

Draylon latched his belt buckle and stood, looking at himself in the mirror. He was whole again. A few hours of recovery from pure hell and he was as good as new. If only his mental state felt the same way. He hadn't heard from Rick. He wondered where his friend was. It wasn't like him not to be a hundred percent involved with his well-being. Maybe it was the difference he'd begun to see lately. Maybe Rick was going through a mid-eternity crisis.

His door opened and there stood Marilyn, black jeans and a tight fitting turtle neck top hugging her curves like a sleek snake. Her hair glowed glossy red against her beautifully pale features. Her emerald green eyes flashed with impish joy.

He turned away from her, and adjusting the cuffs on his sleeves, inhaled her fragrance and fought his inner demon to control his urgency. "I have a bone to pick with you."

"If I remember correctly you wanted to 'kiss my ass,'" she replied casually.

"Try, 'kick your ass.'" He turned to her with serious aplomb.

"Kiss, kick—as long as it's you doing it, I don't care."

He didn't respond. It took every ounce of willpower he had not to take her up against the damn sterile hospital room wall, and in his current state he wouldn't stop at simple foreplay. He was just horny, pissed and sexually frustrated enough to go all the way—morphing be damned.

"Do you know how pissed off I am with you?" She tried to speak but he held up his hand. "No, let me continue. You ran off to go find your mother with no clue as to her whereabouts. You sacrificed yourself to the enemy for what purpose? How stupid could you be? Then when I send Kurren in to rescue you, what do you do? You turn around and risk your life again to come to my aide."

"You're welcome…"

"I. Am. Not. Finished," Draylon seethed between his teeth.

"Oh, yes you are—"

To prove to him he was finished, she forced him up against the wall and ripped the shirt he'd just put on from his torso. Her body pressed into his, taking full control by suffocating his anger with her mouth, devouring any words or thoughts from his tongue and head. Her hands were everywhere, her thumbs scraping across the sensitive tips of his nipples. The heat radiating between them was beyond feverish pitch.

Draylon ripped her knit top from her back, pulling the material around to the front and off so they were skin to skin—

the bra didn't last. Her fingers crawled up his neck and planted themselves in his hair as he lifted her against him, letting her ride his hips, urging his cock to an aching extension, an extension that brought out the beast in him.

Marilyn—I can't—I won't...

He couldn't finish the thought but instead acted on instinct, tossing her away from him onto the bed.

You don't understand. He punched the wall, leaving an indent. *I'm not what you think—I'm...* He left it at that and ran from the room. He ran as fast as he could to get as far away from her as possible.

The openness of Delvante's compound butted up against his former home mountains. It would be the one place he could escape to where no one could get to him—not even Marilyn in her wolf form.

He ran, faster and faster until he took flight. The change in him was a simple transformation as old as time itself. Never did he feel freer than when he could be in his true form. Long ago it had been a blessing to be Zmei, but for centuries, only a curse that caused him heartache and loneliness. He would rather shut himself up in his ancient family home with the bones and remains of his ancestors than to show his true self to Marilyn and have to lose her forever.

Riding the air currents through Dacia to ancient Eskardel, he found the clearing leading to the blocked off tunnel that led to the buried remains. He landed but didn't step further. The air around him turned heavy with a familiar musk, the one that drove him crazy in his dreams, in his nights, in his waking hours.

A long, high-pitched screech echoed off of the mountain range surrounding the valley. On instinct he called back. There, circling above him was the most beautiful creature he'd ever laid eyes on. Scarlet red, sleek serpentine body enhanced by a wingspan that stretched yards on either side. The glint of sunlight bounced off of an emerald lodged in the middle of its high, helmeted skull.

The creature landed clumsily by him, nearly taking a nosedive into a cluster of fir trees. Draylon cocked his head, watching as the creature righted itself and snorted.

Well?

Draylon couldn't believe his eyes or the single uttered word in his head. He had no words to say or even think.

Cat got your tongue? Hello? Are you going to try to tell me that is not you, Draylon? I've dreamed of you like this. It was you I saw flying around in Austria.

Marilyn.

It wasn't a question, just a subtle thought of disbelief.

I've got a problem, Draylon. You see, I'm in love with this guy and I'm not sure if he really likes me. He knows I'm a bit odd but he doesn't realize that I'm...I'm...well, I'm a fictional beast...a dragon. I'm afraid that if we were to ever make love that I would show my true self and send him running for his life...then I'd have to erase his memory and that would just suck because then I would never be able to be with him...

Draylon morphed back to human. Marilyn did too.

They stood there grinning at each other.

"Are you grinning at me because I'm naked or because you're happy?"

"Both." He took a tentative step towards her and another. "You're Zmei? But how?"

She explained the story Nonni told her, even going into detail about Rick and her mother.

"Sonofabitch. Really? All this time and—damn."

Marilyn slapped him on the shoulder. "If all you are going to do is cuss then how can I kiss you and make love to you?"

He grabbed her around her waist, pulling her to him. "You didn't have any problems silencing me in my hospital room?"

"No, but then you took off like a bat out of hell." She

touched his lips with her finger tip. "No more running, Draylon."

"Who, you or me?" He nipped at the finger.

"Both of us. Something tells me I've finally found where I belong."

"Not yet—but you will very soon."

#

"I want to see the sonofabitch!" Diane Reddlin screeched, trying to break free of Therron's hold on her. "You can't stop me, Ron." She breathed heavily.

"Oh, yes I can. We protect our leader at all cost."

"Damn it, he was my husband." Her voice broke into a sob. "He denied Marilyn as his own, saying he was infertile. He literally told me I'd been unfaithful…I hadn't loved any other man but Richard."

"So what do you want from Rick?"

Startled, both Ron and Diane jumped to see Nonni waddling up the corridor to Rick Delvante's office.

"What do you mean, Nonni?" Therron asked.

"She is angry at being deceived, lied to and humiliated by the one man she thought loved her." Nonni tsked.

She walked past them and went right into Rick Delvante's office without any announcement.

Diane and Ron followed tentatively behind. Nonni was as bold as you please and didn't even stop when the receptionist tried to halt her from going further. Nonni pointed her wrinkled, crooked finger at her and the dark, curly haired girl stopped in her tracks.

The elderly woman continued on past the reception desk until she came to the heavy door to Rick's own domain. She turned around. "Come. Come." She waved them forward. "You want to beat the shit out of him? You have Nonni's blessing, my child." Nonni smiled and pushed open the door.

Rick looked up from his desk to see he had unexpected

company.

"You weren't welcomed back, Witch."

"Too bad…I think someone has a bone to pick with you." She motioned to Diane. "The mother of your child would like an apology."

"And if I refuse?"

"She gets to beat the living crap out of you without any interference from us." Nonni turned and glared a silent warning at Ron.

"This has nothing to do with her or you, Nonni."

Stepping unannounced into the room, Diane looked around for her daughter. "Where's Marilyn? What have you done with her?"

Rick squared his jaw. He hadn't aged at all, hadn't changed in features, still looked as virile as he had the day they met. Immortality did that to you, she supposed.

"She's fine. She's sitting in with Draylon right now." His nostrils flared as he inhaled and exhaled sharply. "And I didn't do anything to her. I should be asking you the same question?"

"I didn't do anything…"

"No? Then how can she be a Zmeu?"

"A what?" Diane stared at him as if he might be mad. Hard lines etched into her forehead and she tried to rub them away. "What in the hell are you talking about? You are the one with the immortal genes. You are the one who caused all this."

"Enough!" Nonni muttered something under her breath in ancient dialect. "You both did 'all this.'" She waved her arm, encompassing the situation. She pointed to Rick. "You are Dacian, she is the blood of my loins and that of Drakon, my Zmei mate."

"Sariana?" Therron asked.

"Yes. It's Sariana." Rick sighed. "Still a thorn in Dacia history years later." He grumbled. "She destroyed us by pitting the Romans against us in our worst time."

"No. It was you warring over the broken pieces of medallion that cost you Dacia," she rallied back. "Stupid men with nothing better to do than fight amongst yourselves." She threw her hands up. "Bah! Such foolishness. And Zamolxis gave himself up to the moon goddess for you."

"Zamolxis gave himself to Bendis? For us?" Rick asked. "That's impossible. He told me he would come to me when the time was right and put together that which was torn asunder. He can't be imprisoned."

"Slow child, you do not yet comprehend?" Nonni shook her head. "I was told by Zamolxis to keep the wolf medallion and give it to the *chosen one* upon her twenty-first birthday."

Rick scratched his neck. "The piece Aiden has been looking for all these years? You've had it? He's had his minions infiltrate Dacia off and on this past decade searching for it, thinking I had it."

"Who?" Diane asked. She had no idea what this medallion was but it sounded important.

"I sent it to your daughter. She carries it with her," Nonni said.

"Marilyn has the medallion. What, are you freakin' out of your mind? What possessed you to do such a dumb ass thing?" Rick railed at the old woman. "If she has it and Aiden knows, she's in a great deal of dan—" he stopped. "Wait. Did he know she had the medallion when he sent for her to 'study' with him?"

"No, he didn't," Nonni said.

"I didn't know why she was coming to see him, I just knew she wouldn't be safe around him. But if he knows she has it—" Rick explained worriedly.

"It is fine. We get with Marilyn and she'll have the medallion." Nonni waved it off. "No worries."

Chapter Twenty

Aiden Vamier woke from his sleep to chaos. His fortress was in shambles, his gardens ripped apart as if a giant plow had dug up his earth. Piles of ash that had once been his family met him from within and along the exterior of his fortified compound where berths of dark rooms were now opened to the elements.

Delvante!

He stood in controlled rage over his half-brother's atrocity. Two whole corridors, nearly fifty of his loyalist subjects here in his private domain were gone, dead. He pondered just how to get back at his nemesis. But he'd already tried to get to Marilyn. No—he needed something more, something that would bring not only Rick but his whole clan to its knees. An eye for an eye made the world blind. He didn't want the world blind, just the Dacians.

Walking out into the destruction, nothing came to mind. He could pray to the gods for guidance but that never got him anywhere. He'd sell his soul for a chance to get even with Rick.

The toe of his shoe lit on something in the ground. A

protruding rock caused him to look down. A silver chain lay snagged on the rock. Silver, the known enemy to most of his clan. The newer ones couldn't develop a tolerance for it and perished from it or anything connected to it. He never let them know, it was part of his power-play. Only his devoted elders were given the warning and learned how to protect themselves. For him though, it was nothing more than a shiny substance. He picked it up, curious to its identity.

It was heavy for a simple chain, even for the gage of the links. Was it attached to something? The chain had broken. But half buried under the rubble was a heavier solid piece. He brushed it off, staring at a medallion. He couldn't believe his good fortune. It was almost too good to be true. Were the gods listening to him and answering his prayers?

In his hands he held the most grotesquely beautiful thing he'd ever seen—a half emblem of a wolf's head devouring the tail end of a Balour or dragon, encircling half of the Dacian sun god's symbol. The Dacian half to the sacred medallion Zamolxis had broken to sever the two clans. The two pieces were the key to claiming power of Dacia—the land that rightfully belonged to him

Now he had them both, his piece and Rick's. Aiden wondered how Rick had managed to lose his.

"Very clumsy, dearest brother…very clumsy, indeed."

#

"I always keep it on me." Marilyn fretted as she and Draylon stood before her father, Nonni, her mother and Ron. They were about to explain their unique relationship and needed to know what the gods had in store for them when they were bombarded with the question of her medallion.

"I had it on me the other…it was around my neck…" she placed her hand to her throat. "I morphed into a bobcat and when I turned human again, it was still there. But then—"

"You took on the appearance of the Balour. The necklace

would've broken," Nonni said.

"So it's somewhere over at Aiden's fortress." Marilyn sat down in defeat.

"Let's just pray to the gods that he doesn't find it before we can get it back." Rick sighed. "I'm sending a search party over there first thing in the morning. I can't afford to desecrate any more vampires. I'm afraid the gods are not in favor of me since we went in, destroyed property and killed what minions we could. There is a clause that we are supposed to follow in which we are not allowed to encroach on each other's territory unless absolutely necessary."

"What constitutes as necessary? I happen to think going in and saving Draylon was a very good reason." Marilyn held her head up. "If the gods have an issue with it, they can come talk to me."

"Marilyn...you don't want to egg them on. The gods are not always merciful," Nonni warned.

An alarm sounded throughout the building.

"Sonuvabit—" Draylon looked to Rick.

"What is it? Is there a fire?" Marilyn asked.

"Worse," Rick said.

"What do you mean worse?" her mother asked.

"Vamier has just forced his entry into Dacia. We're under attack."

The lights flickered and went out. Only the emergency lights on battery back-up illuminated the darkened hallways of the compound. That wasn't good. Vamier had powered out the facility, which meant his minions were on the prowl.

"Get Marilyn to safety...now," Rick ordered Draylon. "We're going to head underground." They took off, leaving her and Draylon to use the secret passage through the medical area.

But they were too late.

Two vamps entered the corridor, coming at them, fangs

drawn and bloody from a recent attack. The hiss and howls of matched enemies in battle rang throughout the hallways and open lobbies.

Marilyn put herself between him and the two blond entities.

Damn you, Marilyn.

I've got this...watch! She pushed her hand up against the chest of the advancing vamp, but nothing happened. *I don't understand, they usually disintegrate into ash when I touch them.*

The demons only threw back their heads and laughed, their eyes blazing an overly jaundiced yellow as the one pushed her arm to the side and continued his assent.

Draylon looked around for something to use. *Marilyn, grab onto the metal railing.*

What? Her inner monologue squeaked in fright.

The metal railing...grab it now.

Marilyn grabbed it just as the vampire lunged at her to take a healthy bite. Instead he sank his teeth into her throat and as usual disintegrated. The other, pissed off at his friend's sudden death attacked in retaliation, and they ended up forever tied to one another in an ashy pile of mixed remains.

The silver metal alloy. The younger ones aren't strong enough to fight its power. Even when their victim is only a conductor. To them it's like touching a live-wire and frying from the inside out, Draylon explained breathlessly.

Now knowing what they could use and not having any of his weapons on him, he searched the medical supply cabinets. Gauze, tongue depressors, cotton swabs, latex gloves—not a damn useful thing.

"What about these? Would these work?" Marilyn came up behind him with metal restraints used to help patients through mental detox.

"Perfect! Put one on."

He clamped a loose restraint around her wrist like a gruesome bracelet Frankenstein might give to his bride. He gave her a quick kiss.

"Is this an engagement?" she teased.

"Only if we survive."

#

The hallways were littered with bodies of Dacian medical staff, some were even in mid-morphing. Sadly, there was nothing she could do for them. She followed Draylon onward through the corridors.

They managed to take out three more vampires by wearing the silver bracelets. Now she wondered if it had been the silver chain of her necklace that had been her power and not her own ego. Great. All her abilities and she had no real power? That sucked, royally.

The floor beneath them heaved and buckled. Could her day get any shittier? Just what they needed—an earthquake during a Vamier attack.

"We need to get outside," she yelled to Draylon over the din of alarms and the cacophony of screams and howls throughout the building.

"It's not an earthquake—it's the gods, and they are not happy with something," Draylon replied.

Still, they hurried towards the front entrance to be met by her mother, Therron and Kurren.

"Where's Dad?" she asked, calling Rick by his informal name.

"Your father," Diane hissed the word, "felt the need to confront his brother."

"His brother?" It didn't click at first. "Aiden…Aiden's his brother."

"Half brother to be precise," Therron spoke up.

"We need to stop him before it's too late." She followed Draylon to the main door.

They all stood on the front stoop of the portico into the Delvante Gardens.

It was too late.

#

Rick saw the devastation, friends he'd known for centuries lay scattered about the compound and probably further on through Dacia. He knew what this was. He'd been waiting for this moment in time since Zamolxis first spoke of it, but still, it seemed so sudden.

"Aiden!" he called out. His voice echoed unnaturally through the gardens as storms rallied and Dacia shook under foot. He stood near the alter. He would be ready or as ready as he could be during such a drastic time.

"Looking for me, brother?"

The voice spoke behind him. Sacrilege among the Dacians of old. No one, not even the elders or the prophets, not Zamolxis himself came to the alter from behind. Rick held his tongue though.

"You do realize I have the medallion—both parts in fact," Aiden jeered.

"I didn't doubt it. Otherwise you wouldn't have felt so empowered to attack Dacia."

"You came and desecrated my fortress and needlessly killed my people...I only thought it was fair."

"You captured one of my friends, tortured him and left him for dead."

"Your Zmeu was only being used for bait. I would have released him as soon as Marilyn Reddlin returned to become my apprentice."

"Never," Rick spat out as Aiden began to circle him like prey.

"She's special to you. I wonder why? I know she's the daughter of your chief financial officer at Livedel, that was no problem to find out, but what about *her* in general makes her so important to you and a threat if she is within my company?" He stopped, "As Alice said as she fell down the rabbit hole, 'Curiousier and Curiousier.' What is she to you, Rick?"

"It's not what she is to him that should be a concern, Aiden, my love—"

Both men turned to see the alter once again desecrated by another form coming into the circle from the wrong direction. Nonni stood there hunched over at first, but her voice had taken on a youthful tone. Her body began to straighten and her girth thinned. Her peasant clothing turned into gossamer, nearly translucent, petals of material. Like a Grecian goddess she stood there before them, tall, pale and as beautiful as she had once been.

"Sariana," both men whispered, one in awe and one in hatred.

"That was one of my names. But I am also known as Zamrana…the daughter of Zamolxis."

She stepped forward and studied the two brothers, sizing them up. "Trust me, I had no love for the idea either, but I *am* the daughter of a god." She shrugged and snorted. "You think you have it bad?"

"Marilyn Reddlin is Rick's biological daughter, Aiden." She held up her hand to stop the words from his mouth. "I know…infertile. But it was time, as time has ordained. Rick had no more clue twenty-five years ago than you do right now." She went over and sat on one of the concrete benches.

The goddess's gaze at Rick had him sweating. Her eyes narrowed. Standing, she walked over and stood in front of him.

"And you." She tapped his cheek in a light slap. "You think Marilyn is all your doing?" She threw back her head. "Ha!" Sariana looked back at him under those sultry, gypsy lashes. "You sent me away after I came searching for sanctuary from this idiot." She cocked her head in Aiden's direction. "You wanted nothing to do with me after all the trouble I'd caused, the annihilation of the very species that kept you all safe in battle, the species the gods had gifted your people as a blessing.

"It was all a great plan of the gods. It was a test...I was a test. Could anything cause the greatest race of people to destroy themselves? A simple woman from a privileged home, selected to be the mate of the leader of the Zmei. But there was a twist. Seduce the son of the leading chieftain of the Dacians and see how he responds. If he is a true leader he will understand his lover's need to become the bride of the Zmei, if not..." She shrugged.

"My father knew the outcome. That is why I was sent. I became pregnant with my Zmei mate's heir and managed to keep it with me through the battle and my exile from Dacia. Though no longer Zmei, my child maintained the DNA of the honored ones, and while raised among mortals, passed the gene on each generation until the time was right."

"Marilyn..."

"No. Diane is my offspring. She contained the very seed that you impregnated. Twenty-five years later, the child's true self is revealed...Marilyn is the last mate of the Zmei."

"What will happen?" Rick asked. The world wouldn't be able to handle a rebirth of the Zmei clan.

"That is up to what happens in the next few moments."

"Nothing as far as I'm concerned," Aiden called out as he made his way around to the special pedestal in the center of the garden. "There will not be a future for the Zmei because I will rule Dacia and the ancient ways will be destroyed."

Rick went to stop him, but Sariana stayed him with her hand.

Aiden placed the two pieces of medallion together in the center of the pedestal where centuries ago it had been one. Nothing happened. The earth still shook, the winds and rains still howled around them, lightening flashed over the valley in the distance.

Aiden looked around in confusion, but Rick and Sariana stood perfectly still as if they'd been expecting this. Fellow Dacians began to emerge from the compound to avoid the possible collapse of the building.

The sunlight which was supposed to rise remained hidden behind clouds as dark as night.

"Well, Derzelas is definitely pissed." Sariana sighed.

"What's going on?" Diane stepped forward.

"Wait…wait…he's coming," the goddess instructed with assurance. An old man emerged from the surrounding darkness. He looked as old as Methuselah, dressed in the furs and simple linens of the ancient Dacians.

"Zamolxis." Aiden breathed in awe and shock.

He was smiling broadly until he came upon Aiden standing near the medallion's podium.

"Rick," he started, "you were supposed to be the one to place the medallions together."

Rick bowed low. "I know, my lord. But there has been a change."

"You are giving up the lands and title to your brother?"

Rick shrugged. "It is his birthright after all." He waved his hands around and looked at Aiden. "All of this is now your domain, Aiden. Just like you always wanted. Dacia is now yours." He bowed to his brother.

Aiden glowed, and Zamolxis shook his head in wonder. "Well, now that I've managed to be released by Bendis, she's not going to be happy with whoever set me free."

"What do you mean?" Aiden asked, his smile slowly diminishing.

"Well, she's probably going to deny you her light and power for one thing, maybe…maybe not. She's fickle, but then most goddesses are." Zamolxis walked over to his daughter. "So are you finished with your little experiment of living the mortal life, my daughter?"

Sariana stood up and gave her father a sweet peck on the cheek. "Yes father. It has been a long time."

"Time is irrelevant to us my dear."

"Yes it is," she turned from her father back to Aiden. "Oh, and one more thing…" Sariana waved the crew watching from the steps on over. "Now that the medallion is back together, so is Dacia." Zamolxis stepped closer, too. "Now it is yours to oversee, Aiden. But at a cost. You may not leave the portal to attend to your affairs. And to make sure things are as they should be, we now have the new generations of Zmei to keep watch over your ruling."

Draylon and Marilyn stood together and suddenly morphed into their Zmeu forms with a wave of Zamolxis hand. They took off in flight, screeching their arrival to all of Dacia, representing their place in the land they'd originated from.

The Dacians, and even some of the remaining vamps, ooohed and ahhed over the fictional beasts. They came in for a landing, the black beast easing gracefully into the gardens to stand beside the goddess, but the smaller, scarlet one had a little trouble with finesse and took out the rose trellis and the water nymph on the fountain. Rick winced at his daughter's lack of skill in front of the god.

"These are the Zmei I am sending to watch over Dacia. They will make sure you are treating your subjects honorably and with respect as they help to rebuild the clans," Zamolxis ordained.

"What about my people?" Aiden asked.

"You mean the vampires? Oh they will still be around—unfortunately, the majority are on the outside of Dacia though, except for the few who survived with you this night. They will have to learn to fend for themselves now. If you have true feelings for your fellow vamps, you might look to Rick to help you guide them and help them to adapt and live among the mortals in the real world."

"You mean I am stuck here in Dacia?"

"This is the land you've always fought to have. That is what the medallions were all about," Zamolxis explained. "This is all there is left of Dacia and you are here until you wish otherwise…but 'otherwise' may not be to your liking."

"This is all that I have? But this isn't the real world. This is an alternative timeline created as a sanctuary," Aiden rambled with disgust.

"And it's all yours, brother," Rick said.

"I don't want it. I relinquish my entitlement." Aiden sneered angrily.

Stillness settled in the air as if they waited breathlessly for the fury of the gods to rain down upon them all. Draylon turned from dragon back to man.

Stepping forward he bowed humbly in front of Zamolxis. "My Lord, Dacia is the land of my family. This is the sacred ground of my forefathers. You sent us here to protect the Dacians and that is still my desire in whatever form I can be of assistance. If no one wants this land, I will tend to it as you once ordained."

Rick stepped forward. "Draylon, you do realize that if you do, you will not be able to leave Dacia. Now that the medallion is once again back together the portal will close forever."

Zamolxis looked down at his Zmeu. "Rick is right. Are you willing to give up everything you've had in the last millennium on the outside?"

Having changed back, Marilyn stepped forward and bowed at their god. "Yes, we are."

Draylon looked at her.

"My whole life I've felt I never really fit into society—now I know where my true destiny exists."

"You and Diane did well, Rick. You should be proud."

Zamolxis turned to Rick and then to Diane. "You both should be proud."

He turned his attention back to the young couple standing naked and vulnerable before the all powerful god. "Are you positive about your decision?"

They both nodded and agreed verbally.

"Then I pronounce you, the Guardians of Dacia. You will uphold the truths of our past, secure the vision of the future and rebuild, strengthen and replenish the faith of the Dacians as the laws allow."

It wasn't quite a ceremony, but it was a proclaimed declaration by their god. Rick was still uncertain of what he needed to do. But it looked like Dacia would now be in proper hands.

"What about me?" Aiden stepped forth. "I am a leader of my own people. And I want retribution for the desecration of my property and clan."

Sariana stepped forward, placing a hand on her father's arm. "This was an unfair test all those years ago. And the rules you set down when the Great Divide took over declared that neither clan could kill or destroy upon the other's property. Both parties were wronged here recently, but I do think rebuilding Aiden's fortress is the least you could do."

Zamolxis growled low in his throat and finally relented. "All right. But if that is the case, Aiden will be on the outside again and controlling his vampires." He looked to Aiden. "Sorry, I can't remove the curse—it's not mine to remove. You'll have to take it up with Derzelas. But I don't want you running around without supervision, either.

"I am keeping you confined to Romania. You will maintain your image as professor of Romanian History and Romania's Minister of History. Your clan will have to learn to adjust to their environment. But there will be no more inhumane treatment of your kind. You will learn to have them adjust to the life in a civil manner. And you know what I am talking about. I will have Zamara keep an eye on you from time to time."

Sariana was about to object but a stern look from her father put her lips into a pretty pout.

Zamolxis nodded to Rick. "All right, you know what needs to be done. I will give you forty-eight hours for your people to make their decisions before I close the portal."

Rick held the attention of his clan that stood around. "Zamolxis has spoken. The portal to Dacia will be closed forever in less than two days. You must decide whether or not to stay or leave here and learn to adapt into the mortal world. You are welcome at any of the Livedel facilities around the world for guidance and support."

Marilyn stepped forward. "Wait!" She held up her hand and approached Zamolxis. Rick waited breathlessly. Marilyn hadn't been instructed in dealing with a god.

"You can't close Dacia forever. I won't be able to leave to visit friends or family if they decide to leave."

Rick walked up to her, hoping she hadn't angered Zamolxis by questioning his ways. "Sweetheart, the medallion being placed together on the podium makes it so."

"No. I disagree." She shook her head at her father. "The medallion was supposed to bring the clans together...not shut a portal. The clans still aren't together and may never be. A thousand years didn't make a difference, but it did bring us all to this moment."

Marilyn turned back to their god. "Is it possible to keep the portal open so those true Dacians, whether from Vamier's clan or from the Delvante side, may come here in peace to celebrate, worship and eventually combine their efforts to become united in their own way? This is the land of their forefathers and they may wish to carry on the traditions."

No one spoke. Zamolxis' studied Marilyn as if she had

three heads. She was part Zmei—it wouldn't surprise Rick at all. Zamolxis' turned to Rick.

"I'm sorry, my lord. I hadn't had time to teach her the proper protocol..." Rick began.

The god raised his hand. "No...no...she's right. Nothing has really changed, and yet she's looking towards a peaceful solution, bringing tradition and history as our great connection back into play." He narrowed the distance between himself and the young woman. "What do you propose?"

Marilyn looked around nervously, biting her lip. Draylon stepped up beside her and their eyes met. They were communicating with each other. A quirk of a smile threatened to explode from her, and she nodded at her mate.

At the podium, she carefully removed the two pieces of the medallion. Taking one to Aiden, she handed him half before turning to Rick. "Father, this is yours." She handed him the Dragon piece instead of the wolf. "You are the one who saved the Zmeu. You are the prophet. Uncle Aiden." Aiden looked up when he heard his name. A look of surprise crossed his face. "I've given you the wolf side to remember where your roots lie and also as a reminder that you will be welcomed in Dacia in peace only."

"I'll be damned." Zamolxis laughed heartedly. "Zamara, your mother was right. It takes a woman to keep the peace...or at least try. We men, mortal or immortal, can be hardheaded at times. Hell, it only took me a couple thousand years to figure that out."

"Well that's settled then. The portal remains open, the pieces of medallion are where they need to be and it looks like there's going to be some changes around here. So I'll leave you to it." A knapsack and bedroll fell from the sky and landed at his feet. He blew a kiss up to the faded moon peeking through the thick cloud cover. "I'm off. I've got things to do now that I am back for awhile. Thought I would see how the world has evolved. But I'll be checking in from time to time to see how My People are getting along." He paused. "Just a word of warning, don't piss off any other gods if you can help it."

Everyone still stood around in awe, not sure what to do.

Draylon stepped forward. "I suggest we get our Vamier brethren inside before Derzelas decides to return. There is cleaning up to do after the massacre. But we would like to extend an offer of peace inside the walls until we can come up with a new, modern day reform that is agreeable to all parties in general."

Draylon offered his hand to Aiden. Rick wasn't sure his brother would take it. He still stared at the half of the medallion. "I was given the dragon half of the medallion centuries ago to remind me of my atrocities against the Zmei—the wolf part was our father's emblem." Aiden's voice shook with emotion as he looked up at Rick.

It was the first time he'd said '*our*' father...ever.

"Then it is time you had it, brother." Rick held out his hand, too. Aiden looked at both Draylon's and his.

Aiden tentatively stepped forward, and the three men exchanged hearty handshakes and nods of optimistic approval. "It's been centuries of war and distrust." Marilyn came forth. "I don't expect everything to be resolved...but it looks like a good start."

Epilogue

Marilyn worked right beside some of the Dacian wolf clan who'd agreed to help out in rebuilding Aiden's fortress—the one she'd torn down trying to free Draylon. It was a peace offering they'd agreed on the day of the bonding when Vamier had his people clear the deceased from the Delvante Compound corridors.

"There's a message from your father." Draylon stepped up to her, his dark suit too pristine in this atmosphere.

"Read it to me, I'm in the middle of clearing this pile of rubble."

She directed a bulldozer in to lift another load of stone and concrete as she cleared the last of the smaller debris with a shovel.

"You look so adorable in a hardhat and all smudged—"

"Careful there, Draylon—you're much to pretty to be splattered with a shovel of dirt," she warned. "What's my dad say?"

"Things are going well at Livedel. He's settled into his office and new house. Your mother is finally talking to him in the board room at least but is still torn between coming back here to Dacia and staying in Frederick."

Please, gods…let my mother stay in Frederick.

"I heard that." Draylon smiled. "And I couldn't agree more."

"What about Tina and Mike? How are they doing?"

The last she heard, they'd become rather close. Being kept under surveillance, the two bonded. As excited as Marilyn was at the prospect, Draylon wasn't sure it was a good idea.

"He says here… 'I've hired Tina to go over the accounts of a new merger. Jack Reynolds, a CEO of a technology firm in Dallas, Texas is looking to join forces with Livedel. It'll be good for her since she caught Mike cheating on her." Draylon's voice drifted off, his brow wrinkled, and then nodded his head, as if he knew.

She tossed her shovel to the side. "Cheated on her. Why that low-down, skuzzy, two-bit…" Marilyn could feel her lip curl and a snarl tear from her throat.

"Easy, Marilyn…I'm sure it's not what you think. I've known Mike a lot longer than you have. He has some issues—"

"Yeah, well one of them is being a bastard! Cheating on my friend. Tina doesn't need crap like him. I've worked to get her away from those kinds of relationships."

"Yes, well it's not for us to say. Tina is still young, she needs to find out who she is and what she wants before she can do anything else. And Mike will always be Mike, he can't help who he is."

"I still don't like it." She harrumphed. "What else does Dad say?"

"He says he sends his love and support and will see us for the first delegate meeting of the Dacian Council next month."

"Good. I'm looking forward to that." Still, she was unsettled by Tina's news. She'd always been there when a dating disasters happened. Now she was on the other side of the world…and most of the time in another dimension.

Draylon sashayed his way over to her as he refolded the letter from her dad. There was a gleam in his eye, dangerous, full of fiery passion.

"I'm warning you now…I'm filthy," she said upon his approach.

"I know. You are a filthy, filthy woman."

"I meant covered in dirt, sweat and enough concrete du—"

None of that seemed to matter as Draylon swooped in, stealing her breath away with his heated kisses. She captured his face in her canvas glove covered hands. Some of the crew stopped to applaud and howl their approval.

Draylon waved one hand in celebration to his wolf pack and slowly broke the kiss into smaller, subtle pecks.

He kissed her neck, teasing her unmercifully into heat. "Dinner?"

"Um…Uncle Aiden…and I…and then discussing…history."

Another kiss along her jaw. "But you're dirty."

"I…I…brought a change of clothes."

"Shower?"

"Meet me there in ten minutes—"

"Nope." He picked her up. Her hardhat fell to the ground revealing her auburn hair to the waning sunlight. "I'm not waiting for you to meet me."

"You are such a beast…"

"But you love the beast in me."

She touched his face lovingly. "That I do, my Zmeu."

Coming Early 2015—
Book 2 in The Guardians of Dacia series
Immortal Angel

About Loni Lynne

Born in north-central Michigan, Loni Lynne still loves the quiet woods, lakes and rivers in Otsego County and the Victorian era bay side houses of Little Traverse Bay. But after decades of moving around the country as a child and twenty-five years of marriage to her personal hero, she calls western Maryland her home.

Serving in the United States Navy didn't prepare her for the hardest job ever, being a stay at home mom, to her two wonderful daughters. After years of volunteering as a scout leader, PTA officer, and various other volunteer positions, all while still writing snippets of story ideas, her husband decided it was time for her to put her heart to *finishing* a story. He gave her a laptop, portable hard drive and his blessings to have a finished manuscript, ready to be sent out to the masses in one year. He created a writing monster.

Immortal Heat was her first idea six years ago and has gone through many revisions since then. In the meantime another story took hold, **Wanted: One Ghost** and it became her first published book in 2013. Now with the help of her friends, family and friends of the romance writing community, she's pursuing her love of telling stories written from her heart

Places to connect with Loni Lynne:

Facebook Page for The Guardians of Dacia series: https://www.facebook.com/TheGuardiansofDacia

Loni Lynne's website: http://www.lonilynne.com

Loni Lynne's Facebook Page: https://www.facebook.com/lonilynne

Loni Lynne's Twitter Page: https://twitter.com/LoniLynne1

Loni Lynne's Goodreads Page: https://www.goodreads.com/author/show/7115619.Loni_Lynne

Loni Lynne's Mailing List: http://www.lonilynne.com/mailing-list.html

Acknowledgements

A book is never done without the help of friends, family and fans. I would like to share my appreciation with some wonderful people. To my family, my mother Linda and sister Lissa for their early support, years ago and now. To my in-laws, Jim and Cat, who've been my biggest fans since the first book. To my sisters, Kasie, Marsha and Love for giving me great ideas. To my daughters, Rah and Jen for their inspiration and brainstorming help. To my husband, for being my hero and getting the laptop and hard drive for me five years ago.

I have a great group of critique partners— the Crit Divas (and Devo)— Magda Alexander, Lula Diamond, Teresa Quill, and Andy Palmer, thank you for your honest critiques. Love you guys! My beta readers— Stephanie, Lauren, Sami and Kasie—thank you for double checking and reading. To my amazing editor, Judy Roth and fantastic debuting cover artist, Jenji, thank you for all your hard work. The book wouldn't have life without you.

A special thanks to Magda Alexander for her support and guidance in helping me get my first book in The Guardians of Dacia series out on Amazon. What an awesome woman and great friend.

My fans and readers, all I can say is *thank you so much.* Enjoy.

Remember…***Believe in Fate!***

20020031R00171

Made in the USA
Middletown, DE
11 May 2015